TILDA'S
PROMISE

A Novel

JEAN P. MOORE

SHE WRITES PRESS

Published September 25, 2018
Printed in the United States of America
Print ISBN: 978-1-63152-477-6
E-ISBN: 978-1-63152-478-3
Library of Congress Control Number: 2018938310

For information, address:
She Writes Press
1563 Solano Ave #546
Berkeley, CA 94707

Interior design by Tabitha Lahr

She Writes Press is a division of SparkPoint Studio, LLC.

This is a work of fiction. Names, characters, places, and incidents either are the product of the author's imagination or are used fictitiously. Any resemblance to actual persons, living or dead, is entirely coincidental.

For Sienna, Maddie, and Lilly

"*Being mortal is about the struggle to cope with the constraints of our biology, with the limits set by genes and cells and flesh and bone.*"

—Atul Gawande, *Being Mortal*

"*A purpose of human life, no matter who is controlling it, is to love whoever is around to be loved.*"

—Kurt Vonnegut, *The Sirens of Titan*

Chapter One

HER MUTILATED WORLD

∽

Your membership will expire soon. This was the opening sentence of Tilda's first email of the day, and she hit delete before going any further. Of course her membership to the museum would expire, along with her driver's license in six months, her gym membership, and her subscription to *The New York Times*, among many other things. The milk in the refrigerator had been expired for days. Everything expires.

This gloominess was not customary for Tilda, but it was becoming more common, now that the funeral was four months behind her. The last of her friends' casseroles in the freezer had finally been discarded, and the phone was not ringing as frequently with words of comfort, concern, or just plain awkwardness. It was odd how some people couldn't come out and say they were so sorry that Harold died. Much more frequent were "so sorry for your loss," "so sorry you lost Harold," or, Tilda's personal favorite for irksomeness, "so sorry Harold passed," like a kidney stone. When did forms of *to pass* become so popular? It used to be people said *passed away* at least, like "so sorry Harold passed away." She'd noticed that even newspapers preferred *pass* in their headlines: "Robin Williams passes," Tilda had read recently in the local paper. Passes what? She found this more than annoying, like so much of life. A simple, declarative sentence would do. But unless you've been through it, she thought, unless you've lived with the raw truth, it was much easier to soft-pedal death, to make it something vague and distant, but it wasn't, not in the least.

Just recently, Tilda had read a *Huffington Post* article called "10 Good Ways to Talk about Grief." Right up there was "Tell the grieving, 'I'm sorry for your loss.'" This struck her as inane. The most impressive item, she remembered, was "Don't say anything, just listen." What the grieving need mostly, Tilda knew now, is to be left alone to find their own way out of sorrow. At least that was how Tilda saw it.

"You're depressed, Mom," her daughter Laura had said to her just this morning. "I wish you'd let me make an appointment with Dr. Willis for you."

"Of course I'm depressed. It's how people are when their mates die, when they've been together for over forty years. You don't take drugs for it. You live with it." Tilda had been repeating some variation of this response for weeks. At least Laura allowed that her mother could be depressed for a few months, but even she, dealing with the loss of her own father, felt her mother should be getting on with things now. After four months, she was supposed to be getting hold of herself.

"What about you, Laura? Are you taking something? Or don't you miss him?" She had meant this earnestly but realized, after the words had been spoken, that it had sounded cruel, accusatory. There was a pause. Then Laura said, "I'll be over in a little while. Maybe we can go get a late breakfast. Would you like that, Mom?"

So like Laura. She'd nag and drive her mother a little nuts, but she was a good-hearted, sweet kid. Sweet kid pushing forty.

When, years ago, Harold had asked Tilda if she wanted to break up the party and get married, Tilda had laughed and said yes. They both knew it was time to take on adult responsibility, like marriage. They'd met at a bar, straight out of college. Tilda was there with two of her college friends who, like her, were subbing at a private school on the East Side. Harold was putting back a few for old time's sake with some fraternity chums.

Tilda had her eye on Harold from the start. He wasn't particularly good looking, not in any classic sense, but he moved easily, making him appear both approachable and confident. Nothing too studied, that was the first thing she noticed. His white shirt was loosely tucked into his chinos; his belt sat easily and low on his hips. He wore expensive loafers, she could tell, but they were just scuffed enough to indicate he didn't consider them a fashion statement. He seemed comfortable, with an appealing smile. Tilda watched him repeatedly push an errant strand of his brown hair away from his eyes. His features, Tilda thought, were just off enough to keep him from being handsome, his nose a little too crooked, his lips a little thin. She liked that he would be only a few inches taller than she was in her heels, and that he wasn't too thin. Just right, she thought.

He looked her way, too, but more at the three of them standing at her table, not just at her. Then he turned back to his friends and said something. She could tell he was getting up the courage to come over, so she wasn't surprised when he picked up his beer and headed toward them.

"Here he comes," she said to Lynn and Bev, her friends. "What did I tell you?"

"Hi, ladies," he said, putting his beer down on the bar table. The girls looked down at his bottle and then at him. Harold quickly picked it up, sensing he had been too intrusive.

"Hello," said Tilda in a flirty but sarcastic tone, dragging out the o.

Maybe it was then that he actually noticed her, got it that she was trying to salvage his awkward approach. "What's your story?" she said, looking directly into his eyes.

"My story, hmm. Well, see those two guys over there? Really nice guys, I might add. We thought maybe you three ladies wouldn't mind having a drink with us."

Straightforward, certainly not too clever, thought Tilda, but she was in, if she could have Harold.

After a few awkward moments and more unremarkable exchanges, the six of them did end up having a few drinks. No one went home with anyone, but phone numbers were exchanged. Tilda wrote her number on Harold's cuff at his insistence.

They started dating after that, but not exclusively. That had taken a few years. During their more serious time together, Harold went on for his master's in accounting at City College, and Tilda took a fifth year getting her teaching certificate in English. She was offered a job at the Upper East Side private school where she had subbed. The day Harold landed a job with a big firm downtown, they celebrated with dinner at Sardi's. Harold flashed two tickets to *Hair*, which had just moved to Broadway—a very hot show, he assured her.

Their adult day jobs left them hungry for playtime on their off-hours. They went dancing, to dinner and the movies, and to Broadway shows, and they took weekend trips before settling into the daily routine of work each Monday morning. Some weekends they joined protests and marched. They were passionate about civil rights and sympathetic with anti-war protesters, but they loved having fun together more than anything. And they had fallen deeply in love. "My green-eyed beauty," he called her. "My eyes are hazel," she said in return, deadpan, but enjoying the thought that her eyes were, to him, maybe, a mysterious, exotic green. "And I'm no beauty." Here she firmly believed her position. But she was cute; she'd accept *cute*. A gymnast in high school, she hadn't changed much after college, still standing at five foot five, weighing 120 now, five pounds over her college weight, hair still short and sandy blonde. She wouldn't win any beauty contests, but she never fretted about her looks.

They had a smallish wedding under the chuppah in his mother's backyard in Queens, married by a renegade rabbi.

They called him that since he had agreed to do the honors even though Tilda wasn't converting. The Jewish wedding had been more for Harold's mother since Harold thought of himself as a cultural Jew, not a religious one. And Tilda had given up on Catholicism several years after her confirmation, finding it remote and out of touch with the reality of her life. (Was it really a sin to have impure thoughts? Was thinking about sex really so bad?) She had been agnostic ever since. So having an untraditional Jewish wedding seemed to please everyone, including Harold's mother. Harold smashed the glass, and a catered dinner was served under a tent. Harold and Tilda's friends were there, the same ones who had been at the bar that evening six years earlier, in fact. They toasted the couple and said it was about time.

The newlyweds rented a small apartment on the Upper West Side, worked, and, while they still liked to have a good time, they began to settle down. It took them a few years before they decided to start a family, but it wasn't that easy. Low sperm count, they were told. Then, a few years later, Laura was born. Harold wanted more, a son, another daughter, it didn't matter, but by then Tilda was already thirty and wanted to go back to teaching as soon as the new semester started. They could try again, she said, but later. In the meantime, everyone was tickled with Laura, the cutest baby ever. Everyone said so, not just Tilda and Harold.

Gladys, Harold's mother, was more than happy to care for the baby, taking the train every day, like a nanny. The arrangement lasted for ten years, until Gladys got sick, but by then it was too late anyway. The years, it seemed, had a way of piling on. In spite of trying, there were to be no more pregnancies. Laura was destined to be an only child.

⚬

The doorbell rang. "Hello. Anybody home?" Laura's voice rang out, cheerful but a little tenuous.

Laura and her family—her husband, Mark, and their fourteen-year-old daughter, Tilly, Tilda's namesake—lived in Longview, Connecticut, one town farther north on the I-95 corridor. Tilda and Harold had left the city in the early '80s so Laura could grow up on a tree-lined street, ride her bike, and walk to school. It seemed a dream at the time, but New York was on the verge of a resurgence, and Harold and Tilda sold their place on the West Side easily and bought easily, too, in Water Haven, a small town north of the city on the Long Island Sound, a mere fifty minutes from Midtown on the Metro North.

"I'm in here," Tilda answered, not getting up from her desk, where she had been re-reading a poem she used to teach, wondering if there would be some comfort in it now. *Try to praise the mutilated world. Remember June's long days, and wild strawberries, drops of rosé wine.* Not comfort so much as a feeling of closeness to Harold—the words provided that, she had to admit.

Laura wandered back to the third bedroom, her mother's office ever since she'd retired from Water Haven High five years earlier.

"There's no light in here, Mom. Do you want to ruin your eyesight even more?" she said, flicking on the overhead light.

Tilda shielded her eyes. "Oh, don't do that," she said, putting down the lid of her laptop. "I'm done. Just turn out the light."

"Where would you like to go? I'm up for an omelet. You?"

Tilda got up and pushed her chair under the desk. "You pick," she said, grabbing her bag and following Laura out.

Best to leave the organizing to Laura. Having her say was important, a need for control, Tilda always thought. She wasn't sure where this had come from. Neither she nor Harold had ever been particularly controlling, she thought. They knew when to go with the flow, to use an expression from their younger days.

From early childhood, Laura liked to be in charge, to make the decisions, and, as an adult, she was very competent, always called on to head committees and to organize school fund-raising projects. The enigma, though, was that Laura, beneath her together exterior, was very sensitive. Anything sad she heard on the news involving humans or animals could and often did reduce her to tears. Problems in the lives of her friends, and certainly within her own family, would leave her weeping until Mark stepped in to reassure her that all would be well, even when it was clear it would not.

So it was surprising that she was holding back so much regarding Harold's death. Surely Laura too was feeling the pain, but she seemed to be putting all her energy into hovering over her mother, and Tilda, more weary than annoyed, wanted her to back off.

Tilda's need for relief from her daughter's intensity probably summed up the friction . . . no, not the right word . . . the *tension* that existed sometimes between them. Tilda often wanted to be left alone when Laura wanted to take charge. Even when Laura was growing up, Tilda would often yield. If Laura wanted to back out of gymnastics for editing the school newspaper, she would do it, rarely consulting her mother and father, until the forms had to be signed. Then Tilda would sign, no arguments, and that was that. When it was time for college, Laura gave up a four-year scholarship to UConn to go to a local community college. Why? She and Mark were dating. Marriage was imminent, Laura announced. This had caused some conflict in the family, but in the end, Tilda and Harold reluctantly agreed. After two years at the college, Laura became a dental hygienist. Shortly thereafter, Mark proposed. A year later, they were married. Laura continued to work for a time—until she got pregnant. She had not worked a day since. Was it just Tilda's imagination, or had Laura turned her back on so much of what her mother and her generation had worked to achieve?

Tilda tried not to take it personally, Laura's giving up on gymnastics—which had been Tilda's strength—and then Laura's eschewing college to get married and become a mother. Tilda had pursued teaching and worked while Laura was growing up. Time passed, and there were no brothers or sisters. Laura, on the other hand, gave up on furthering her education and on a career to get married and to rear a single child, a child to be doted on. Laura seemed to be completely focused on Tilly, leaving no inclination for a larger family. From Tilda's vantage point, for all Laura's competence, she seemed to be overwhelmed with the tasks of motherhood. And no wonder. She fretted over most things Tilly-related. She wondered whether the food she prepared and served was healthy enough. What was better—organic or locally grown? She checked in daily with Tilly to be sure she was up-to-date on all her assignments. She worried that Tilly's AP classes kept her too isolated from a more diverse circle of friends. And she practically ran background checks on the friends Tilly did have. Laura spent hours organizing carpools to soccer and swimming. Then, mercifully, when Tilly settled on dance, they both enjoyed a little breathing room in their hectic schedule.

It was no wonder, then, that motherhood left Laura either stressed or exhausted—sometimes both.

Mystified, Tilda tried to make sense of the contradictions: a competent take-charge daughter, a natural leader (it seemed at first), who opted for home and family instead of, say, the boardroom. Tilda, a child of the '60s, thought her daughter might take up the mantle, be whatever she wanted, president, even. And she had done whatever she wanted. She had decided to be a stay-at-home mom. Tilda tried not to judge, but it seemed to her that the women's movement had produced a generation of supermoms, rather than freeing them from the single role in life that had limited so many generations of women before them.

It had all worked out in the end, though, she said to ease her mind. Laura and Mark and Tilly were a close-knit and loving family. Tilly was flourishing, a fourteen-year-old excellent student, excelling in dance. Tilda couldn't be disappointed if this were the result.

The night that Harold died in bed beside her was, ironically, the first night in months that Tilda had been able to fall into a deep sleep. She had been having trouble ever since she learned that their pharmacist's fifty-year-old daughter had died in her sleep, choking on her own blood after oral surgery. Then an old teacher friend she had known for years died in her sleep after knee-replacement surgery proved so painful that she had become hooked on pain meds. And she had liked her martinis in the evenings, but the combination had proved to be too much. Despite the reasons attached to these deaths, Tilda had decided sleeping could be dangerous.

Every night she'd wake up at three, eyes wide open, staring at the ceiling. This went on until the night Harold died. Tilda had read her book until becoming drowsy, which was her routine. Before turning out the light, she looked over to see the rise and fall of Harold's chest accompanied by a light snore. She turned out the light, pulled up the covers, and fell into a deep sleep, not waking until seven, squinting and catching a glimpse of light just beginning to show through the open spaces in the night shades. She had made it through the night.

Tilda told Laura later that she knew immediately something was wrong. It was too quiet. Then she realized it was Harold. He wasn't breathing.

Laura and Tilda had gone over this many times, Laura trying to fathom why her mother hadn't called immediately. Tilda, too, in retrospect, wondered why she had been so removed. She didn't cry or scream, or if she had, if she had shaken Harold and implored him to wake up, if she had cried hysterically, it was someone else who had done those things. She herself had gone someplace far away, to a place where there was no Harold, to someplace where she knew she was without him and that she would be from then on, but she didn't know where that place was. She was moving, pulling on a sweater, calling the ambulance, she must have, but she wasn't there, not in the bedroom with Harold lying near her, not breathing. After all, Harold wasn't sick. He was healthy.

He was supposed to be waking up, getting coffee, reading the paper—for years to come. He was supposed to be with Tilda for their morning routine, always. And beyond that, he was supposed to be there for Tilly's milestones, her graduations, for all the triumphs surely waiting for her—all those things in the future—he was to be there, not here, lying so still.

When the ambulance came to take Harold away, Tilda must have been dressed. She must have followed, to take care of all that needed taking care of, but before she walked out of the now-empty bedroom, she must have turned to look at the bed, still unmade. She must have walked over and put her hand on the pillow, felt the mattress. Yes, she remembered, where the pillow met the mattress, it still felt warm. It couldn't have been Harold's warmth, but it was the closest she would ever come to his warmth again. She remembered stepping out of her shoes and getting back into bed, nuzzling into the warm place. Harold's smell. Not aftershave or cologne, just Harold. Home. She couldn't remember getting to the hospital after that or calling Laura, though she had done both.

Tilda, who had taught the concept of irony to her high school students ("One cannot escape the irony of the sinking of the *Titanic*; it was proclaimed to be unsinkable"), was now forever linked to the word. It was grimly ironic to her, all that instruction years ago into the meaning of the very word that she would never be able to shake in her late years, the *irony* inherent in the night Harold died.

❧

Laura suggested they go to the diner on Waterton Avenue, and Tilda agreed. They sat in the booth near the door, which had been left open to catch the fresh breeze that had blown into town overnight. Saul's was one of the few mom-and-pop businesses remaining on the avenue. Where once there had been a Woolworth's with a soda fountain, an Asian produce market, a hardware store, and a real non-chain department store, there were now a Saks and a bank—no, ten banks, on a shopping strip of about half a mile in length. There was no hardware store anymore, only Restoration Hardware, which was no hardware store at all. On a street where once you could get groceries, home supplies, and shoes at a reasonable price, there were now boutiques with clothes only celebrities, sports figures, and hedge fund families could afford. The avenue offered nothing to sustain life, unless you could eat Tiffany jewelry or light your home with a Baccarat crystal lamp for a mere two grand.

Back in the 1980s, Waterton Avenue was a reasonable place to shop. There had always been wealthy people, but they were out of sight on their estates. Now it was the poor who were out of sight. The Escalades and Suburbans ruled, driven by stay-at-home moms who shopped in yoga clothes and pushed double-wide strollers down the street, daring anyone to get in their way.

Tilda wasn't sure about her beloved town anymore. She had to admit to being less tolerant of what she thought to be the folly around her, especially now, without Harold. Since his death, she could barely stand what she observed in her neighborhood. Just last week, she had reached her limit. She had pulled her Subaru into a parking space clearly marked for small cars only. She deposited her quarter for twenty minutes of parking time and walked to the cleaners to drop off a few things. By the time she returned, a huge Navigator had managed to maneuver itself right next to her car—not too successfully—into a spot meant for a compact, had hit the meter next to hers on the shared metal post, and then narrowly avoided lopping off the side-view mirror on Tilda's appropriately small car. The mammoth car in question was of course over the line, it being a habit of these monstrosities to always take up two spaces because of their unseemly girth. It was clear Tilda couldn't possibly get into her car. There was no room to even open the door. She thought about trying to squeeze in on the other side and climb over the gearshift to make it into the driver's seat, but the car on her passenger side was pretty close, too. She might be able to make it, but her lumbar spine began to twitch at the thought of it.

Tilda looked around, trying to spy the social miscreant who could do such a thing and then wander off to enjoy the day—or at least the next two hours. No luck. She looked for the parking-ticket guy. No luck. A cop? No luck. So she pulled the writing pad she always carried with her out of her bag and wrote: *Dear driver, please note that you have made it impossible for me to get into my car. Please learn how to properly park your car, which technically is not a car, but a truck masquerading as one. And do you really need a vehicle of this size? Many generations before you have managed to raise kids, brave the elements, get to work, and shop, etc., in actual cars.*

Writing the note had taken the edge off her anger. And it was anger. Her generation had worked and raised kids, had done it all—and with cars that were fuel-efficient. Why had this generation forgotten so much? She wished she could go home and tell Harold. They would've talked about her experience, been mildly incensed, and then they would've found the humor in Tilda's reaction, in that note. They would've laughed together until the anger vanished.

She put another quarter into her side of the double-headed meter, which miraculously was still working, and went to CVS to use her 25 percent discount coupon on a few household items.

⌒⌒⌒

"You should eat something, Mom," Laura said, watching her mother crumble the bun on her plate. "Aren't you going to at least taste your soup?"

"Hmm?" answered Tilda, remembering the ride home that day, after she had returned to see the monster car gone and her own car unscathed, with plenty of room for her to open the door and drive away. "Yes, of course, I was just . . ."

"Just gazing off into space?" offered Laura.

"No, just thinking."

"You do that a lot these days, gaze off and go someplace in your mind. I feel like you're not really here," said Laura.

Tilda saw the concern in her daughter's face, but instead of feeling the need to reassure her, Tilda sighed and looked down.

"I need to talk to you, Mom, but I don't know if this is a good time. Do you want to talk to me?"

Tilda pulled herself up in the green leatherette seat that had been part of the diner's decor for as long as she could remember. She looked into Laura's brown eyes, just like Harold's, soulful and kind. She folded her hands on the table and resolved to give Laura her attention.

"What's on your mind?"

"Okay," said Laura, pushing back her brown hair, where a few strands of silver were beginning to shine through. "I don't want to upset you, just promise you'll hear me out."

"What is this all about, Laura? I'm fine. Why are you so focused on me these days?" Tilda felt her resolve begin to fade as her heart started to beat a little faster.

Laura leaned in over the table and spoke softly. "Please don't get annoyed. I'm beginning to think you do it on purpose so I'll stop, and then we never get to talk."

Tilda took in a breath and said, "Okay, I'll try, I promise, but you have to know I'm all right. It's just August. It's only been four months."

"I know, I know, but even before Dad, the house was getting to be too much . . ."

"Oh, Laura, this isn't where this is going, is it? Honey, please. You know I love that house. Now more than ever, I could never leave it."

Laura's eyes filled with tears, and she fumbled in her bag, looking for a tissue.

Tilda paused and looked at her daughter. She remembered the time in the school auditorium when Laura, who was ten, stood in front of the audience and forgot all the lines of "Paul Revere's Ride" she was supposed to recite. After a few painful seconds that seemed like hours, Laura hung her head without saying a word and then dove her hands into her pockets, looking for the tissue her mother always made her carry.

A sensitive child, and a sensitive adult, she did manage to be very efficient and productive, and to be a good mother in her own right. Just too hovering at times, as a mother and as a daughter. That was it, not so much a helicopter parent (or daughter) as a hovercraft. Tilda smiled to herself at the thought of it. She remembered reading somewhere that the hovercraft's design, enabling travel over land and water and ice, made it most useful in missions of search and rescue—and here was Laura, seated across from her, on a rescue mission.

Now it was Tilda who leaned in over the table. "Honey, it's okay, really. Look, I'm eating my soup." Tilda picked up her spoon and took a big dramatic slurp, the smell of chicken and oregano alone whetting her appetite. Tilda's noisy slurp made Laura laugh—a response Tilda had learned to extract from her daughter over the years during hard times.

As Laura put her tissue away, Tilda took the lead.

"What if we made a deal? What if you gave me a year to get back on my feet? You know, that year of getting to acceptance. Isn't that what they say, that you need to go through the five stages of grief? Then we'll talk about what to do with the house and with me." Tilda wasn't being entirely forthright with her daughter. She had spontaneously devised a tactic to buy herself some time, to get out from under Laura's hovering. Tilda, in fact, did not expect her grief to be handled so tidily. She expected to mourn for the rest of her life, but Laura certainly didn't need to be in on her true feelings on the matter.

Laura was quiet, pondering. For a minute Tilda was afraid she was about to start sniffling again.

"Do you remember the last night of shiva?" Laura asked.

"Yes," answered Tilda, wondering where Laura was going now. The whole shiva experience had been, in the opinion of the family (that is, Tilda, Mark, and Tilly) a bit forced. All Tilda remembered definitely about that period was how insistent Laura had been about it. "We need to sit shiva, and not just one or two days. The whole seven. For Dad."

Mark had receded into the background on this, as with all things pertaining to Laura's need to uphold the rituals belonging to the Jewish side of her family. Not being Jewish himself, and knowing Laura's need to express her own Jewishness, however untraditional her Jewish background and conversion had been, he knew better than to offer any alternative. Tilly, also not Jewish (although Laura hadn't given up hope that maybe one day . . .), just rolled her eyes, but since she was a teenager and did this about most things, her parents ignored her. Tilda tried to remind Laura that her father had not been a practicing Jew since they'd moved to Connecticut. Tilda also threw in that she was not sure how she felt about seven days of mourning in front of a bunch of people she probably didn't even know that well—and that being the widow gave her more than a little voice in the matter—even if the weeklong occasion would be at Laura's home and not her own.

Laura had finally won the day, however, by bringing up her father's ties to his past, adding that while he had given up on religion after his mother's death, his cultural roots were deep. Tilda knew this was true. Harold was full of stories about his parents, whose families came from Lisbon. "My family, on both sides, can trace our roots in Portugal back for centuries," he told Laura. "And I can tell you—they didn't have it so easy. During the war, my parents were here, but we had relatives still in Portugal, under Salazar, and he may have offered a safe haven against Hitler, but he was no friend of the Jews. He just wasn't interested in world domination."

Laura used to sit for hours, listening to her father's stories of the old country, more history lessons than true family history, always sprinkled with tales of forbidden Jewishness dating back centuries, of hidden identities, of lighting Shabbat candles in darkened rooms and praying over unleavened bread in hushed voices.

One day, when Laura was twelve, she came home from her Catholic elementary school and asked her parents, quite ceremoniously, to meet her in the living room. Once they were seated before her, she announced, "Mom, Dad—I've decided to become a bat mitzvah."

Tilda had been mystified by the request, but Harold's smile gave away his pride. He may have given up on his religion, but his daughter, for reasons yet unknown, had found it. He quizzed her to be sure she knew what she was asking. "You want to formally enter the Jewish faith, to become a member of the Jewish community, on your thirteenth birthday. Is that right?"

It was clear she had given it thought. When Harold asked her why, she answered that it was her heritage, and she felt a need to claim it. Parental discussions followed behind closed bedroom doors, beginning with the most obvious questions: "What is this all about?" and "Why now?"

But Tilda knew why. It was because of Harold and his stories. Later she'd tell him, "If I had been telling her stories of my Italian grandparents and the history of their suffering, she'd have wanted to be a nun." And yet, there was no argument, never any doubt, really. If Laura was serious (and apparently she was), if she wanted to be Jewish, then she would be. While supportive, neither Tilda nor Harold was interested in taking up the cause, meaning Harold didn't renew his faith and once again Tilda didn't convert. What they did do, however, was find a rabbinical student, Amy Geller, who for a period of one year took Laura through her studies and helped her prepare her haftarah. Laura never waivered. Her commitment was a marvel to her parents.

Without joining a temple, the family held the service and the party at the local veterans' hall, which was much nicer than anyone expected, the caterer's plants and decorations making all the difference. The whole affair—friends and Laura's entire seventh-grade class—was a success. On Monday morning, Laura's teacher, Sister Sophie from France, led a discussion on the meaning of becoming a bat mitzvah.

Although the school's policy clearly stated the school provided an education "for students of all faiths," Tilda and Harold weren't so sure. But the principal, Mother Marie Clare, ensured them that Laura, a fine student, was welcome to complete her education at St. Madeleine's. And so she did, with honors.

She continued to practice her Judaism, and Harold finally joined the small temple in Water Haven, which held services in the Congregational church, so Laura could be a member in good standing for High Holiday services. But Harold never reaffirmed his faith, although he did continue to regale Laura with tales of his family's struggles in Portugal.

And so in the days following his death, to honor her father, Laura made sure all the principles of sitting shiva were upheld. She prepared her house for guests to arrive, so that after the service, all she had to do was turn on the coffeemaker and uncover the dishes. Before the first guest had arrived, she had placed a bowl of water and white paper guest towels on a table by the door. Inside on the mantle she lit the Yahrzeit candle. While she didn't hold the family to it, she herself didn't bathe, she covered mirrors, and she wore a torn piece of black ribbon on her dark dresses for a week. She let Mark know—as well as the rest of the family, albeit rather unnecessarily, Tilda thought—that in no uncertain terms, there would be no sex during that time, either.

All this Mark endured and Tilda, too. She and Mark and Tilly had forged a bond during this time. Being a proudly agnostic trio, they took comfort in their mild amusement while, at the same time, going along with Laura's wishes. At the end of the week, though, after the last guest had left, Tilda hugged Laura. "Thank you," she said to her daughter. "I know I wasn't for it, and maybe I was a little unenthusiastic . . ." Laura then had put up her hand to stop her. "No, dear, let me finish," Tilda insisted. "It was, the whole thing, really, it was a big comfort. I mean it. Your father would have been proud." She had meant it. During that week, Laura's house had smelled of coffee and cookies, of brisket and cabbage, and of wax burning. There was something primal, archetypal about the ritual that went beyond the brain, directly to the heart, Tilda now remembered.

⸎

"Mom, shiva, remember? The last night?"

"Yes, what about it?" Tilda said, pulling herself back into the present.

Laura looked at her mother.

"I told you then that the period of mourning is called *shneim asar chodesh*, when a child mourns the death of a parent, for twelve months. Laura drew her eyebrows together, deep in thought. "I've been wrong about all of this."

"All of what?" asked Tilda, almost afraid of what she might be unleashing by the question, a long introspective soliloquy, something Laura was prone to in her quest always to be a better person.

"This morning on the phone you asked if I missed Dad. I didn't answer. I didn't think I could, really. I think I've been afraid to let go, to admit . . ."

Tilda reached for a tissue and handed it to Laura. It was a kind gesture, but oh how Tilda did not want to proceed with this line of thought. On the one hand it appeared that Laura was on the verge of finally expressing her grief—a good thing—but Laura's grief could prove overwhelming, for her and for Tilda, who struggled mightily every day for control over it, for a semblance of normalcy.

Laura began to sob quietly. She stopped and tried to talk, several times, before she was able to continue.

"I miss him every day, a lot, so I try not to think about it. I just get busy. The busier the better, because if I think about it, I can't stand it. I can't *understand* it. It wasn't supposed to happen. He wasn't sick; he wasn't old. He wasn't supposed to die."

The waitress came over and began to clear the table. "Is everything okay?" she asked. "Can I get you anything?"

"It's okay, really. We'll just be a few minutes," said Tilda.

"No worries. Take your time." The waitress brought over a water pitcher, refilled their glasses, and left them alone.

"I know, I know," said Tilda, in an effort to comfort her daughter. "I try not to think about it either. So unfair, so fucking unfair."

Laura looked up. She had never heard Tilda use the F-word, and the shock registered on her daughter's face.

But Tilda acknowledged Laura's response with a laugh.

"Something you should know about your mother, Laura. I swear now. A lot. To myself, mostly. I think it's a passing thing. I'm sure I'll get over it."

They both wiped their eyes.

"So I'm with you, Mom. We're both entitled to a year," she said, crumbling her tissue. "You, to get through the five stages, and me—*shneim asar chodesh*. I promise I won't bug you anymore. And then when we reach Dad's Yahrzeit—the time of one year—we'll talk. Is it a deal, then?" Laura asked, reaching across the table.

Tilda grabbed her daughter's hand. "It's a deal, I promise." Laura's brown eyes brightened. Harold's eyes. *Remember the moments when we were together in a white room and the curtain fluttered. . . . Praise the mutilated world*. If only she could.

Chapter Two

"I GOT A GIRL . . ."

❧

On a Friday morning in September, Tilda sat at the kitchen table intently reading the orange juice container in front of her. After several attempts to reach the 800 number listed on the carton, she gave up in her quest to discover why, if the juice was not from concentrate and it was "100 percent fresh squeezed," it didn't taste anything like fresh-squeezed orange juice. "Oh fuck it," she said and hung up.

Looking out the bay window, she saw the first harbinger of fall, a yellow maple leaf softly gliding to the ground. The goldenrods at the property line were glowing vividly in the morning sun of a bright, clear day. Weeds, really, she thought, but she had always lived in harmony with the wild plants and flowers at the edge of their expansive lot at the beginning of a conservation area, one of the main attractions when they first saw the house all those years ago. In late summer the gold-enrods paired beautifully with the purple asters that nuzzled in next to them. Her own beds, though, the ones she always tended so carefully, were languishing, some with roses, others circling trees with astilbes, cornflowers, and black-eyed Susans.

She could barely look at her vegetables these days, planted on the far end of the patio. One day in the midst of her mourn-ing, she had rushed to Tom Pride's Nursery, had loaded up on her usual seedlings, and had planted them in a fury only to neglect them for the remainder of the season, Laura and Mark occasionally watering the patch on their visits.

How lucky she had been. No deer or voles had ever gobbled up her luscious vegetables and herbs. Despite her neglect, the tomatoes were still coming in plump and juicy, even as the vines began to wither, but the herbs had dried up, including the basil. Basil was her favorite. Her father nurtured thick clumps of it outside their kitchen door when she was a child. She loved the cool feel of its slightly curled and rounded deep green leaves. Pinching a few from their stems and crushing them with her fingers, she was transported by the immediate and overpowering scent, both sweet and pungent. "It's good in the tomato sauce, and it's like toothpaste, for your breath, when you want to be kissed," her father used to tell her. This was delivered with a playful nod and smile, quickly followed with, "But not you or your sister. You're too young." For him, they would always be too young. Nevertheless, she never left home without first chewing a few sprigs—from her first parties, where there was sure to be a game of spin the bottle, to her first dates, when there was bound to be a good-night kiss at the door.

Now she pushed the juice container aside and sprinkled granola on her yogurt. The house was quiet except for the sound of her own chewing. The silence was bringing on the dark mood, the name she had given her feelings these days. Was this darkness the same as Churchill's black dog? She didn't think so because that would mean she was depressed, and she didn't think that missing Harold so much she could hardly breathe at times was depression. It was grief, and that was different. The dark mood was the overpowering sense of absence: absence of Harold, of comfort, of happiness, of any sense of joy. Surely there was no joy; maybe there never would be again.

Ever since the immediate shock of Harold's death had passed, she'd experienced life as though enveloped in a thick gray cloud where everything was the same, dull and uninteresting. When Tilda and Harold had breakfast together there had been little conversation—Tilda usually sat at the kitchen table with a cup of coffee and the *New York Times* spread out in front of her while Harold sat in the screened-in porch off the kitchen listening to NPR—but she could be happy. She even felt joy, seeing him there, chin lifted, staring into space, as though he could see the news in front of him.

She sat in the kitchen this morning as she did most mornings, with her coffee and granola, but today the paper was on the driveway where the carrier had thrown it. She didn't have the energy to get dressed and walk the few steps out the door to get it. Her neighbor next door, Amanda, often tiptoed barefoot out her own front door to retrieve the paper in nothing but a skimpy, short robe.

When Harold happened to notice, which he often did, he'd comment, "There she is again, sans panties," causing Tilda to laugh. Tilda was never jealous, even though Amanda was at least twenty-five years younger and a real looker, as Harold would say. But Harold and Tilda had grown old together, and they knew each other's boundaries. Harold did not stray. He might look, but he didn't stray. "Go on," Tilda told him one morning as he watched Amanda bend down. "Go help her get the paper, so she can keep her clothes from falling off. And if you get anywhere with her, I'll be the first to congratulate you, you old coot."

"At my age, I'd rather have the paper," Harold said in return, a variation on the punch line of a familiar joke he often told: "A man is met at the door by a beautiful woman who asks if he would like super sex. The man replies, 'At my age, lady, I'd rather have the soup.'"

Her world without Harold was a foreign place, where the distraction of grief mingled with the burdens of ordinary life. Tilda thought about the storm windows that would have to be put up soon, something Harold did reluctantly every fall, trying to make it to Halloween before having to close up his porch. There were a lot of things yet to be done—accounts to be closed, taxes to be sorted out, an office full of files and closets full of a lifetime of accumulation to be confronted. But she didn't have the energy for all that yet.

Just then the phone rang.

"Mom, you got a minute?"

Tilda recognized Laura's anxious voice under her casual words.

"What's the matter? Is everything okay?"

Laura paused and took a deep breath. "It's Tilly. She's all right. I don't want to worry you, but . . ." And then she paused again.

"Just tell me. You said she's all right. So just tell me."

"She's cut herself . . . well, not cuts exactly."

"How? Is it serious?"

She heard her daughter draw a breath, "No, not really, but she did it on purpose."

"Well, was it cuts or scratch marks?"

"It didn't look deep."

It took a moment for the words to register. Tilda knew about cutting. She had a student once, a girl named Zelda, a creative and talented writer who cut herself. In those days, troubled or unhappy students often turned to Tilda for guidance or for attention, sometimes both. Her friend Bev once said it was because she made them read *Catcher in the Rye*—and then stood her ground when some parents objected. "Your students think you're a kindred spirit," Bev had said.

"What happened? Tell me how you found out. Did she tell you?" Tilda's thoughts were racing. It took many more rounds of questioning her distraught daughter before she finally learned that (a) Tilly was at home, not at school, where her actions would have triggered a series of events including possible expulsion; (b) she used a safety pin and barely drew blood, so it appeared to be superficial; and (c) she'd willingly told her parents. With these key points in mind, Tilda was able to calm her daughter down.

"I'm not trying to minimize this, dear, honestly. It's just that a lot of kids who do this do it for a long time and hide it from their parents—and sometimes the cuts are deep and need stitches. The fact that she talked to you, that's very significant."

"Do you think so? We're so worried. She told us she did it, but she hasn't said why. She doesn't want to go into it. We don't know what to do, but we're looking into counseling. That's the obvious first step."

Tilda didn't want to rule out the possibility, but she was also afraid that what appeared to be a minor version of a more serious act might escalate unnecessarily. She had seen it happen during her teaching days. When cases of self-harming were revealed, the school had no choice but to act, no matter how superficial the injury. Such incidents were cries for help. At worst, the student might pose a danger to others, putting the school at risk. Students who injured themselves at school could be barred from returning, their parents having to find alternative schools that would take them. Once labeled as "troubled," students were invariably consumed by the "system." Tilda could not accept any scenario in which her granddaughter became a troubled kid.

"Maybe not just yet. Maybe now the best thing is to keep talking and keep an eye on her."

Tilda knew that wouldn't be hard for Laura, the hovercraft. She wondered if Tilly was acting out under the pressure of too much attention at home, giving her mother something to really worry about instead of the usual grades, friends, appropriate hair, clothes, behavior, and all the rest.

"Would you like me to talk to her?" asked Tilda. "She talks to me sometimes about things." It was true. Tilda took pride in her relationship with her granddaughter, the fact that Tilly called her or sent her text messages, asked for her opinion. Then, of course, there were days and weeks when Tilly went dark, no word, when talking to her at all was difficult. Tilda always chalked it up to typical adolescent behavior.

"She does talk to you about things, doesn't she," said Laura.

"Maybe that would be a good idea. She wants to go shopping for dance stuff tomorrow. Maybe you could take her."

"That would be great. I'm here all day. Ask if she would like that and let me know."

After they hung up, Tilda remembered that Tilly had just made the dance team. She found it hard to reconcile the cheerful dancer with the sullen self-cutter she was contemplating now. She hoped Tilly would say yes and that she would be able to take her to the mall for whatever she needed to help restore her to her cheerful self.

Tilda opened the sliding doors and walked over to one of the shelves on the porch where Harold kept the radio he'd had for years. They had a new one in the living room, a fancy digital affair that Mark had set up for them so they could listen to a radio without static, and Harold had been sure to tell Mark that he was a good IT guy, for a financial planner. But Harold remained partial to the Panasonic he'd had since the '70s, the one Tilda said looked like a small boom box. She turned the power switch to on and sat in Harold's rattan wingback with the deep floral cushions and put her feet up on the ottoman. The room was a little chilly but still comfortable enough for a respite from her morning's conversation with Laura.

She listened to the morning news, an interview with a young woman who was explaining a bill that was expected to become law about sexual consent on college campuses. The young woman made a lot of sense, as far as Tilda could tell, not being all that familiar with the story. Instead of "no means no," the new bill was about affirmative consent, or "yes means yes." The woman quoted wording from the bill explaining that lack of protest or resistance didn't constitute consent.

Tilda was reminded of her own days on campus when girls would invariably come back to the dorms with horror stories of having to physically fight their way out of being raped. Even screaming *no* didn't mean *no* back then, she thought.

But here was this reporter talking about a bill about to become law that would put the woman in charge. *Yes, I like that. You can do that. No, not that, the other thing, more of that.* If Tilda understood it correctly, that's what a young woman could expect; it would be the law.

Her thoughts turned to Tilly. There was so much ahead of her. At fourteen, she was on that cusp where childhood felt close, and yet she was looking forward to the woman she'd become. Tilda knew it was daunting. She could barely remember her own feelings at that age, when boys were both appealing and frightening. And there was so much more. Today girls were told they could be anything—an electrical engineer or a well-educated mom in yoga pants with a doublewide baby stroller. It was called choice, the real accomplishment of the women's liberation movement, or so the story went. There was nothing wrong with choice, but Tilda knew it wasn't that easy and never would be.

The next morning, promptly at ten, Tilda heard the doorbell ring.

"Coming," she called, rising from her chair in the kitchen where she had been reading the paper. She ran her fingers through her hair on the way to the door, hoping to tame errant strands. She was always careful about her appearance in front of her granddaughter, not wanting to look too frumpy or too old. When Tilly was no more than five, she had announced to her grandmother that she loved her even though she had wrinkles.

"Tilly Willy, come in," she said, opening the door, grabbing her granddaughter and waving at Mark, who was in the car waiting to be sure it was okay to take off.

"It's okay, Mark," Tilda called. "I've got her."

"Jeez," said Tilly, pulling away. "I'm not a package from the UPS guy."

"Oh, come here, you. Don't be such a sourpuss." Tilda pulled her granddaughter to her and gave her a big hug. Folding her into her arms, she took in Tilly's shower-gel scent of vanilla and orange, like a Creamsicle. Tilda felt the dark mood that constantly dogged her beginning to lift. This wasn't joy, but it was as close as she could come.

Tilly let her grandmother hold her for a second, even hugging back a little, but then she pulled away. In the living room, she plopped down on her grandmother's white downy sofa with a defiant thud. She began to pull her phone and earbuds out of the little bag she had slung across one shoulder and over her body. Tilda gave her a look as if to say, *Do you have to?* Tilly put them back and closed the bag.

Tilda stood above her, taking a moment to admire her granddaughter. All arms and legs and lithe, she had a dancer's body. Her blonde hair was pulled back into a ponytail, accentuating her hazel, almost green eyes. Now an inch or two taller than Tilda, Tilly had inherited her height from her father, but she had her grandmother's eyes and hair.

"And another thing. I'm not Tilly anymore," she said, crossing her arms over her blue plaid shirt.

"What do you mean, you're not Tilly anymore?" Tilda was laughing, but she was also gearing up to be a little hurt. She liked that Tilly was named after her. There had been some confusion after her birth. When considering names, Laura wasn't sure it was customary in the Jewish faith to name a child after a living relative, but Harold, plugging for his wife's name, reminded her that his family was Sephardic and that to the Sephardic Jews, it was an honor to name a child after a relative, living or dead. Laura herself had been named after her paternal grandmother's family name, *Lara*, and after that Laura embraced the idea.

"No offense, Grandma, but Tilly is a terrible name for a kid my age. Too many words rhyme with Tilly: *silly* or *chilly* or *pilly* or *killy* . . ."

"*Killy* isn't even a word," said Tilda, settling into the upholstered chair across from her.

"And you call me Tilly Willy. See what I mean? It's a dumb name. I want to be called Harper."

"Harper? No one in our family is named Harper."

Tilly sat up and turned to Tilda. "See, that's it, right there. Why does a name have to come from someone else in the family? I just like Harper." She settled back down into the sofa, pulling the nearest throw pillow close to her chest and crossing her arms over it.

Tilda smiled and said, "Okay. I see, I guess, but can I tell you a little bit about how you got your name? You don't have to change your mind, but you might find it interesting, to know the history."

Storytelling was Harold's domain, not Tilda's, and, more to the point, her family was adamant about keeping a tightly pulled curtain over their history. No window into the past for them. "We're Americans now," her parents repeated. "Nothing good comes from rehashing the past." In fact, it was painful trying to drag information from her mother or her father, as though some bond with the dead would be broken if they said too much.

"I'm Tilly because you're Matilde, and I was named after you."

Tilda couldn't help but notice how glumly her granddaughter and namesake recounted this truth.

"Well, yes, but there's more to it." Tilda waited to see if there might be a reaction, but Tilly only looked at her with eyebrows slightly raised, as if to dare her grandmother to say something she might find remotely redeeming about her ill-gotten name.

"Have you ever heard the song 'Waltzing Matilda'?"

Tilly frowned, pulled her lips to one side, and shrugged.

"Well, my mother loved that song, so my mother named me Matilde, even though no one in our family had that name."

"That's it? That's the story, Grandma?" Tilly threw the pillow aside. "Okay, let's go to the mall."

Tilda ignored her. "My mother loved the song because her mother loved it. It was popular with the soldiers during the First World War, 'the war to end all wars,' only of course it wasn't."

Tilda looked at her granddaughter to see if she still had her attention. Tilly may have been thinking about chicken wings and ranch dressing, her favorite at the food court, but she seemed to be listening, so Tilda went on.

"Grandpa was Portuguese, but my family's Italian, so my name—and yours—the one on your birth certificate—is spelled M-a-t-i-l-d-e. That's the Italian variant of the name. The name in the song is spelled with an *a* at the end, like in Saint Matilda, which is Germanic. I should probably be Tild*e*, but I've always been Tild*a*, and you're Tilly." Tilda smiled at her granddaughter, hoping she would be amused by this plunge into etymology.

Now Tilly was clearly sighing and rolling her eyes.

"Grandma, it's Saturday, not English class."

"Okay, kiddo—you're right. I'm not your grandpa when it comes to storytelling. Let's get going."

◌◟◞◌

In the car on the way to Stamford on I-95, Tilly, who had been quiet, asked, "What was your name when you were growing up? What did the kids at school call you?"

Tilda stole a glance at her granddaughter, not believing she was interested in the subject, yet here she was, bringing it up again.

Looking back at the road in front of her, she replied, "First, I've always been Tilda, but by the time I was in junior high, I was Bones, even to my friends."

"Bones. That's terrible, Grandma," said Tilly. "I'd hate it if my friends, or anyone, actually, called me that. But I do get teased for being skinny. The boys at school call me Tic Tac sometimes, but I don't care." She lifted her chin as she looked out the window. "They're such a pain."

"Are they a pain? Really? You're not interested in boys?" Tilda asked, feeling as though she were skating on verbal ice that might crack at any moment.

"I don't know, Grandma. Can we talk about something

else?" Tilly began shifting uncomfortably in her seat, tugging on her shoulder strap, as though it were too tight. Tilda thought that was the end of the conversation, but then Tilly continued.

"I don't know about boys, about liking them, I mean. But they don't like me, that's for sure."

"How do you know? What makes you say that?"

"They make fun of me. I look like a boy. That means I don't have boobs. That's what Tic Tac means, no boobs. They're a pain, boys. That's all. That's what I mean." Tilly turned to look out the window again.

"Is there anything else you want to tell me?"

"No, Grandma. I don't want to . . . I mean, there's nothing else to say."

"You know you're still growing, right? You know you're not through developing."

"There's nothing more to say, honestly," said Tilly.

Tilda was pretty sure that wasn't true, but she knew not to push her granddaughter. Laura had always talked about whatever was on her mind at that age, but Tilly was different. She talked when she wanted to let you in, but she could and would just as easily shut you out.

As they neared their exit, Tilda said, "My maiden name was Marrone. Did you know that? Pronounced as though it had an *i* on the end, so the way I got to be Bones was that at first I was Bony Moronie. Have you ever heard of Bony Moronie?"

"Um, yeah. Grandpa had an old record of it."

"Wow. Good memory, Tilly."

Harold had an extensive collection of old albums and 45s. He and Tilly used to go through them for hours. Tilda found it hard to believe a young girl like Tilly would be interested in Harold's "oldies but goodies." But there she was with Harold as he took his old Jensen out of the closet, and he'd let Tilly put the yellow disks in the 45s so they could listen to his singles. She seemed to be fascinated by the cumbersome process and the old machine.

"Yeah, Grandpa told me about it. Now I remember. He

said it was your nickname, but I never thought about it as being something the kids called you to be mean, about you being skinny."

"Well, it didn't bother me so much," said Tilda. "Grandpa had all those old rock-and-roll songs. He liked 'Bony Moronie' even before he knew it was my nickname, but once he found that out, he couldn't stop playing it, over and over, every time we were together at his place before we were married.

Tilda saw Tilly looking at her out of the corner of her eye.

"You used to go to Grandpa's when you were dating? Wasn't that . . ."

"It was the '60s, Tilly. You know about the '60s, right?"

"Oh, yeah, 'drugs, sex, and rock and roll.'"

"Well, drugs, not so much."

"Grandma. You're shocking me."

"Okay, okay," said Tilda. "Anyway, Grandpa used to call me Bony Moronie all the time. Still does . . ." Tilda caught herself in one of those familiar moments when, for her, Harold was still very much alive.

"Still did, I mean, until recently," she said, correcting herself. "Oh, there's the exit," she said, swerving a little too quickly into the exit lane.

Tilly was silent as they got off the highway and continued on toward the mall.

When they got out of the car, she grabbed her grandmother's hand, something she never did anymore, not since she'd become a teenager, anyway.

"Thanks, Grandma," said Tilly, "for our talk and all that stuff about your name. It was pretty interesting." Then, spying a few teenagers heading for the entrance not far from them, she quickly dropped Tilda's hand.

A few minutes later, as they walked toward the dance store, Tilly said, "Will you think about it, Grandma? About Harper, I mean? I may need your help when I talk to Mom. I'm thinking about legally changing my name."

Tilda agreed to think about it, but that was all.

After a successful spree at the Barre Store, the duo decided it was time to eat. Tilda decided on salad and Tilly, wings. They sat down at a table at the food court. When Tilly pushed up her sleeves to eat, Tilda saw it. The red scratches on her left arm. She thought she saw a dim rendering of a word, but she couldn't make it out. Laura never described it, just said it was a scratch. Her heart pounding, she knew it would be a mistake to act impulsively, and yet, in that instant, she decided on the direct approach, not for any sound psychological reason, but because she was alarmed.

She reached over and held Tilly's exposed arm. "What's that, Tilly?" she asked, sounding less calm than she had hoped. "Did you . . . is that a word? Were you trying to . . ."

Tilly immediately pulled her arm away.

"Grandma, stop," she said, loudly enough to draw attention from an elderly couple at a nearby table.

Tilda let go. "I'm sorry," she said, waiting to see what Tilly might say next.

But Tilly didn't say anything. Instead she rewrapped her wings, put them back in the carton, and stood up. "Can we go, please? I want to go."

Tilly wasn't one for drama, but she was visibly upset.

"Okay, let's go then," said Tilda, looking through her bag for her keys while her granddaughter stood above her impatiently.

They rode home in silence, all the way to the driveway, and then Tilly said, "Don't come in, Grandma. I'll just tell Mom you had to get home."

Tilda shook her head and started to open the door. "It's okay, Tilly, I won't say anything. Honestly, I don't even know what I would say."

Tilly reached over to take Tilda's hand from the door. "Please," she said. "I don't want to talk. I just want to go in myself."

Tilda took a deep breath. "Okay, but your mother is going to know something is up, and then she's going to call me, and then we'll talk. I just want you to know that."

"Sure. Fine." Tilly gathered up her packages, and, before getting out, she quickly said, "Thanks, Grandma. For the stuff, I mean."

At home, Tilda poured herself a glass of wine and sat on the porch in Harold's chair. The dark mood had settled in with her again. When the phone rang, she decided to let it go if it was Laura. She couldn't face a call with her daughter right now, even though she had questions of her own to ask. She glanced over to see who it was, and when she saw it was Bev, she answered, relieved to know she could unburden herself with her old friend.

"So on top of everything I feel like an idiot for thinking I could just waltz right in and get her to confide in me. Instead I made a mess of it, but when I saw the cut into her skin I wanted to scream. I couldn't control myself." Tilda was relieved to be admitting not only to mission failure—not getting any information out of Tilly—but to a worse grievance, hubris. She had to admit, she was proud thinking that Tilly would tell her what she wouldn't tell her own mother.

"What's wrong with me? There's a real problem here, and I'm patting myself on the back about what a great grandmother I must be."

"Okay, enough," said Bev, who had known Tilda for so many years the two were more like sisters than friends. "All you did was show your real concern. If anything, your reaction proved to Tilly she was messing around with serious stuff."

"That's true, but how do I know she won't go entirely underground where her family is concerned, me included? At least before she was talking to her mom. Now she may not talk to anyone, and that will be my fault."

"Will you please stop blaming yourself?" Bev hardly got the words out before Tilda interrupted.

"There was a word spelled out, I think. The scratches were pretty shallow, and they could've been made with a safety pin, but still they were deep enough and red enough to spell out a word."

"A word? Are you sure? That sounds different from cutting. I thought cutting meant deeper cuts, done a lot, like, repeatedly."

"I don't know—I'm not sure. And that's another thing. When Laura first told me what Tilly was doing, I was so sure of myself, like I knew all about it, but I don't know anything. I didn't even tell Laura that Tilly should see someone when she was thinking about counseling."

"Okay, I see where this is going," said Bev. "No matter what I say, your comeback is to dig yourself into a deeper hole, a guilt hole."

Tilda sighed. "You're right. I've got to call Laura. I don't want to, but she needs to hear from me what happened."

"That's not even what I was saying, but yeah, you should probably call her. But before you do, take a minute to give yourself a break."

It took Tilda another hour or so to gather the resolve to call her daughter, but Laura called first, and the two talked through the whole food-court episode.

"I think I saw . . ." Tilda paused to gather courage. "Did you see anything besides the scratches on Tilly's arm? I think I saw a word, like she was trying to write something."

Laura was stunned. "A word?" she asked. "What word?"

They discussed it further but came to no revelations, and after they hung up, Tilda was left wondering if she had seen anything written on the inside of that pale, soft arm. She wanted to forget the whole thing. Let it be morning again, before the doorbell rang, when Tilly was just a taller, ganglier version of the darling little girl she had always been.

Tilda had special memories of her granddaughter that

she returned to over and over as she contemplated the miracle of her growing up. She saw her at three pushing her little plastic lawnmower all over the carpet, again and again, until she was sure she had mowed every strand. She saw her at two, in the picture on the change-of-address postcard that Laura sent out. Tilly in a red, pink, and orange wool cap kissing Mark as the snow coming down over them looked like magic dust. She saw her in backward time, when she was just born, swaddled in pink in her hospital bassinet, before the years could bruise her, hurt her—cut her.

Chapter Three

SO FELL EXCALIBUR

〜ⱷ〜

Tilda's reaction to the death of Excalibur, the rescue dog euthanized in Spain for fear he might transmit the Ebola virus, took her by surprise. She was undone. Alone in her office, she read the news online, sinking her head into her hands. With long, racking sobs she could not control, her rational self told her this response was beyond all reasonable proportion. *I know*, she replied to the rational voice, *but it's overwhelming, such unnecessary death and cruelty.* But for Tilda, the Ebola crisis, with its horrific and terrible deaths and the irresponsible and fear-mongering reporting, all seemed to be mixed up with the fate of this poor animal. She allowed herself this vulnerability. It was all right, she reasoned, to give in to this. *I'm crying for the dog, yes, and for the victims of this horror, but also, I must admit, for Harold and for me.*

She had steadfastly refused to give in to her most wrenching sadness, choosing instead to "stay busy," so this relenting was unusual. When Laura and friends inquired after her, she answered with, "I manage to stay busy." And she did, volunteering at the food pantry, reading, walking on the beach, keeping up with her family, even the occasional lunch date with friends. Crying and grief were so painful to her she tried to avoid them. The nights were the worst. She had given up trying to sleep, and her night prowling—walking around the house aimlessly, eating, trying to read or watch late-night TV—was beginning to feel ghoulish, like the goings-on of the undead. Lately Tylenol PM was doing the trick, but for how long? She had declined when Dr. Willis offered to help soon after Harold died. "I can prescribe something to help with sleep," he had said. "Nothing too strong, just to help you relax, so you can get your rest." But she had said no.

Her eyes fell on a photograph on the far end of her desk, almost hidden behind the green-and-blue ceramic bowl Tilly had made in the third grade. The photo was of Tilda, Harold, and Bully, their exuberant black Lab named after Theodore Roosevelt, taken at the beach almost ten years ago now. They asked a passing stranger to snap the shot. Taken in winter, when dogs are allowed at the Water Haven beach, fresh white snow is mingling with gray sand. Tilda and Harold are sitting on a bench, Bully on the ground between them with a big smile on his face. It was definitely a smile, Harold always said. "You can just see how happy he is." And Tilda had to admit, Bully always seemed to be smiling.

Bully, a rescue, loved being off-leash, running with the other dogs in and out of the frigid water. But his favorite thing was playing Frisbee with Harold. Bully never missed, jumping so high onlookers at the beach often gasped. Strangers called him Frisbee, and, indeed, at home, that was his nickname, that and TR. Tilda and Harold, usually reserved in company about the special attributes of their dog, were shameless at home, calling him "genius dog" because he seemed to understand their every word. If one of them said, "We're not going out right now," Bully would lower his ears and walk back into the bedroom and curl up on his bed. If either asked, "Do you want to eat dinner?" Bully would circle them excitedly and rush into the kitchen, skidding to a halt right in front of his bowl, sitting, waiting for the pleasure beyond all, mealtime.

But Bully's most endearing quality, Tilda and Harold both agreed, was his appreciation for having been rescued. They bestowed upon him their belief that he had this special knowledge—that he had been saved by two senior citizens who were committed to making this lost and forsaken mature black dog the center of their lives. And aside from Tilly, he was.

For a while it appeared the three of them were growing old together, but then Bully outpaced Tilda and Harold. In his geriatric years, Tilda "seniorized" the house for him, putting down pads for accidents and multiple beds for his ever-increasing naps. She cooked rice and boiled chicken as his digestion grew more delicate, finally pureeing his food. Bully, ever the good-natured fellow, died quietly one morning several hours after not getting up for breakfast. Tilda and Harold, realizing a missed meal was significant, had stayed by his side all morning, petting him and telling stories about his wondrous deeds and good, sweet nature. When he took his last breath, they sat longer, cried and consoled one another, and told more stories before calling the vet about what to do.

Tilda and Harold buried his urn in the backyard near Tilda's roses. Tilda later added a little marble marker that read, *Bully, An amiable dog, born c. 1997. Died August 13, 2010.* So of course she cried when she heard news of Excalibur's death. When Bully died, Harold had been there to console her. Who was going to console her now, to soften the blows of an often cruel and senseless world?

⟞ ⟝

It had been several weeks since the Fucking Mall Misadventure, as Tilda referred to it to no one but herself. In the meantime, she held her breath, hoping there would be no further cutting incidents. Maybe Tilly was over this particular type of adolescent malaise. Maybe the cutting had been a one-off kind of thing, experimentation, done and over. The other possibility was not as reassuring, that Tilda was no longer a part of the family inner circle, no longer to be consulted on this or other growing pains, by Laura or by Tilly, who had been ignoring her grandmother since that awful afternoon. Tilda was hurt by this, but she was trying to be patient, knowing as she did about teenage mood swings, having seen more than one of Tilly's in the past.

To fill in the gap, Tilda began following Tilly's every move on Instagram. She had become a follower several years ago, when Tilly first started posting. At that time Tilly was happy to have as many followers as possible, even her grandmother. At first Tilda joined in the fun, "liking" this or that post—even occasionally commenting. As time went on, though, her involvement lessened. She began to observe but not participate, wanting to get the uncensored straight scoop, hoping that Tilly would forget she was even there. That seemed to work, and so Tilda would dip in once or twice a month to see what her granddaughter was up to.

But since the mall incident, Tilda had become what could only be described as an online stalker. If she was online paying bills, answering emails, or googling the title of a new book, she'd first go to Instagram, seeing what Tilly was posting—and Tilda was doing this once or twice a day. She was compelled to peek, telling herself it was all right to snoop in this way. She couldn't help but be worried; it was her granddaughter, after all.

Fortunately, on this fall afternoon, her worries seemed misplaced. Tilly's latest posts were selfies with smiles, shots of friends at dance-team practice, and photos of Tilly with friends at the movies. Feeling relieved, she closed her laptop at the same time the doorbell rang. She rose from her chair and went to the front door. Leaning in to look through the peephole, she saw Darren Esmond, Amanda's husband, glancing over his shoulder toward his house and straightening the collar of his rather wrinkled plaid shirt. Tilda opened the door.

"Hi, Darren, come in. Everything okay?" she asked.

"I'm sorry to bother you," Darren said, stepping inside, "but I have some business to take care of, and I was wondering if Lizzie could call you in case she needs anything. She's okay to stay home alone for a little while. I'd like to let her know you'll be around, just in case. She's getting a ride home from school and should be here in a little while."

Lizzie was Amanda and Darren's fourteen-year-old daughter and a friend of Tilly's. "Of course, Darren, and tell her she can come over any time when she gets home. She doesn't have to stay alone." Tilda motioned him to sit down on the sofa in the living room.

Darren sat but seemed anxious, on the edge of the seat, his elbows on his knees. He lowered his head. "Thanks," he said.

"Is everything okay?" she asked again, increasingly aware that things were not. Darren bore a strong resemblance to a young Jeff Bridges and was generally unflappable in a quiet, unassuming way. She saw him every morning climb into his truck, and most days he was home by five, though sometimes he came home late, seemingly doing whatever it took to bring the job in on time and within budget. "That's why he's a successful contractor. You can count on him. That's his reputation," Harold often said of Darren after one of their many "over-the-fence" conversations. Harold and Tilda hadn't been close with the Esmonds, but Harold and Darren seemed to like one another, and Harold respected him. Today as Darren sat in Tilda's living room, staring at the floor, shoulders rounded, hands now rubbing his jeans, it was clear something was up.

"It's Amanda. She's gone."

"Gone?" asked Tilda. "What do you mean? Where?"

"Well," answered Darren, meeting Tilda's gaze before turning away. "That's a hard question to answer. She left a note—just for me. I know she didn't want Lizzie to find it."

Tilda thought this was the preamble to a more revealing explanation, but Darren paused, as though he didn't know what to say next.

"It's personal, Mrs. Carr . . . Tilda." The *Mrs. Carr* was the tip-off. Although they'd been neighbors since Lizzie was a baby, Tilda was still Mrs. Carr to him. No wonder he was having trouble talking to her about something "personal."

Tilda could surmise what was going on, and that would have to be enough. Darren was not giving anything more away. If Harold had been there, she would have left the two of them to talk, but, without Harold, it was up to her.

"Of course, Darren. Do what you need to do, and take your time. If it gets late, I'll have Lizzie come for dinner, or, better yet, I'll take her out for a bite. Don't worry."

Darren got up and put out his hand. "Thanks, Tilda. I'll try not to be too long," he said, heading for the door.

Before he left, Tilda lightly put her hand on his arm. "Darren, these things, they take a while sometimes to work themselves out. Try not to worry."

Darren looked at Tilda before gently moving his arm away from her. "It's not that simple, but thanks." As he walked outside, he turned and said, "Look, I'm sorry I can't talk about it, but I appreciate your help. Oh, and Lizzie has my cell phone number if you need me."

⌒~ᘒᘒ

Tilda busied herself watering the begonias on the back porch, passing time until she would call Lizzie and invite her over. Now that Mark had put the storms up, the begonias would be comfortable during the cold months ahead. After adjusting the fluorescent light over the top of her euphorbias, she dug her finger into the soil to be sure she hadn't overwatered. Thinking about her conversation with Darren, she remembered the last time she had spoken with Amanda. It was just after the mall episode with Tilly, in fact. Amanda waved Tilda down as she was backing out of the driveway the following Monday morning. Rushing over, she wrapped one arm around her body, keeping her light robe in place, and with her free hand motioned for Tilda to lower her window.

She seemed a little frantic and rushed for time, Tilda recalled now, as she waited for the window to open. She'd brushed her unruly auburn hair back away from her face and asked if Tilda had a five-dollar bill she could borrow. "It has to be a five, exactly," she explained. "It's for Lizzie. They have a field trip today and they need not only the exact amount, but only one bill. Of course she just told me today."

"Of course," answered Tilda, rummaging through her bag. "Where are they going?"

Amanda looked puzzled. "Um, I guess I don't know. We're so rushed. She only told me about the money, and now she might miss the bus."

Taking her cue, Tilda quickly passed the money through the window. Amanda grabbed it with a barely audible thank-you and turned toward her house. "I'll pay you back later." But she hadn't paid it back yet, Tilda suddenly remembered.

The incident of the five-dollar bill was very typical of other Amanda moments, so she hadn't thought much of it. She was always in a rush, it seemed to Tilda, never giving herself enough time to make it through the day without just narrowly getting by. It was behavior that Tilda found hard to understand, having spent her working years in the classroom, where promptness and planning were necessities. But there was something else about Amanda. Her haphazard life seemed emblematic of her dissatisfaction in general.

Unlike Laura, Amanda didn't hover over Lizzie. In fact, just the opposite. She seemed not to know what was going on in her daughter's life. There was always the rush out the door in the mornings to make it to school on time and the last-minute dash to the store for supplies for whatever school project Amanda didn't know was due. Darren always seemed in the background of whatever chaos was going on around him. Tilda never made much of any of this, observing from the safe distance of next-door-neighbor behavior, polite but not involved.

But now, after her conversation with Darren, she began putting pieces together in a different pattern. There was the time Tilda was leaving the house and saw Amada carrying an easel and several shopping bags. She stopped just long enough to set her things down inside the front door and to walk over to Tilda to catch up for a minute as they sometimes did. Waving an arm toward the house, Amanda said she was finally getting back into her painting, something she had set aside years ago when Lizzie was born and they had left the city to move into the "burbs," as she called their neighborhood in Connecticut. She had said it so wistfully that Tilda had imagined her pining over her lost life as an artist in the making.

"What kind of painting?" Tilda had asked.

"Oh, oils. Abstract expressionism. The stuff that is out of style today, it seems, unless you're Jasper Johns or someone else famous. I did drip painting. Are you familiar with that type of art?"

Tilda thought immediately of Jackson Pollock's huge canvases and the impressiveness of his technique although she was never quite sure what to make of it. But she had fallen under the spell of *Autumn Rhythm* when she saw it at an exhibit in the city years ago.

"Yes, I know his work," she answered. "It's intriguing, isn't it? Where did you study, Amanda?" A not-quite-innocent question, she knew, designed to find out if Amanda had a serious background or if she just splattered paint around on canvas.

"The Art Students League for a while. I had a studio not far from there. Well, several of us did. We shared. It was a great time."

Now Tilda set the watering can down on the shelf next to the begonias and wondered if Amanda's disappearance was in any way related to her desire to reclaim her art. At first Tilda thought maybe it was another man, but now she thought this seemed more likely—that Amanda's disappearance surely had to do with her need to find a room of her own, to pursue a long-dormant dream.

It wasn't unusual for women in their forties to begin questioning their decisions, wondering if they had closed doors prematurely. In Tilda's day the prospect had been raised repeatedly in popular culture. Then it was about women needing to "find themselves." Tilda was part of the conversation, certainly with Bev after seeing movies like *An Unmarried Woman* and *Kramer vs. Kramer*, great movies, they both thought, but Tilda never needed to find herself. She was content with her life, with Harold and Laura, her teaching job. She was a feminist, but she never felt the need to leave home, to escape as apparently Amanda had done.

Tilda looked at her watch and decided it was time to check in on Lizzie.

At first Lizzie was reluctant to leave whatever it was she doing at home to come over, and Tilda could understand that. At fourteen, she was probably still a little thrilled that she was old enough to be left at home alone, if only for a little while. Certainly that was true of Tilly. But as the evening wore on, Darren still wasn't home, so Tilda called again, luring her with the promise of homemade mac and cheese and chocolate chip cookies. This was the meal Tilly usually wanted when she came over for dinner. Tilda would slip in a little serving of green beans and salad to add some nutritional color to the steady diet of white and brown food most kids Tilly's age seemed to crave.

Sitting at the kitchen table, happily eating a second serving of macaroni, Lizzie bore little resemblance to Tilda's granddaughter. Lizzie wore distinctly un-skinny jeans, apparently oblivious to the latest in teen fashion. She wore baggy green cords and a bulky white sweater that Tilda, no expert on such matters, was nevertheless pretty certain she hadn't seen since the '80s. Lizzie's long brown hair hung loosely over her shoulders, one side pulled back with a bobby pin so she could eat without getting hair in her mouth. Tilda was sure she was not on the A-list at school, but there was something charming about her. She seemed completely at ease.

"I'm surprised Dad hasn't called in a while," she said, reaching for a cookie.

Tilda poured her a glass of milk and said, "Well, I'm sure he'll be here soon. We could play Scrabble if you'd like, when you've finished eating."

"Sure. I may be here longer than you think, Mrs. Carr. I think Mom has taken off."

Tilda nearly spilled the milk before putting it on the table in front of Lizzie. She pulled out a chair, the dragging noise on the wood amplified as her senses perked up.

"Taken off? Lizzie, what do you mean?" She sat down across from her.

Lizzie lifted her napkin and wiped her mouth slowly. "Well, I guess it's okay to say, but Mom was acting kind of funny this morning at breakfast, and then she gave me an extra hug when she dropped me off at school, like it was a special good-bye."

Tilda wasn't sure if she was more amazed by Lizzie's calm retelling of her mother's "taking off" or by what she was actually saying. "But where would she have gone? She wouldn't just leave you and your father."

"Honestly, I'm not too worried. Mom is, well, you have to know her. She's not like other mothers. She likes to follow her bliss. That's what she says everyone should do. But the funny thing is, I guess she hasn't really followed hers, until now, I mean."

Tilda, suddenly aware that her mouth had dropped open, closed it so suddenly she heard a little snap. Torn between wanting to learn more and taking Lizzie in her arms, she realized that the girl was not in need of comforting.

"It's her art. She tries to paint, but there's always something stopping her. She blames it on all the stuff she has to do, but I think she's afraid she can't anymore—I mean, artistically—like maybe she's lost her vision or something. So I think maybe she had to go to figure this out. It might be scary for her, too, you know?"

Tilda leaned back in her chair, scratching the back of her head. "Well, no, Lizzie, I don't think I do know what you mean. But if your mother has purposely left you and your father, aren't you . . . doesn't that bother you?"

Lizzie moved her mouth from side to side, her eyes on the plate in front of her, and thought about this for a minute before looking up at Tilda. "No, not really. I mean, I hope she finds what she's looking for, but I think she's doing what she thinks she needs to do. And besides, I know she loves us, Dad and me, and I know she'll come home when she's ready."

Tilda was up from her chair now, leaning over to hug Lizzie before she knew what she was doing. Lizzie was undaunted. She allowed herself to be embraced and then gave Tilda a little pat on the back.

"It's okay, Mrs. Carr, really. It's Dad I'm more worried about."

Chapter Four

CLOSER YET I APPROACH YOU

∾

"You've got to love her," Tilda said to Bev on the phone the next day, after the mac-and-cheese dinner with Lizzie. "She's like this wise old soul in a fourteen-year-old body. There I was, worried about her being completely in the dark about Amanda, and yet there she was with her finger right on the pulse of what was going on with her mother, and completely accepting, by the way. The only person she's worried about? Her dad. And why? Well, apparently, he isn't as together as his teenage daughter. It's a riot," she concluded, and then added, "If it weren't so sad, really."

"Yes, it is sad," Bev said. "She's still a child, after all, no matter how together she may appear, and that's not right. But men disappear all the time, and while it's terrible and all, when a woman does it, it's considered far worse. 'How can she abandon her child like that?' Isn't it just as bad when a man takes off? Anyway, she's not the first woman who left home to find herself. Remember *Kramer vs. Kramer*?"

"Yes, of course I do, but we don't know for sure that's what's happened. Probably, though."

"And no doubt there's a man involved. What is she, early, midforties? You know . . . the flame that's about to go out is the flame that burns brightest, premenopause and all that. It's all hormonal, anyway."

"Oh, God, Bev, you're so cynical."

"I'm not cynical. I've lived through it, and so have you. But ultimately, these are the problems of the privileged. No one is starving or wondering where they will sleep tonight. No one is sick or dying without insurance."

"Well, yes, but . . . well, you're right." Tilda realized she would get nowhere trying to convince Bev this wasn't about class struggle, the prism through which Bev saw most things. While Tilda and Harold were having a grand time in the '60s, Bev was out marching, licking envelopes, and passing out flyers on street corners about the pressing issues of the day. Whether it was the war in Vietnam, the war on poverty, racial inequality, women's rights, anti-nukes, or world peace, Bev was there, inexhaustibly there.

For a few years she had been happily married to Dave, Harold's old college buddy, until "radical feminism" (Dave's label for their problems) came between them. Dave wanted a family and a "normal" life. Bev, raven-haired and sleek, had stopped shaving her legs and had begun wearing long, shapeless dresses with clunky sandals. Her abandonment of feminine cultural norms—emblematic of how politicized his previously chic wife had become—was all he could see.

Dave grew depressed. They divorced. When he remarried within a year, Bev never looked back, and though she never remarried, she did have her flings. Bev and Tilda remained friends through it all, and Tilda admired Bev, knowing she could never match her friend's resolve and commitment. And yet, she never wanted more than what she had, her life with Harold.

Now with back problems, exacerbated by weight and arthritis, Bev limited her volunteerism to phone calls. Recently she'd been trying to secure microloans for women in the Democratic Republic of the Congo.

"Besides," continued Bev, "why are you becoming so involved? I mean, it's better than having you moping around, no offense, but this is out of character for you."

"Thanks for your compassion," Tilda replied, unfazed by her friend's directness. Their bluntness—and sarcasm—back and forth with one another was one of the most cherished features of their relationship, a habit of long-standing. "Maybe it's because of Lizzie. She really got to me. And Darren, good grief. He's so lost. I agree with Lizzie; I'd be worried about him, too."

"Hmm. When's the last time you talked to Tilly, or Laura?"

"I haven't talked to Tilly since the mall, over two weeks ago now. I think she's ignoring me. Well, she's more than ignoring me. She's pretty much shutting me out, but I haven't said anything yet—to her or to Laura."

Tilda paused and looked out the window toward her rose bushes, now bare.

"I have to admit, it bothers me. But I have to give her some time, probably. Whatever is bothering her, she's holding it against me for prying, I guess. But Laura? I talk to her almost every day, although not that much about Tilly."

Bev was silent.

"Why are you asking me about my conversations with Tilly and Laura?" Tilda asked. "Do you think I'm sublimating with another family because my own has disowned me for being so insensitive to my only granddaughter's serious issues?"

Tilda was reaching for some dry humor, but the squeezing in her chest told her she hadn't hit her mark. Just talking about Tilly let her know how much she missed her.

"I wouldn't go that far, but you may have a point, except for the insensitive part. You were being a grandmother—a loving, concerned one at that."

"Thanks for the vote of confidence. And anyway, I'm not overly involved with Darren and Lizzie. I just had Lizzie over for dinner, that's all. And Darren called this morning thanking me for yesterday. He didn't get back last night until after ten.

He didn't say, but I don't think he found out anything about Amanda's whereabouts."

"Okay, enough about your neighbors," Bev interrupted. "Listen, have you heard anything about the new movie at the Quad on the women's movement? I saw a review yesterday in the *Times*. It looks pretty interesting. I can't believe Gloria Steinem is eighty. Should we go? What do you think?"

Tilda's first impulse was to say no, her reflex reaction to anything that took her astray from home. She hadn't thought herself ready for fun with friends, but then maybe going into the city with Bev wasn't such a bad idea. She and Bev hadn't had a day together in a long time.

"That would be okay, I guess," she said. They decided on the day, and since Bev lived in the Village, not far from the theater, they agreed to meet for lunch before the movie at a restaurant Bev liked. "It's Italian vegetarian, if you can believe it, but it's actually quite good. Good seafood, too, so it's not actually vegetarian."

It was chilly but clear the day they met up for the movie. The week since their phone call had passed quickly. During that time, when she wasn't thinking about Tilly, Tilda fretted about her decision to join Bev on this no doubt ill-conceived venture. She wondered if she would be too gloomy to be good company. She hated pity, even though she knew Bev wasn't the pitying kind. She worried about the weather; what if it was terrible? What would she wear? What would still fit, after her "widow's weight loss"? (There actually was such a term.) She had lost ten pounds within a few weeks after Harold died, and even though she was slowly regaining it, her clothes still hung on her, so much so that she was careful, especially around Laura, to always wear several layers with extra-full scarves that she looped around her neck and then let flow around her.

But when the day arrived, there was no need to worry about the weather: the sun was shining, and it wasn't too cold. Just a light jacket would do. No coats, scarves, or gloves would be required. She hoped Bev wouldn't notice or comment on her weight. She simply wanted to enjoy the day.

Walking to the train from her home, Tilda took in the fresh air, realizing how much of life she had been missing. On the train, instead of reading, she sat by the window and watched the towns and trees passing by. When the train made its stops along the way, Tilda eagerly looked into the faces of strangers boarding, feeling a little like a shut-in who had recently reentered the world. In fact, she thought, that's what she was, with the exception of several outings with Laura and the fucking mall misadventure with Tilly.

When the train pulled into Grand Central, Tilda decided she would take a taxi rather than deal with mass transportation. Today—her first real venture out—she didn't want anything to disturb her sense of calm enjoyment. And she was enjoying herself. A strange but welcome feeling.

After paying the driver, as she was getting out of the cab, Tilda caught a glimpse of an auburn-haired woman across the street. She was wearing a long dark green wool sweater, black leggings, and black ankle-length boots. The clothes and the hair, the look of the woman, were so familiar. Just then the woman turned into a storefront that looked like an art gallery. Tilda stopped and tried to shield her eyes from the glare, but she had lost sight of the woman, and she couldn't make out the wording on the window. Had she just seen Amanda go into an art gallery? She felt in her bones it was true, but she couldn't be sure. She heard someone calling her name. Tilda turned and saw Bev in front of the restaurant, waving her arms.

At Tilda's insistence, they took a table by the window. All through lunch Tilda kept looking out the window and across the street. Finally, Bev put her glass of pinot grigio down with a decided thud. "What is so interesting out there?" she asked.

Tilda turned her attention back to Bev. She had been

staring out the window into the bright light of day, and now she had to wait for her vision to readjust to the darker room before she could see the frown on Bev's face.

"Was I staring . . . out there?" she said evasively. "I guess I haven't been out much lately, and this is my first trip into the city . . . in a long time." This struck the right balance, she thought. It was true, if not entirely forthright. She didn't want Bev to know the source of her distraction, that she may have seen Amanda, who was still AWOL from husband and daughter after a whole week. Bev already thought she was getting too involved in the plight of her neighbors, so why bring up what was probably an imaginary sighting?

She picked up her glass of wine and commented on the lunch, which was, after all, quite good. She never drank wine during the day, and it was going to her head a bit, but in such a pleasant way that she was thinking about ordering another to go with the rest of her baked sole, something else she never ordered for lunch, but today everything was different. Her senses were alive and she took everything in: the fragrance of the lemon and Italian parsley in the white wine sauce, the crackling sound of the crisp bread as she tore pieces to dip into her plate, and of course the light reflecting on the glass of the storefront across the street, the one thing she kept returning to.

Leaving the restaurant, Tilda wondered if there was time for her to cross over to see if the store was a gallery and if indeed she had seen Amanda, who might still be there. She hadn't seen the auburn-haired woman leave, and she'd been keeping her eye out all through lunch.

"We'd better hurry. We don't have that much time before the movie starts," said Bev, as if she were anticipating Tilda's possible defection.

"You do still want to see the movie, don't you?" asked Bev.

"Yes, of course I do," she replied as they both picked up the pace.

But during the movie Tilda was distracted. Her second glass of wine had left her a little dizzy and drowsy, and she couldn't stop thinking about Amanda. Every so often Tilda's head would bob, and she would drift off, seeing Amanda waving to her from the store across the street. Then she would sit up only to feel Bev's glance in her direction. Tilda would then try to focus on the film. In one frame she saw suffragists in long dresses and big hats from the early 1900s marching for their rights, looking determined and happy. In another, police hauled them off to jail. In one, the camera homed in on a political cartoon of a man with his foot on the back of a fallen suffragist, and the sympathetic caption read, "Where there is no vision, the people perish."

"No shit," Bev muttered under her breath. Tilda looked in her direction and smiled, letting Bev know she was paying attention.

In footage near the end of the film, the members of Pussy Riot, at their punk-rock-protest best, were attacked by Cossack militia members during the Sochi Olympics. "You've come a long way, baby," the announcer intoned somewhat sarcastically, but then she made the point that men and women around the world had supported the feminist rioters. It was all very upbeat, followed by the usual there's-still-work-to-be-done coda.

"Sort of obvious, wasn't it?" said Bev as they left. "I mean, yeah, there's a lot to be done, but as far as I can tell, not much is happening these days." She stopped and looked at her friend. "If you saw enough to form an opinion. You kind of nodded off for a while, didn't you?"

"The second glass of wine. I shouldn't have had it, but I was with you, it, the film. I saw most of it, and yes, it was obvious, but also good, don't you think?"

They stopped for coffee at an old diner nearby to do a debrief of their own, from the '60s to the present day, both wondering where and when the fire had gone out of the movement but agreeing there had been progress.

"The fight now is equal pay for equal work. And don't even get me started on the minimum wage. Unless women are willing to organize, to fight, nothing is going to change," said Bev, ready to launch into the cause currently taking up her remaining volunteer phone time.

Tilda, while sympathetic, decided not to encourage her. "It's been a long day. I'd better think about getting home."

Bev walked Tilda to the corner where she would grab a cab to Grand Central. They hugged good-bye with promises to stay in touch, and Tilda watched as her friend continued on toward home. Instead of a taking a cab, though, she walked in the opposite direction, back a few blocks toward the store where she had first seen the auburn-haired woman.

It was in fact an art gallery. Tilda walked in and began looking around. A young woman in black with matching big-rimmed black eyeglasses and a black asymmetrical haircut asked if she could be of service. Tilda didn't quite know what to say but quickly decided to appear interested in acquiring some artwork.

"I'm looking for the work of an artist I think you have. She may have been here earlier today, a medium to tall woman with thick auburn hair?"

"Oh. No, that's not one of our artists, but there is a woman who looks like that who makes arrangements for one of our clients. Are you looking for the work of Emile Baptiste by any chance, the Saint Lucian artist? He lives in Brooklyn and exhibits in one of our galleries there as well. We have some of his work over here, if you'd like to see, this one hanging," she said, pointing to what appeared to be a color photograph of a nude couple swimming in water of intense clarity. "And here are a few others." She began walking in her stilettos to a far corner of the room, where she began pulling out works of island scenes, dramatically vivid, Tilda thought.

"He's one of the best hyperrealists around. Aren't these striking?"

"They're beautiful, but I thought these were photographs. And the woman I'm looking for is a painter."

"They're paintings, not photographs. And no, Ms. Esmond,

if that's who you mean, is Mr. Baptiste's rep. She may paint as well, but we don't carry her work."

The woman turned sharply and walked back to her desk.

Tilda did not notice the woman's loss of interest. She was focusing on one word, *Esmond*. Tilda had found Amanda. Surely this was more than coincidence. Tilda didn't believe in fate, but what were the odds, she wondered, that she would have found her missing neighbor on her first full day out of the house and into the city since Harold had died? She left the gallery prepared to make a parting comment about the vivid paintings, not photographs, but the woman in black barely looked in her direction as Tilda left. Brooklyn, she thought. She hadn't been there in a long time.

⌒～๑๑

October continued to be mild and pleasant, just as it had been the week before when Tilda and Bev met in the city. Since then, Tilda had started taking long walks in the park, the spice-colored leaves in the sunlight and the riot of the goldenrods tugging at her heart. Harold had never tired of the change in seasons, always calling Tilda to his side to look out the window with him at whatever sign had captured his attention. In spring it was the forsythia, in fall the goldenrods.

Her melancholia persisted but not her depression. Her grief was becoming more a companion to be accommodated than an enemy to be feared. These long walks were both sad and comforting, a distraction from the troubled world she encountered whenever she turned on the news, which was rarely, but one did have to keep up. At least that brave Pakistani schoolgirl had not only survived but had persisted in her fight for education in the face of unspeakable ignorance. Tilda, remembering her teaching days and her dismay when students failed to value their educations, was particularly drawn to Malala Yousafzai's story. And this month she had won the Nobel Peace Prize.

Speaking to Laura, Tilda had said, "Who am I to feel sorry for myself when that child can be shot in the face and then show the world she won't be stopped? It's amazing, isn't it?" Laura had conceded it was, but then she turned the topic to Tilly.

"You need to come by more often, Mom. She's not ignoring you, you know. She's just busy with her life. The longer you stay away, the worse it gets, this impasse."

Tilda felt her chest tighten. She didn't want to make too much of it, but Tilly's rejection was unfounded, she thought, and she could not bear it. The subject upset her, and she struggled not to let it, but here was her heart struggling for space in her chest.

"She may not be ignoring me, exactly, but she has shut me out, don't you think? I mean, she definitely doesn't want to go out or come over anymore, and when I'm there, she finds any excuse to leave the room." The more Tilda thought about it, the worse she felt, but then another thought came to mind. Maybe Tilly wasn't doing so well after all.

"How is she doing, really?" she asked.

"What do you mean? She's fine. I never should have said anything—she's fine. No more incidents, if that's what you mean."

Tilda thought about this. She was relieved to hear it, but not entirely certain that what her daughter said was true. Laura seemed to be treading lightly, not so much hiding information as maybe not wanting to believe anything was wrong—or not knowing.

"I hope you're right," she said.

"I'm right. There's nothing going on, and you need to come over more often."

Tilda agreed, and they settled on Friday night.

"We'll have Shabbat together."

"That would be nice. I'll see you then," said Tilda, hoping it would be, and then she said goodbye.

There were several days remaining before the Friday night dinner. Tilda knew it was useless to argue with Laura. And Tilda had to believe her when she said all was fine. If not, she would have packed Tilly off to counseling by now. Her daughter never saw a problem that couldn't be cured with a little intervention, and her efforts now were directed at getting grandmother and granddaughter together again.

Tilda, on the other hand, didn't have much to do until then, and she hadn't been able to get Brooklyn out of her mind. Ever since she had seen Amanda in the gallery, she knew she would have to go—to see for herself what had become of her neighbor. When she thought of Darren, she became uneasy, wondering if she should let him know what she had uncovered. But she also worried that she might be lifting the lid from something she could not control. Who knew what Amanda was up to—or with whom? She didn't want to be responsible for unleashing a domestic confrontation gone wrong. No, she would find out more before deciding what to do next. That was that, then. She would go to Brooklyn. And why not? She had a right. The weather was good. She needed to get out more, and she hadn't been there in years—to the place where her mother and father had met, married, and started their family. The old family home had been at the juncture of Williamsburg and Greenpoint—not far, it turned out, from the gallery where Emile Baptiste exhibited his work. It was amazing what a little online researching could reveal.

So, she told herself, she had every reason to go—two, actually. And the visit to her old hometown provided cover for the other, if less fully formed, motive—finding Amanda.

❧

The day after the phone call with Laura, Tilda took the train to Grand Central and then the subway to Williamsburg. When the train arrived, she took a moment to get her bearings, and then, as she was coming up the subway stairs into the old neighborhood, she was surprised by, she realized, the *absence* of feeling. There was no sense of coming home. She had told

Laura she would be gone for the day, visiting the place where her parents had lived and where she and her younger sister had been born. And it was true, that's what she was doing. This was the neighborhood where her parents had begun their lives together as a married couple. But she had few memories of the place. Her only pleasure would come from trying to picture her parents walking these streets, but the Italian neighborhood of her parents' time had changed dramatically with trendy shops and assured young people everywhere.

This neighborhood was also very near the street where Emile Baptiste's paintings were exhibited, in a gallery just off Metropolitan Avenue. And that gallery, it was clear, was Tilda's true destination. In the two weeks since Amanda's disappearance, Tilda had continued to make herself available in case Darren and Lizzie needed her. She had prepared dinner for Lizzie several times, and they'd played Scrabble together. Tilda had challenged her use of *za* but had to concede. Lizzie had been right. "It's an accepted shortened form of *pizza*, Mrs. Carr."

"Please call me Tilda," she had responded.

"Okay," said Lizzie, adding up her winning score, "but just *Tilda*, not *Miss Tilda*, the way kids are supposed to say today. I think it's so lame."

"That's fine." But Tilda didn't think it would stick. Lizzie seemed like the kind of kid who would always call adults by their last names.

They didn't talk all that much during these visits, and Lizzie preferred to stay away from the subject of her missing mother, although she still seemed confident her mother was fine, just not wanting yet to be found. Tilda didn't know how she could be so sure, but she found Lizzie's certainty to be reassuring.

A subject she did want to raise with Lizzie was Tilly, but she restrained herself, not wanting to take advantage of her new friendship. Occasionally Lizzie would mention Tilly herself.

"Tilly's in my math class. Did you know that?" she had asked during their last dinner together.

"No, Tilly didn't mention it. She's been so busy with dance and her schoolwork, we haven't had much time to talk." She looked at Lizzie, hoping she would say more.

"Yeah, she is pretty busy—with friends, too. I mean, she hangs out with the whole dance team, and the cheerleading and football people, but she's also friends with the people in black . . . well, that's what I call them."

Lizzie went on to explain that she didn't hang out with either of these groups, her friends being among the vanilla people, another of her own terms, Tilda thought.

"And who are the vanilla people, and who are the people in black?"

"The vanilla people are people like me, sort of bland, I guess. I mean, we don't try to be one way or the other. We're just us. But the people in black are very serious. They dress in dark colors, and some have belly button piercings. Tilly's friend Andrea has one, but not Tilly, I don't think."

Now Tilda began to worry again—not only about Tilly but also about the company she was keeping.

"Is she very serious, Andrea, and Tilly, too?" she ventured.

"Well, I guess, sort of. Maybe sort of artistic, too. Andrea writes poetry."

"Oh, that's kind of serious," said Tilda, relieved.

"Yeah, and it's apocalyptic and weird, actually. And they're anti a lot of stuff, but they like art and culture, too. I can be anti sometimes, actually, but they're way more intense than I am."

Apocalyptic and intense, that can't be good. But just as Tilda was about to go off on a negative tangent, Lizzie countered with a more hopeful observation. "But Tilly hangs out with the dance kids, too, and they're pretty smart. They study a lot."

"Oh, good. Tilly is a good student," Tilda responded.

"Uh-huh."

It went on like this until Lizzie went home. One comment was encouraging, another discouraging, until Tilda figuratively threw up her arms and realized if she wanted reassurance, she would have to go see Tilly for herself.

But for now she was here in Brooklyn, following the directions she had written down before she left home. Turning off Metropolitan Avenue, she took a deep breath and walked, with purpose (not entirely sure what that purpose would lead to) into the Backdoor Gallery. The walls were covered with paintings that looked like photos or photos that looked like paintings, she couldn't tell. But she was sure of the paintings she saw of island scenes, both vibrant and sad, clear-eyed yet conveying a sense of loss, like a lost Eden maybe. These were the same as the ones she had seen in the Village.

A thin woman with angular features and severe bangs began walking toward her. Then Tilda noticed another woman in the far end of the gallery whose back was turned. She was leaning over a table with a canvas stretched out in front of her. When the woman stood up, Tilda saw her toss her auburn hair as if to shake it away from her face in order to get a better view of the image in front of her. The thin woman approached, but before she could say a word, Tilda quickly turned and walked out. It was Amanda—and Tilda couldn't face her.

"Shit," she said, walking briskly away, her sense of purpose gone. "What a chicken shit."

She walked a few blocks before going into a coffee shop, or coffee bar, or whatever they were called in Brooklyn. The shop was full of people in their twenties, men with beards and women with long straight hair, all of them texting or working on computers. She had a hard time trying to imagine her parents in this place. All the black-and-white photographs in all the family albums seemed to have been taken in a distant land, long ago. Not here.

She sat at a corner table in the back facing the wall and waited for her server, or barista, no doubt.

What was she doing here? Seeing her old home? Where her parents had lived? That had been a ruse from the beginning. No, she had come to find Amanda, and when she did, she left. What was that all about?

I found her and I chickened out, afraid she'd be furious with me for butting in. She continued fuming over her behavior until she heard the waitress coming up behind her. Tilda was about to order a cup of coffee—or maybe a double shot of espresso would be better. But when Tilda looked up, it wasn't the waitress. It was Amanda, with a perplexed look on her face.

"What are you doing here?" Amanda asked.

Tilda wondered for a moment if Amanda hadn't seen her earlier. Maybe this was another crazy coincidence. Maybe Amanda just happened in and had never seen Tilda turn and run from the gallery. Then she realized this notion for the fantasy it was.

Tilda felt a surge run through her body from her stomach up to her lungs. Flight. That was what she wanted, not confrontation. Confused and embarrassed, Tilda had nowhere to hide, and Amanda was there, in the coffee shop, wanting an explanation.

In the midst of her embarrassment at being caught snooping, she was suddenly calm. Better own up. Simple as that.

"Please, sit down, Amanda," she said, pulling out a chair.

Over coffee, Tilda tried to answer Amanda's question. "Darren came over and asked me to watch Lizzie when you first left. He's been frantic. It's Darren and Lizzie, Amanda. I've known Lizzie since she was born. I'm concerned."

Amanda listened, her alarm growing. "I don't know what to say. Have you been tracking me, for them?"

"No," said Tilda. "It's not like that." She explained how she'd first seen her in the Village and her uncanny feeling that it was meant to be. "It was too much of a coincidence just to let it go. I know it sounds weird, but I almost felt as though I was supposed to find you."

Amanda, who wasn't adverse to notions of fate, nevertheless did not seem too satisfied with this answer. "Did you tell Darren you had seen me?"

Tilda shook her head.

"You could have. He could have taken it from there, just as you did, dig a little deeper. That's how you were led to Brooklyn, isn't it? Why haven't you told him?"

Tilda was thrown completely off-balance. Why had she taken this on herself? Her reasons now seemed flimsy.

"I don't know. I suppose I wanted to make sure you were all right, to protect you—and Darren and Lizzie—from what might follow. But honestly, I guess I hadn't really thought it through."

"Protect me? Them? Why on earth is that your role? Isn't it really just curiosity then?" Amanda asked.

"That makes it sound like prying, nosing around in other people's business, being an old busybody. If that's it, then I apologize. I didn't mean any harm. I was concerned, that's all."

Amanda was silent, letting Tilda's words hang in the air. Meanwhile Tilda was stung by the notion that she was a busybody. That seemed to be the verdict that was sticking.

"Maybe I should have told Darren," Tilda said. "He's sick with worry. He may be suspicious, but I don't know if he knows about Emile, and I don't think I should be the one to tell him."

"Keep Emile out of it. You don't know a thing about him."

This triggered a rapid response from Tilda, who said more than she even realized she knew.

"I know more than you think. He's an artist, a hyperrealist, from Saint Lucia. He's been in this country exhibiting his work for ten years. I know he lives in Williamsburg. I know the galleries where he exhibits, I know you represent him, and I know . . ." Here Tilda stopped for a second, and then, what the hell, continued, "And I know you live with him."

Then she stopped, half expecting Amanda to either jump up out of her chair and strangle her or to storm out. But she did neither. She sat quietly and looked Tilda in the eye.

"I guess this is what happens when an old woman has nothing to do but sit home and google. This sounds all the world like stalking. Don't you have anything better to do with all that time on your hands?"

Tilda took this like a punch in the gut. "Oh," was all she managed.

Seeing Tilda's reaction, Amanda shifted her gaze away and

bit her lip. Then, turning back to face her, she said, "I'm sorry, Tilda. I shouldn't have . . . after everything you've been through."

Tilda knew what was coming next, and she wasn't sure how she would handle it.

"Harold, I mean. I shouldn't have said that."

Tilda put her elbow on the table, her hand to her head, took a deep breath, and let it go. She distinctly felt a headache coming on, right behind her eyes, which were suddenly very tired. She put down her arm and looked at Amanda.

"Forget about me and my motives for a minute. What about your family, Amanda? They're hurting, especially Darren. You've got to care."

Amanda was quiet, reflecting, Tilda thought, and maybe letting her guard down a little.

"I know I'm causing them pain, but I can't go back," she said. "And I can't just call, not yet. But I will, honestly. I just need more time."

She took a sip of coffee. Tilda didn't say anything.

Amanda put her cup down. "I don't know what I'm doing. Half the time, I want to run home, but the rest of the time I feel as though I'm living the life I was meant to live. You can't know what it feels like to live every day as though it should have been different. And it isn't that I don't love them. Lizzie? My God, I'd die for her, gladly, but what about me? I want my life. How many more years do I have? And then what? Lizzie goes off to college, and I'm struck with dreams of what might have been?"

She stopped to look at Tilda, who sensed she wanted to say more.

I'm in it now, so what the hell, she thought. "What about Emile?" she asked. "Is this for real? For the long haul?"

Amanda glared at Tilda, who thought the conversation was over. Continuing to stare, Amanda finally answered, "Do you think you could understand? Why I'm doing this? Can you grasp the sense of how empty I've felt, for so long, and that now I have a new feeling, of a great connection with this man?

I met him in the city when I was having drinks with some old friends from my days at the Art Students League. He is such a powerful presence, inside and out. He exudes strength, but he is as kind and patient as anyone I've ever known."

"You have that with Darren," Tilda blurted out.

"Darren is a good man, a good husband and father, but it's not the same. And Emile isn't taking any of this lightly. He knows I have some things I have to work out. He's giving me space to do that. And, I . . . I'm enormously attracted to him. There's a pull there that . . ."

"You don't have to . . . I don't need to know."

"Oh, please, Tilda. You asked. Surely you get that there's more to this than just playing around. I'm passionately drawn to this man. I don't feel whole when I'm not with him, and when I am, I'm completely distracted. We can't make it through dinner, we're that crazy for each other."

"Amanda, you're talking about sex. It's not a mystery. It's sex. Do you wreck your family for it?"

"So you've never felt this way, about anyone? Then I feel sorry for you, because I wouldn't miss this for anything."

"You're assuming a lot that you don't know anything about. You think that because I'm old, I don't know about passion?"

Amanda shook her head. "You don't even know what I'm talking about—not this kind of passion."

"Please. Of course I do. I was young once, but by your age I guess I was fortunate. I was satisfied. I didn't have a sense that life was passing me by. I felt that Harold and I were going along together, that whatever happened, we'd have each other. But that didn't happen either, did it?"

"I'm so sorry, Tilda. Really, I am. But don't assume that because you've never been in my situation that I'm throwing everything away for sex. Give me some credit."

Tilda nodded. It was true. They were both making assumptions and coming up with empty judgments, solving nothing.

"I'm sorry, too," Tilda said. "I don't know what I was thinking. Maybe I was trying to get out of myself, and when

Darren came by, I was able to help, something I hadn't been able to do for myself—or for anyone for that matter."

"But what about your family, Laura and Tilly? You're so close to them."

Tilda drew a deep breath. "They're fine, really. Everything is fine. Just forgive an old woman with too much time on her hands, as you said. Look, Amanda. This is your business, yours and Darren's—and Emile's. I'm not passing judgment, honestly. Or I don't mean to. Maybe that's more honest. You've said you need more time, so that means to me that you haven't closed any doors."

Amanda nodded and agreed. And that was how they left it.

⌒∽૭૭

Shaken and tired, Tilda retraced her steps to the subway, then to Grand Central. On the train home, as the sun faded and the lights in the train came on suddenly, she felt her familiar dark mood descend. She missed Harold to her bones. She wanted to put her head on his chest and tell him what a fool she was. He would stroke her hair and say something kind while defusing her self-pity. "You're a fool, but you're my fool, and I love you." That was what they did for one another, especially as the years mounted. They gave each other a safe harbor. Each was home to the other. And now that home had been torn away, as though in a violent, unpredictable storm.

Sitting on the train among the other passengers, her calm exterior not betraying her inner turmoil, she had never been more alone. *No one knows what I'm thinking, how I'm feeling*, she thought. She watched the young mothers tending to their children, older women reading books or staring straight ahead, a man in a suit speaking into his phone, issuing orders just loudly enough so that everyone would know he was someone's superior. Tilda was set apart from them, yes, but she knew what held them together. They too would have their dark days. *No one escapes, and now it's my turn.*

As soon as she got home, Tilda tossed her bag on the nearest chair and called Bev to reveal the entire Amanda encounter. Bev took it all in without much pushback, just letting Tilda talk, even though Tilda was certain Bev had plenty to say.

The most forceful thing Bev said was also the truest. "You've involved yourself, and now this thing is going to eat at you. Every day that passes, the gnawing will get a little stronger."

Chapter Five

GREETING YOURSELF ARRIVING

∽

About a week and a half later, Tilda turned the calendar page to November. She sat at her desk as the late morning sun cast its weak light on her papers: bills and assorted correspondence she had put off answering until completing all the paperwork associated with Harold's death. Who knew the furious bureaucracy a death could unleash? Now here she was, also having to face what she had been dreading most: the holidays and short, dark days. She knew that everyone in her inner circle would be worrying about her and extending invitations. The thought of going anywhere, being with anyone, even Laura and Tilly, was painful. All she wanted to do was pull the covers over her head and emerge in the spring, like some hibernating bear.

Things between her and Tilly were thawing just as the wind was turning colder, but they still weren't back to where they had been when Tilda, the proud grandmother, would get phone calls and texts from her granddaughter. Tilly was polite but distant. The Shabbat dinner had been a turning point. That was true. Tilly didn't run off and even engaged in some conversation, all very light and superficial, though. Tilly didn't push or probe. Outwardly Tilly seemed fine, but Tilda still sensed something hidden in her behavior, the way kids act sometimes around adults, as though they have another life that doesn't include anyone over their own age. Maybe this was to be expected, but Tilda couldn't shake her intuition that appearances were cloaking a less favorable story. *No, not intuition,* she told herself. *Just worry, maybe just worry, nothing more.*

And then there was Darren. He had come to rely on Tilda, to appreciate her growing relationship with Lizzie. Absent now for over three weeks, Amanda hadn't yet fulfilled her promise to call home, and Tilda was burdened by the knowledge she couldn't share with Darren. Lizzie was still certain her mother would come home in due time, but Tilda thought Lizzie was beginning to grow a little sullen. A preternaturally cheerful girl, her glow was beginning to fade.

These problems, other people's problems, were heaped on top of Tilda's still too-raw emotions. She would think she was handling things well and then a scent of aftershave, fresh and clean, like Harold's, would catch her attention, a tune would play in the background, a stranger in the store would bear a strong resemblance, and she would become undone. One day in the CVS on Waterton, she actually followed a man around the corners of the aisles, trying to get a better look at him. Of course she knew it wasn't Harold, but it would have been enough just to be in the presence of someone who looked like him. When the stranger turned toward her as though wondering why she was following him, Tilda was mortified. There was no comfort in this man's presence at all, just humiliation. She ran out of the store and sat in her car sobbing, waiting until she was composed enough to drive home. Emotions were tricky, she had come to understand. They could change in a heartbeat.

Checking emails, she saw her sister Barbara's message, asking why Tilda hadn't returned any of her phone calls. *Time to face the music,* Tilda thought before hitting her sister's number on the phone.

It wasn't that she didn't love her sister. She did, and they had always been close—they still spoke every few weeks—but the truth was that Tilda didn't want to talk to anyone, and she knew this phone call would come with an invitation.

Two minutes into the conversation, Barbara asked, "Why don't you come for Thanksgiving? The change will do you good, and you know the weather will be better. It's perfect in Phoenix now, right on through, well, until summer."

Tilda wanted to tell her baby sister (younger by four years) that she loved the Grand Canyon and Sedona, but other than that, she wasn't a fan. She didn't understand how Barbara could live there. Tilda may have suffered from sun deprivation from November to March in Connecticut, but if Arizona was the answer, she'd take depression. But she knew this wasn't the time for this familiar diatribe, and she knew Barbara was happy there with Mike, her dependable and loving husband, and with her two grown sons, Jake and Nate, nearby. Instead she told Barbara she would stay put. "You know I can't leave Laura this year, and I want to be with Tilly and Mark. You can understand, right, Barbs?" Off course Barbara would understand, even if Tilda weren't being completely honest. She just wanted Thanksgiving to disappear.

"Hey, I was in the old neighborhood not long ago," she said, changing the subject. "You wouldn't recognize it."

"I wouldn't recognize it anyway. I was a baby when we left."

Of course that was true. "Yes, that's right."

Brooklyn may have been their parents' home and where the sisters were born, but they'd been raised in an apartment on Miami Beach, another area neither would recognize today. South Beach in those days was rundown, and rent was cheap. Two blocks off Ocean Drive, not far from Nikki Beach, the Marrone family lived in the Neptune Arms. They had a sprawling, hot, third-floor apartment where in the summers their mother, Maria, kept the lights off, the windows open, and the fans on. If they were lucky, they'd catch an ocean breeze that made the heat bearable. Tilda and Barbara shared a bedroom and slept in cotton underwear on cotton sheets, waiting for the fan to rotate in their direction for a little relief.

Their neighbors were Jewish, mostly retired, from New York, and their grandchildren only visited in the winter. Tilda and Barbara waited each year for the kids to arrive so they'd have built-in playmates for daily outings to the beach.

The beach was the center of their lives once they learned to swim. One of Tilda's favorite things was to swim away from shore until the water turned colder, letting her know it was deep. Then she'd flip onto her back, stretch out arms, and let the waves rock her as she looked up at the blue sky, feeling the salt beginning to tingle her face and chest as the water evaporated in the sun.

The summer between sixth and seventh grade, Tilda's boyfriend, Jonny Langer, called to tell her he was having a beach party. Jonny was the cutest boy in her class. He was fun to be around and had the best blue eyes. She'd had a crush on him all year. Apparently he felt the same way because at one of their class parties, he asked her to go steady. She wore his ring around her neck on a long, silver-plated chain, often reaching up to cradle the ring in the palm of her hand, proudly bearing its weight. Her friends could barely contain their envy.

On the phone he told her there would be hamburgers and cold drinks, even volleyball at the party. As soon as she hung up, Tilda knew what she would wear: her new two-piece pink-and-white-striped seersucker bathing suit. It had a hint of padding in the top.

On the day of the big event, Tilda was unaware of the hours she'd spent in the sun until the sand between her bathing suit and skin began to itch and burn, until even raising her arms to hit the ball back across the net set off prickly pain in her shoulders. Tilda was ecstatic when Jonny asked her to run into the water with him one more time before his mother would call for him to help pack up to go home.

As they plunged into the surf, he grabbed her hand, and with heads underwater, eyes open, and only surfacing to get a gulp of air, they kicked their way out until the water was just deep enough so they could touch bottom.

"Let's see how long we can hold our breath," he said. "And when we're under, let's open our eyes and look at each other to see who can stay under the longest."

"Okay," said Tilda, quickly taking a deep breath and diving under the water. Soon Jonny was in front of her, with his eyes open, looking at her. Then he pulled in closer, putting his hands around her head, and he kissed her on the lips, their bodies floating out behind them, until they could stand it no longer and had to surface. Tilda wanted to grab him and hold him against her body. She felt so strange, as though nothing but holding him to her would help.

"Want to do it again?" he asked.

"Okay," she answered.

But the strange feeling grew stronger and a little frightening. After the third time, Tilda said, "We'd better go back now."

As they started to swim, he grabbed her hand again, and they kicked their way back, heads submerged, only popping up to take a breath. No one could see he was holding her hand.

Soon after, when Jonny's father, a violinist in the Miami Orchestra, got an offer for first chair in Philadelphia, Jonny and his family moved away, breaking Tilda's heart.

She had had a terrible sunburn after the beach party, forever sealing the day in her memory with thoughts of both pain and longing.

"In the end, it was a pretty colorful childhood, don't you think?" asked Barbara. "I mean, we had the beach right there, and we had a lot of fun. It was probably a good thing that we left New York."

It was true. There were good reasons to leave. A plumber and loyal union man, their father, Aldo, had plenty of work on the hotels going up on Collins Avenue. But that wasn't the whole story. While Tilda and her sister were enjoying their years growing up on South Beach, while Tilda was experiencing first love and first kisses, there was a brother who had been left behind in Brooklyn.

Two years before Tilda was born, Maria gave birth to a

baby boy, cause for great celebration in this first-generation Italian American family. Anthony, as they named him, after Aldo's father, was destined to become everything Aldo had envisioned for himself. He would not only graduate from high school, he would go to college. He would become a doctor, as Aldo had once wanted to do, before financial realities meant work and no higher education.

But soon it became clear there was something wrong. Anthony did not grow and develop as he should have. At four months he was still not raising his head when Maria placed him on his stomach in his crib. At six months he was not sitting up. At eight months, he lay in his crib not smiling or able to focus attention on his parents or on anyone. He cried and could not be comforted. Maria and Aldo were devastated to learn soon after his first birthday that he would never progress. "He has Down syndrome," Dr. Geminelli told them. "You are both young. For your sake—and for the sake of your children to come—put the boy in an institution where he will be cared for, and get on with your lives."

And that is exactly what the young couple did. It was what parents did then to escape the heartache heaped upon them by a cruel and indifferent world, often including those closest, even family.

With Maria and Aldo's consent, Dr. Geminelli made the arrangements. One night, after Aldo had returned home from work, a nurse from a new "home" outside the city rang the doorbell, while a driver remained in the car, staring into the distance. Maria let her in, gathered Anthony's belongings, and handed over her son. Aldo held her to keep her from collapsing. Somehow the two found the strength to stand in the doorway and watch as the car carrying their firstborn son disappeared into the night.

Tilda could never clearly envision that scene. It seemed too impossible to be real. Nor could she imagine that she would be born a year later—the baby meant to make up for Anthony. She had never felt that way growing up, but surely that is what she was intended to be. Four years later, Barbara was born.

As an adult, learning her family's history for the first time, Tilda was left wondering how her parents had found the courage to try again to create a family—and how they had amassed the power to forget their firstborn son.

Around the time when Anthony would have been six, Aldo learned about all the work in Florida, where the weather was warm year-round. The family packed up and left for Miami. Tilda and Barbara would never know their brother. In fact, they were not supposed to know of his existence. While his sisters were frolicking on the beach, Anthony lay abandoned in Brooklyn.

Every month Aldo and Maria received a "progress" report from the Children's Division of the Rockland County Asylum for the Mentally Infirm, but there was never any progress, just doctors' notes on height and weight and diet, a note from the infirmary whenever he had a fever or other illness. These reports were then secreted away in a large envelope tucked under papers in her father's desk—as Tilda would discover after his death.

We had a lot of fun, Barbara had just said about their Miami childhood. And that was true, Tilda had to admit. They were a tight-knit family unit, their family of four that should have been a family of five.

Tilda never would have known about Anthony had she not volunteered to go through her father's things after he died unexpectedly of a heart attack at fifty-five. By that time, Tilda had moved to New York. She'd gone for college and stayed, while her parents had remained in the family house in North Miami Beach, where they moved before Tilda entered high school. Maria, too overcome at the time of Aldo's death, either forgot or never knew that Aldo had kept all of Anthony's records in the bottom drawer of his desk. There was a final letter in the stack informing the parents of Anthony Marrone of their son's illness and death at age thirteen, in 1954. The letter requested the parents' attention to the funeral arrangements. If not, the letter read, Anthony would be interred on Hart Island, New York's potter's field. Anthony had died, the letter said, after a brief illness, of peritonitis.

Reading the letter left Tilda with rage and guilt. How could her parents have left him, never telling her or her sister about Anthony?

"How could you?" were Tilda's very words when she confronted a still-grieving Maria.

"You can't judge me, Tilda," Maria had said in her own defense. "You have no idea on God's earth what it was like for us, and you don't know what it was like in those days."

Maria told her and Barbara how Anthony's condition caused them not only great sorrow but great shame. His condition was a dark secret. When the asylum people came to take Anthony away shortly after his first birthday, it was in the dark of night for a reason—to shield them from prying eyes. Later the young couple told their friends and neighbors that Anthony had died.

"It was easy to pretend he was dead, because of our real grief. We stayed in our house with the curtains drawn for days. We would have starved if our families hadn't brought us food." Maria was inconsolable in the retelling of it.

Tilda, too, was desperate. She had come home to help her mother and to mourn her father. Instead, she had discovered a brother, who she would mourn now too. Her sorrow overwhelmed her and became anger directed at her mother. Her mother's pain, she would realize much later, was doubled by Tilda's rage. Not only was Maria forced to relive the greatest sorrow of her youth, but she was also struggling with the unexpected death of her husband. Years later, Tilda would see herself in her much younger mother and recognize their new bond.

"It was cruel, yes," her mother had said then. "But we weren't the cruel ones. It was how it was then. You didn't keep these kids at home. Don't you think it tears me apart every time I see parents who have children with Down syndrome or other problems—and they're coping; they're not hiding in shame? Don't you think I say to myself maybe we could've done that? The guilt never goes away."

Barbara and Tilda made their separate peace with their parents' tragedy. Barbara readily forgave and felt it best to let Anthony's memory rest in peace. "We can't undo the past," she had said soon after their father's funeral. "We only hurt Dad's memory and cause Mom more pain if we don't let it go. Let it go, Tilda," she advised.

Tilda had a harder time. She began to see a fuller picture the more she looked into it. She learned that her mother had been right. Young parents were almost forced to institutionalize their children deemed too damaged to lead normal lives. But the more she learned about the harsh treatment inflicted on the children in the often overcrowded and understaffed institutions, the harder it became to "let it go." She began to understand how her father had carried this burden until he died, a burden bound in an envelope inside his desk, never to be discarded, as if by keeping the contents, he had somehow kept a part of his son with him. Maria, too, had died carrying the pain of her lost son, her firstborn. Tilda believed, like them, that she would never be able to let Anthony go.

"If you change your mind about Thanksgiving, we're here," Barbara said before they ended their call.

"Remember how Dad always talked about Harry Houdini?" asked Tilda.

"What? Why are you bringing that up?"

"Oh, no reason really. Just that I always thought he represented escape to Dad, like maybe he wanted to escape, but then later I thought, no, it was because Houdini died of peritonitis."

"Look, sis," Barbara said, not wanting to go down this road with her sister, Tilda knew. "I want you here, but do me a favor and make sure you're with Laura's family. Please don't be alone. You're not cooped up in that house all day, are you?"

After assurances that all was well, Tilda was able to get off the phone. *Just don't be alone*, Barbara had repeated before hanging up.

Tilda didn't tell her what she knew to be true: *I'm always alone now, no matter who I'm with.*

Tilda hadn't thought about her brother in a while. Before Harold's death, she'd made it a point of going to the cemetery where Anthony was buried every few months to leave a pink rose, her mother's favorite. And now she realized she hadn't been there since late March.

It had comforted her to learn that the weekend she and Barbara had stayed with neighbors, when her parents had "unexpectedly been called home to Brooklyn," an event never fully explained, they had actually been attending Anthony's funeral. "He's buried at St. James Cemetery," Maria told Tilda soon after she discovered Anthony's envelope in her father's desk drawer.

I'll visit again soon, Anthony, Tilda promised her brother. Even when she was in the throes of her dark mood, she never wanted to push Anthony out of her thoughts. *He's part of my life, in my heart, where he belongs,* she thought to herself.

⸻

Trying to get a better grip on the day, Tilda went to see if there was something she could put together for lunch, but the cupboard was bare. *Better steel myself for a trip to Nature's Food,* she thought, a venture sure not to lift her spirits. The parking lot was always crowded, the prices always too high, and the aisles, jammed. But she went anyway because there were certain things she could get there that she couldn't get anywhere else, like the dark-chocolate-covered goji berries she had become addicted to ever since Tilly had shared some of hers on an outing to the movies, one of the last the two had enjoyed together before Tilda's life had fallen apart.

Sure enough, the parking lot was a disaster, with giant SUVs vying for spaces wide enough for nothing larger than a Volkswagen bug. Tilda was lucky enough to scoot in behind a car that was leaving without setting off a major rumble among competing drivers. She'd seen it happen, usually male drivers getting out of their cars and engaging in some major chest bumping before the Dominican lot attendant could good-naturedly break it up. The women usually just shook their long ponytails vehemently at the offending driver to express their indignation.

Tilda thought the ingredients of a good fruit salad would do, so she wouldn't have to navigate the entire store with a cart too large for the cramped aisles, full not only of shoppers stopping in the middle to read every word on every label, as though no one else existed, but also, invariably, employees stocking shelves from dollies piled high with huge boxes from which they replaced old products with new ones. It was a bumper car ride, getting through it all, and making it to the backed-up checkout lanes required finesse and patience. Of late, Tilda was definitely lacking in the latter.

Finding herself miraculously alone among the melons, she began diligently assessing the quality of the cantaloupes to see if the jacked-up price was worth it. Most were green (not a good sign), they were tough to the touch, and they had no smell. Eventually, she found one, nice and beige, tender to the touch on the bottom, but not too soft, and it had a sweet, not-overpowering aroma. She had a moment not entirely sad remembering that it was Harold who had taught her how to buy fruit.

She rolled it over in her hands several times trying to determine if it was worth the price.

"That looks like a good one," she heard someone say, as she looked up from the melon in her hands.

A man had come up near her, but she hadn't noticed. She looked at him, not answering, her mouth skewing a bit to the right. He looked friendly enough, but she didn't like strangers thinking they could just strike up an uninvited conversation.

"They're expensive, but they're also out of season, probably from Guatemala."

"Uh-huh," replied Tilda, putting the cantaloupe back.

"Aren't you going to take it?"

Tilda didn't answer him and began walking over to the strawberries. *Now I'll probably get a lecture on these,* she thought, as he walked over to the raspberries.

"The prices here are ridiculous, but the quality is generally good, don't you think?"

"Not particularly," replied Tilda. "I take stuff back all the time, tomatoes at the bottom of the container that are moldy, grapes that are sour, that sort of thing." She noticed that the talkative stranger was about her age. He didn't look a thing like Harold, except he was about the same height, and while heavier, he looked straight and healthy. Not as good-looking as Harold, not now or ever, she was sure. But he had a nice smile. Good teeth, if they were his own. And nice brown eyes, but nothing like Harold's.

"Sure. Produce is tricky anywhere, but I keep coming back for the organic stuff. I do a lot of juicing, and . . ."

"That's nice," said Tilda, "but I need to get going."

"I was just going to the juice bar across the street. Would you join me? Maybe?"

Tilda was taken aback. What was going on here? Was she being picked up over the berry counter?

"I don't, um, juice," she said.

"Sorry to impose." He bowed his head to her and turned to walk away.

Maybe it was the gesture, so inoffensive, sort of old-world sweet, that got to her.

She laughed and said, "No, please, you're not imposing. I've just been a little grumpy lately. You're fine. Thanks for the offer, but I . . ."

"It's okay. Maybe another time."

Tilda gathered up some berries, a pineapple, and bananas before going back for the cantaloupe. Then she grabbed a container of cottage cheese and headed for the checkout. She put down her bag, placed her items on the counter, and said hello to the cashier, a manager-in-training who was having trouble getting the scanner to scan. A young woman with Down syndrome began putting the produce in Tilda's bag. Tilda had seen her before and was glad to see that she was employed and probably living on her own. Maria had been right. Things were very different today. Tilda paid the cashier as the young woman put her bag in the cart. "Thank you," said Tilda with a smile. When the young woman didn't answer, Tilda said it again, but a little louder, and she put her hand on the woman's shoulder, startling her. She began to scream, "Don't, don't, don't!"

Tilda kept saying, "I'm sorry, I'm sorry," but the woman was not comforted. The real store manager came over as Tilda kept apologizing.

"Excuse me, ma'am," he said.

"She won't get in trouble, will she? It was my fault. I shouldn't have touched her."

"No, of course not." Then he turned to the young woman. "Brenda, would you like to come with me? You can sit in my office for a while if you'd like."

Brenda quieted down and followed the manager. Order was restored, except for Tilda, who was mortified as everyone within earshot stood listening—and watching.

The stranger from the cantaloupes came up behind Tilda and whispered in her ear. "This might be a good time to try a good green juice."

Tilda gathered up her bag, holding it to her chest, and let him guide her out of the store, his hand gently cupping her elbow.

Chapter Six

SEEKING TO REPAIR WHAT IS BROKEN

∼

"It wasn't exactly meet-cute, was it?" said Bev when Tilda told her about the incident at the store.

"Not exactly. I really should've known not to touch her. I don't know what gets into me sometimes. I'm usually so standoffish and then suddenly I turn into some version of the touchy-feely, dotty old grandmother."

"Well, no. First, you're not that standoffish, and second, no one will ever accuse you of being dotty—well, not unless you get demented in your old age. But enough about that, tell me about organic man."

"Okay, first of all, let's get serious. I think I know where you'll be going with this, that I've *met someone*, as in someone I'll be interested in. That's what happens in those movies with old actors, our age, right? I saw one on TV the other night with what's-her-name. You know, still beautiful—did a lot of movies in the '60s? Anyway, her husband dies, and next thing you know she's talking all warm and fuzzy with her other old friends, who are really actresses from old sit-coms. Their conversation is supposed to be funny because they sound like fourteen-year-olds teasing their newly widowed friend about having a crush. I had to turn it off, it was so wrong."

"Right. And everybody's rich, and they all live in beautiful houses and have lots of eligible old actors hanging around."

"Why does this sell? First of all, most widows I know don't have money to burn, or friends with perfectly highlighted hair. And they're either so shell-shocked by loss that men are the furthest thing from their minds, or they're like Midge—you remember. She was so lonely that she joined all those dating sites. Most of that led to constant disappointment, remember? I think she finally found someone with mild dementia, and she's happy taking care of him. So good for her, but she went through hell because she was so terrified of being alone. These are not movie stories. Well, maybe Midge's story would make a decent indie, but it probably wouldn't sell. No, people want to see old actors, looking great, in love and starting over."

"Okay, I get it. So who's the guy you're not interested in?"

"His name is George. He's a retired librarian. He was at the library over in Longview, Laura's town, and he was there for twenty years, he said, after he retired from the military. I bet Laura knows him."

"A military man. Did he see action? God, don't tell me he's a Vietnam vet. That would be tragic."

"He is, but he was against the war. Well, he wasn't when he went, but that's how it ended up. He was posted in a place called Phu Bai doing radio research. I'm not sure what that was, but I don't think it was as innocent as it sounds."

"A lot of guys wouldn't do anything that supported the war."

"I know, Bev, but he was career Army. His whole family was. Telling them he was against the war, and he did, was a big deal for him."

"You got all of that out of one juice-bar date?"

"It wasn't a date, but he was very easy to talk to."

It was true. He had been very understanding after the store incident. So much so that Tilda wound up telling him about Anthony, something she would ordinarily never mention to anyone except those closest to her. He then told her about his brother who had died young and how every time he saw a boy about as old as his brother had been, he felt a pang of regret and sometimes a desire to reach out and engage the kid in conversation.

"Maybe that's why I tried to get you out of there, because I had an idea about what you were feeling, not that I knew you had a brother, of course not, but that I saw that you were trying to make a connection."

"But why did you talk to me in the first place, a perfect stranger?"

"That was kind of forward, wasn't it? But you remind me a little of my wife, the way you were so intent on those cantaloupes. That was something Joyce would've done."

Joyce was his wife of forty years who had died eighteen months ago of lung cancer. Never smoked a day in her life, he told Tilda, who had asked if it ever got any easier.

"Not exactly. You just learn how to accept it better," he'd answered, "how to keep going."

"Does he have kids?" asked Bev.

"Two daughters and three granddaughters, all in the Boston area."

"Well, he ought to be pretty sensitive to women, then," said Bev. "What's next?"

"Nothing's next, Bev," said Tilda. "We exchanged phone numbers, but nothing's next. Even if I see him occasionally, just to talk, it will be as someone who understands what I'm going through, who's been through the same thing."

And Tilda did think she might see him again for those reasons. But she was definitely not interested in anything more. Harold would always be the one true love in her life.

⁊～ᴖ

By Thanksgiving Eve, Tilda had been invited to dinner not only by her sister but also by Bev, and even George (whom Tilda had seen twice casually and strictly for company since the Nature's Food incident) had asked her to join him at his daughter's. "You need to be with family, even if it's not your own," he had said.

Tilda wasn't sure why everyone thought she would be alone. She kept reminding her would-be hosts that she had a family, who were also missing Harold terribly, and that of course she would be with them (as much as she was still dreading it and the whole damn holiday season, she said to herself more than once).

Just as she was ready to call it a night, she thought about Darren and Lizzie. She had assumed they would be going to his mother's in White Plains for Thanksgiving, but she thought she should call to check.

The phone rang several times before Darren answered, sounding disappointed. "I hope I didn't wake you," she said.

"No, it's early yet. I was just hoping we'd hear from Amanda."

Tilda bit her lip and felt a quick punch in her gut even though there was no one there to deliver it. *She hasn't called yet—after promising me she would?* Those were the words that were uppermost. But of course she couldn't say them.

"She still hasn't called?"

Darren said no and went on to tell Tilda all the reasons why he was not going to his mother's. Mainly because she cried every time she saw him and Lizzie, making them feel worse, like abandoned puppies, having to be nurtured and *seen to*.

"I can't put Lizzie through it," he concluded.

She pictured Amanda with her artist friend, the one she couldn't keep her hands off of, and felt a flash of anger, like lightening rise to the top of her head. She took a few breaths to calm down and said, "Well, then come to us. It will be fine, and no one will be making anyone feel one way or the other. We'll all be dealing with our own issues, and besides, it would be so good for Tilly and for Lizzie to have each other."

Tilda imagined Darren had been preparing his refusal, but when he heard the case for Lizzie being with Tilly, he let her continue.

"You know," she pressed, "it would cheer her up, and it would make Tilly happy. I know she misses Harold. Thanksgiving was his favorite holiday. He always said it was the only one not devoted to religion or any other cause, just family and friends getting together to eat. He made it fun for all of us, especially Tilly. Being with a friend would help her out."

Darren was still quiet, but Tilda could tell he was coming around. "Are you sure it would be okay with Laura? It's sort of late for more people."

"Laura has been cooking for days. We always have so much food left over, we spend the next day packing it up and delivering it to the Ezra Farnum House. She'll be delighted, but if it will make you feel better, I'll call her right now and make sure and then call you back."

He agreed, and of course Laura said yes. It made her happy to be inclusive on her father's favorite holiday, just as Tilda had expected.

⌖

Tilda arrived at Laura's in the morning to help with last-minute preparations. The smell of roasting turkey hit Tilda as soon as she walked in the door, making her clutch the grocery bags she was carrying to her chest. Without warning, the tears came and flowed down her cheeks. Laura saw her predicament and took the bags so Tilda could reach into her purse for a tissue.

"You see, this is why I've been dreading this. It's too soon, Thanksgiving. It meant so much to him."

"I know, Mom. It's okay. It's going to be okay. Just take a minute to . . ."

Tilda knew Laura was struggling, too, and didn't want to make it harder than it already was, but there was nothing to be done to change the situation or to ease anyone's pain, so she continued.

"It would have been better if I had gone to Barbara's, where I would have been miserable for entirely different reasons,"

Tilda said, wiping her eyes. "There I would have been dying for a drink to escape their cursed cheerfulness, the original Ozzie and Harriet." This was Tilda's less than complimentary description of her sister's conservative teetotaling family. "But here, I'm just dying." With this, Tilda's overly dramatic rendering of her misery, she burst into tears all over again.

Laura, to Tilda's surprise, maintained her equilibrium, and she led her mother to the sofa in the living room, where Tilda collapsed, her head in her hands. Laura sat beside her and took her mother's hands in hers.

"I know. This is so hard, for me, too. I keep feeling as though Dad is looking over my shoulder, ready to dip a finger in the cranberry sauce or to ask for a little scoop of stuffing, the way he always did. But I'm doing okay." Laura dug into her pocket. "Here, Mom, take these," she said.

Tilda stared at the two white pills in her hand until Laura came back with a glass of water.

"Why am I taking these?" Tilda asked, not waiting for an explanation before swallowing. "They look like Tylenol."

Laura nodded yes. "There's a good reason," said Laura. "I was so gloomy, and you know about how the holidays make depression worse, so I did some research because I wanted to be sure what I was feeling was in the normal range for a recent loss."

This was so like Laura, thought Tilda, who herself never doubted for a minute the legitimacy of her grief, fully expecting to live with it on and off for the rest of her life.

"I found out that emotional pain, like grief, activates the same part of the brain as physical pain. So they did experiments and gave acetaminophen, basically Tylenol, to people with emotional pain, and it worked. They discovered that their brains showed less activation in the region that registers pain, whether it's emotional or physical. Makes sense, right?"

"Well, I don't know. It sounds kind of simplistic."

Laura nodded and said, "I know, but it was worth a try, and you know what, I think it does kind of dull the pain. I mean, of course I still know he's not here and won't ever be again, but . . . anyway. A little better, Mom?"

"I'll be okay. What about Tilly?"

"Well, she's been quiet. Not her usual holiday self."

"Yes, of course. This was a special time for the two of them." Tilda remembered last Thanksgiving, when it seemed as though their lives together would go on as always. No one foresaw this future, not when they were happily making their separate wishes as Tilly held the two ends of the turkey wishbone in her hands, something they had done together since she was five.

It had been Harold's idea that year. "It works like this," he had told her. "You hold the wishbone all by yourself, both ends, one in each hand. See, Tilly, like this," he told her, demonstrating. "And then you pull both ends while we all make a wish, silently, and you pick one side of the bone or the other to win. No one's allowed to tell what their wish is, or it won't come true, right, family?" Everyone nodded as though they had been doing this little ritual for years before Tilly had come along.

"Now, the trick is, you have to pull both ends, like this, out and away, until one side breaks. Okay, Tilly?"

"But what about me? Don't I get to wish?"

Harold had seemed to contemplate this for a minute and then said, "Oh, of course you get to. You get to make two wishes, so no matter which side breaks, you still have a wish that will come true."

This seemed to satisfy Tilly. "So," she said, "I can make whatever wish I want to come true. I'll just break the other side."

Her grandparents and parents nodded in approval, ignoring that she would be in effect gaming the game, but choosing rather to marvel at her precociousness.

Tilda still remembered her wish that first time, that they would all be as healthy and happy as they had been at that moment, the same wish she made every year. Tilly had told everyone she had wished for a trip to Disney World, and when

Harold told her she wasn't supposed to tell, she cried until her parents told her they were all going to the Magic Kingdom for Hanukkah and so had to spoil the surprise.

"Tilly! See, it works. Your first wish and it came true, even though you told it," Harold said. She rushed into his arms, delighted that Grandpa's game had already yielded so much pleasure. This had been the beginning of the special Thanksgiving bond they shared.

"Where is she now?" Tilda asked.

"In her room. She'll be down soon to help with the candied yams and the mashed potatoes. Are you feeling a little better, Mom, really?"

"Yes, thank you, honey. It must be the Tylenol. We'll all be okay, I'm sure." Then with great earnestness, she patted her daughter on the knee and quickly rose. "C'mon, kiddo, let's get started. I've got everything for the pies in the bags, and they're just about ready to go in the oven. I just need to do some assembling," she said, thinking how similar *assembling* and *dissembling* sounded.

⊂～౿౿

By early afternoon when the doorbell rang and Darren and Lizzie arrived, Tilly had still not come down. Laura stood at the bottom of the stairs and called for her. When that didn't work, she looked for Mark and realized he was still out back raking leaves. Tilda looked out the kitchen window to see Laura standing with her hands on her hips saying something to Mark, who put down the rake and followed Laura into the house. Laura came back into the kitchen and smoothed her hair back with both hands.

"Honestly, I've got one who won't come down and one who won't come in. Mom, you'd better go make sure our guests are comfortable."

"I'm bringing them some sparkling water and something to snack on."

"I have some nuts and also crackers and cheese. I'll be out in a minute to say hello. I haven't seen them in a while, since the funeral, I think." Laura kept to her task, peeling the potatoes, Tilly's job.

Tilda, who had felt all day as though some unseen gremlin had been pummeling her stomach, took a deep breath. "My God, Laura, we're quite a pair, trying to get through this, aren't we? And I bet Tilly, too. That's probably why we haven't seen her all day."

"I don't know," Laura said, "but this isn't right." She pulled the apron over her head and walked toward the stairs again.

Tilda picked up the tray she had been preparing for Darren and Lizzie.

When Tilly finally came down, she was wearing jeans and her plaid flannel shirt, her hair back in a ponytail, a stark contrast to Lizzie, who was in a pink tulle party dress. If there had been a teen magazine article rating what to wear to a family Thanksgiving, ranging from underdressed to over-the-top, each girl would have been on opposite ends. Neither one seemed to care or to notice.

"Hi, Grandma," Tilly said, giving Tilda a tight hug around the waist. It had been so long since she had shown any affection that Tilda was nearly undone. The hug had been tender, and sad, Tilda thought. "Hello, Mr. Esmond. Hi, Lizzie," she said. Then, turning specifically to Lizzie, she asked, "Would you like to help me with some things in the kitchen? I always make the mashed potatoes and the candied yams. It's not too bad, kinda fun, actually."

Tilda noticed that Tilly's eyes were a little red. With her shoulders slightly rounded, her gaze down, she seemed on the verge of folding into herself. She was Tilly, but not the same girl who bounced through space barely touching ground when she walked. This was an earthbound Tilly, and it broke Tilda's heart to see her.

Once they were alone in the living room, Darren told Tilda there had been a breakthrough.

"Amanda sent us cards. After you and I talked, I realized I didn't check the mail yesterday. I always figured she'd text or call, but she sent cards to us both," Darren told her.

Tilda's head jerked back, her chin tucking into her neck, a maneuver executed unintentionally, and she hoped Darren didn't notice, but she was surprised at this news. Who goes AWOL over the holidays and then sends cards?

"Mine didn't say much," he explained. "A lot of words, but still, just how sorry she was, that she was okay, and that she couldn't come home."

Listening intently, Tilda was surprised yet again, this time at Darren, who was opening up on his own, without Tilda having to pry loose each word. Had he come to trust her, believing he had a friend to confide in? The thought made Tilda cower with shame, knowing his trust was misguided. She was still sitting on information because Amanda had promised to call, not to send fucking cards.

"Those were the main points, but she filled up the whole space, mostly about how she knew she was causing so much pain. Frankly, it made me madder than hell."

Tilda certainly understood Darren's reaction. It was callous and bordering on cruelty for Amanda to have sent a card for Thanksgiving, with no explanation and no hint of her intentions, just that she was gone and sorry.

Tilda steeled herself and asked, "How did Lizzie take it? If you don't mind talking about it, that is."

"No, it's okay. She didn't say much, just that she was happy to finally hear something and that she was glad her mother was okay. But she's been sort of depressed, I think, not really herself lately. It's gotten worse with the holidays coming. By now the two of them would have been shopping already and would've had wrapped presents hidden around, in closets and under the bed and stuff."

Tilda thought it best just to listen, but the more Darren talked, the angrier he became.

"Honest to God, I don't know what she's thinking. I

don't think I'll ever be able to forgive her for this." And then he stopped, abruptly.

Tilda was quiet, too, not sure what to say.

"I'm sorry, Tilda. I try to keep it together—for Lizzie. But really, she helps me. Without her, I don't know what I would've done by now."

Now Tilda felt even worse for holding back essential information, and just as Bev had warned, it was gnawing at her.

"Darren, how hard have you tried to find her?"

His back seemed to straighten at the question, as though he were considering the idea for the first time.

"I guess I really haven't. I mean, after that first night I haven't gone out looking for her. I've called her friends and talked to them, but I believe them when they tell me they don't know anything. But if you mean hiring someone, no, I haven't even considered it."

"No, I didn't mean you should've been doing more. It's just, I guess I was curious, wondering if you could find out where she is." *The way I have*, she wanted to say, but she stopped herself.

"Honestly, it's the fact that she left. That's it, really, not where she is. I'm not sure I care where she is. I can't believe she was careless enough to have done this to me—but mostly to Lizzie. Her leaving us, what she's done, it's unbelievable. At this point, I don't know if I even want her back. And if there's a guy involved, I'm done. She hinted at something in her letter to me, but I'm not sure. I just keep hoping it's about something else, getting it out of her system, her lost art or whatever. She was always talking about her art-school days. Christ, I've had it."

Tilda needed to be done with this conversation; she felt she risked telling Darren everything she knew, and part of her wanted to so badly. When Laura appeared announcing dinner, Tilda was a little less apprehensive about her own family and its problems.

There were toasts around the table, a little formal, Tilda thought, but at least no one cried. Mark went first. "We are happy to have Darren and Lizzie joining us. Welcome to our home. Even though our hearts are heavy this year, let us be grateful for the love we have, and happy Thanksgiving to us all." Then Laura said, "Welcome to our home. In the Jewish tradition, it is always a mitzvah to welcome others to share in whatever food and drink there may be, whether meager or bountiful. As much as we miss our father, grandfather, and husband, may we all be happy for our blessings."

Having found the strength to say these words, Laura was about to sit down, only to rise again to say, "Lizzie and Darren, you knew my dad, and Mom says you had a warm relationship—as neighbors—over the years."

Tilda nodded in agreement, not very forcefully, not sure where Laura was headed with this impromptu speech, but fairly certain it would end calamitously, no matter how much Tylenol had been consumed.

"So I want to share some things about this holiday and what it meant to my dad. Mom may have told you, Thanksgiving was his favorite holiday. He loved the inclusiveness of it. We often had guests he invited, people who, before he retired, came to him to do their taxes, who maybe had just lost a spouse or who were alone during the holidays. One year we set five extra places for these friends of my father's. And, you know what? It was wonderful. We had the best time. Everyone was happy. There were jokes and stories. No one was depressed or sad that day. When everyone left, my father said, "That was a true mitzvah, Laura. Thank you."

Darren and Lizzie looked up at Laura, and Lizzie smiled a little quizzically.

"It's a long story, the meaning of the word, but basically today it refers to an act of kindness. In the best sense, as my father saw it—not necessarily as rabbinic scholars would see it—but to him a mitzvah should be freely given out of love and not out of a sense of duty. So coming from him that day, it was the greatest compliment he could have given me, but it was really him. He was the reason we had that wonderful experience."

Now Laura sat. She reached for her glass and took a long sip of water.

Tilda raised her own. "Thank you, Laura." She wanted to say more, but all she managed was, "You captured the moment beautifully." She, in turn, took a big gulp of wine to calm the unwelcome swell of emotion that was brewing. She looked over at Tilly. Though her eyes were downcast, she was not crying. They were getting through it, this dinner, this day. Maybe these were the things to be thankful for this year, Tilda thought.

After what could have been a rocky start, the holiday meal went smoothly. There were no tears, no one was sullen, and all seemed to be on course for an uneventful conclusion to a day Tilda knew everyone around the table had been dreading. Lizzie seemed returned to her cheerful self, saying over her second helping of pumpkin pie that she was adding *mitzvah* (singular) and *mitzvot* (plural), additional information Laura had gladly provided, to her growing list of killer Scrabble words. Tilda challenged the word and its variants as foreign and therefore not acceptable, but Lizzie looked it up on her smartphone and found the words were indeed allowed. Even Tilly joined in the fun, saying her grandmother had finally met her match.

And so it went, as though a magic bubble had descended, if only temporarily, to protect the family and its guests from further sadness on this, Harold's favorite day of the year.

After more helpings of pie and coffee, Tilly and Lizzie offered to clear the table. Tilda enjoyed a private moment of hope when she saw the girls deeply engaged in conversation in the kitchen. She couldn't hear them over the clatter of dishes, but from her vantage point, it looked as though they had been close for years.

Later, when the dishwasher could be heard humming away, signaling the true end of the evening, no one seemed eager to have it end. One by one they found their way to the living room to engage in more after-dinner conversation.

Maybe it was inevitable that someone would go too far, push too hard. Maybe the bubble was more fragile than anyone had thought.

"Tilly, look what I've got," said Mark, pulling the cleaned-up wishbone out from behind him. "Let's make a wish. The way we always do."

Tilly turned from Lizzie, seated beside her on the couch, to look at her father. "No, Dad, I don't want to," she said, turning back to Lizzie, but Mark persisted, saying it wouldn't be Thanksgiving until she made a wish.

After two or three more of Mark's attempts, Tilly again turned in his direction. "Okay, Dad. Here's my wish. I wish you'd stop."

Mark looked surprised at his daughter's vehemence, which only made Tilly object more strenuously. "I said I didn't want to. This was my thing with Grandpa, okay? I don't want to, not this year. Or ever, probably."

Everyone was quiet. The bubble had burst, that much was clear, and Tilly, probably sensing she was responsible, felt she had nowhere to go but away. She got up off the couch and ran to her room, leaving Mark fumbling for something to say. But it was left to Laura and Tilda to make the obvious excuses—emotions were still raw, holidays were difficult. The words sounded rote, yet true enough. After a few awkward moments, Darren and Lizzie said their thanks, their genuine thanks, and left.

When Mark said he was going up to talk to her, Tilda asked if she could. "Maybe it's a grandma kind of moment." After all, reasoned Tilda, it was Grandpa that Tilly was missing.

Chapter Seven

CLEAR ALL HISTORY

Tilda knocked lightly on the door. There was no answer. She opened it a crack and knocked lightly again. She peered in the opening and saw Tilly rise up onto her elbow and turn in her direction, a look of disbelief clouding her face. Disbelief at her overreaction to the events downstairs, Tilda surmised. But more, disbelief at how her world had turned so suddenly from lightness and ease to darkness and pain—the stuff she had only read about in the books Laura had thought intense but age-appropriate: that stuff was now happening to her. It was beginning to make sense, all the troubling behavior, the cutting, the withdrawal. She began to see Tilly's world through her own world of grief. She began to see that perhaps her granddaughter was avoiding her because she reminded her of her grandfather, whose death had brought down her carefree world.

Tilda had wanted to protect her granddaughter from life's harm for as long as possible: no injury or sickness (please, God), no heartbreak (keep boys away as long as possible, she hoped), no major disappointments (she made the dance team, yes, thank goodness). But here her granddaughter was, dealing with the worst pain human life had to offer: death. Not the death of a long-lost, remote relative, or even of a loved family pet. No, this was the death of someone revered, who was a connection to a time long ago that made the past easier to understand and in so doing made life easier to grasp. All those stories her grandfather had told her had taught her that. And now that source of love and gentle easing into the ways of the world was gone.

"May I come in?" Tilda asked.

Tilly sat up on her bed by the window and folded her arms around her raised knees. "I guess so."

As soon as Tilda sat down, Tilly embraced her and sobbed. "I'm sorry, Grandma. I've been a bitch to you, and I don't even know why, really. And I don't know why I was so awful downstairs just now. It's just that nothing is the same anymore."

Tilda stroked her granddaughter's hair, released from its ponytail and hanging around her shaking shoulders.

"You know what?" she said. "You don't even have to apologize. You get a pass because this is just so shitty. This bites. I mean it."

Tilly pulled away to look at her grandmother.

"No, really, Tilly. We get to say what we never say, and the world will just have to deal with us because this is so different from anything we've gone through before, and so damn hard. Everyone will just have to wait until we either feel better or figure out what to do about how god-awful we feel."

"It just doesn't go away. Some days I don't even think about it, but now with the holidays—everything is definitely not awesome. Everything is awful."

"I wish I had a way to make you feel better, honey. I don't. Everyone says what we're feeling now will pass, but that doesn't help, really, does it?"

"I don't know anything anymore. I hate life. I hate myself. I don't want to be me anymore." Then she said, "I'm sorry about that day, Grandma. I was touchy about the scratches."

Tilda knew to go lightly here. This was the territory that

had led to their troubles in the first place. She didn't say anything, waiting to see if Tilly wanted to talk.

"I don't know. It's all so confusing. I miss Grandpa so much, and I, I hate myself. I don't even know why."

Tilly looked at her, bewilderment in her eyes. Tilda wanted to hold her for as long as it took for this darkness to pass.

"But I haven't done it again," Tilly said.

Tilda took some comfort in this. Maybe Tilly was reaching bottom and would begin her climb back to her known world.

"I'm glad, Tilly."

But then Tilly said, "It wasn't just cutting."

"Do you want to talk about it?" she asked, treading carefully. She knew this was a delicate moment, and she didn't want to press her.

Tilly looked at her, held her gaze, not answering. *She's waiting, but for what?* Tilda wondered.

"No," Tilly said, and she turned away.

"All right, honey," Tilda replied as she rose.

"Grandma, wait. I mean, do I have to know who I am . . . just now?"

Tilda wasn't sure what Tilly was thinking, but she felt certain she knew the answer. "No, Tilly, you don't, not yet," she said.

"I love you, Grandma."

"I love you, too."

Tilda took her granddaughter's chin in her hand, looked into her puffy eyes—more hazel than green today—drew her into her arms, and kissed her on the cheek, taking a moment before letting go.

She got up and walked out of the room, closing the door gently behind her.

Their love of Harold was their bond now, thought Tilda on the way home. It wasn't that Laura wasn't mourning, for surely she was, but if there was anything for the foreseeable future to bring Tilly to her grandmother, Tilda knew it would be her love for her grandfather. Just when Tilda thought her bruised heart could hurt no more, here it was aching anew when she thought of her granddaughter crying in her room, struggling to understand her own behavior. Surely just being an adolescent was challenge enough, but Tilly was coping with grief, too, so it was no wonder that she didn't know who she was. And yet Tilda couldn't deny that Tilly's comments and her question had been troubling. There was a story there, but she wasn't ready to tell it.

Tilda held the steering wheel tightly. *Or was I not ready to hear it?* she asked herself, remembering how Tilly had turned away. No, she thought. It was best to be patient. Tilly would talk when she was ready, and then Tilda would be there for her to help ease whatever was troubling her granddaughter, who was surely struggling with problems too big for her. *One thing at a time*, thought Tilda. *She needs to get over her grief. We both do.*

With Thanksgiving behind her, in spite of the way it had ended, Tilda felt some relief in knowing one holiday was done with, even though that left two to go. In fact, Christmas/ Hanukkah and New Year's looked like thick forests to lumber through before she could just hibernate the winter away. The only good thing about the season so far was that the Ebola crisis seemed to be easing and the media had taken a drubbing for its national fear-mongering.

Thanksgiving may have been Harold's favorite holiday, but Tilda had always been like a kid during Christmas and Hanukkah. Getting to celebrate two holidays that kept the darkness at bay, both with wondrous light and song, both with baking and food preparation that kept the house smelling sweet and alive no matter how the wind might blow or the snow might fly—what could be better? When Tilda was growing up in Miami, she and Barbara used to dream about cold, snowy Christmases with carolers and hot chocolate, just like the commercials on TV, but once she actually experienced it she decided it wasn't so enticing after all. Growing up in Florida had instilled in her a love of light and open space, of ocean breezes, and of sun coming up on the horizon.

But Harold had made it better. He put lights on the hedges under the window in front of the house, and they told themselves they were winter lights—and ecumenical—not suggesting any particular holiday at all. Inside, there was a small tree with twinkling lights of red and green and white by the fireplace and a huge menorah on the mantle—and white and blue lights framing the hearth. They listened to the Mormon Tabernacle Choir on Christmas and played Hanukkah and klezmer music during Hanukkah. They cooked brisket and potato pancakes for Hanukkah and turkey for Christmas, the smells permeating every room.

This year the boxes with the lights and other decorations Tilda and Harold had acquired over the years, the dreidels and stockings with everyone's names on them, even one for Bully that they still hung every year in his memory, all remained in the closet.

Laura had suggested that the menorah, little tree, and hearth lights might comfort her mother, but the effort seemed too much for Tilda. Laura tried to get her to read up on SAD. "It's a real thing, Mom. It's not just you. It's called Seasonal Affective Disorder. You can even get special lights for it." But Tilda hadn't responded, and Laura, maybe remembering the deal they had struck about their year of mourning, had backed down.

And so now, after Thanksgiving, at the true start of the holiday season, the house was dark: no lights, no tree, and no menorah.

She sat on the side of the bed. On the night table were a glass of water and a bottle of Tylenol PM. She took a tablet with one long swallow, pulled the quilt up over her, and waited for sleep to take her away.

Her team was in the circle. The opposing team had the ball, a brown playground ball that hurt when it hit, when it was thrown with force, the way Danny Blix, her first-grade nemesis, threw the ball. It was so random, the ball coming at you, you trying to stay out of the way, trying your best to be the last one standing. Tilda ran and ran, from one side of the circle to the other, with no clear strategy guiding her. When the whistle blew, she stopped. She had made it, the last one on her team still in the circle. She let out a sigh of relief and was about to take her place on the outer circle, but before she could leave, she noticed that her teammates weren't out of the circle at all. They were instead sprawled on the ground, arms and legs at strange angles. They weren't moving, they weren't breathing, and they weren't her teammates anymore. They were older, grown. And then she was on the ground, kneeling over a body. It was Harold. Leaning over him and screaming, she had morphed into the young protester in the famous photo after Kent State. That was when she woke up.

She sat up and turned on the light. It was only a dream, she told herself, her heart still racing. She thought about how Kent State had led to her and Harold committing to being more active, and how Bev had offered her support as well. They had all written letters protesting the war and supporting the protests that followed. Harold even had a letter to the editor published in the *New York Times*. It had all been so upsetting, those unprovoked deaths. At least one of the students killed had been walking past and was not even part of the protest. Tilda hadn't thought about Kent State in years.

She looked at the bottle of Tylenol PMs and thought of taking a second one but decided on something stronger. She went to the medicine cabinet in the bathroom where she found the Ambien Dr. Willis had prescribed but that she had never taken. She popped one into her mouth, turned on the faucet, scooped up some water, and swallowed hard. *Maybe I'll wake up in an hour and start eating compulsively, or take the car for a spin. Whatever. At least I'll get some sleep.*

Tilda went back to bed and slept until the morning light crept through the crevice in the blackout shades.

The night of the Ambien dosage proved uneventful. There were no midnight snacks, drives, or other odd behaviors associated with pharmaceutical somnambulism. Tilda was simply able to sleep through the night with no more troublesome dreams or interruptions. There were, however, lingering effects from the dodgeball dream. Simply put, Tilda couldn't shake it. It stayed with her, causing her to tremble when she thought of it, something that occurred at odd moments—in the grocery store, at the bank, at home in the kitchen and the dining room. The trembling, lasting for a minute or two, would be the first of several other physical reactions; next a chill would start from her stomach and radiate outward until her arms and hands tingled. If she was out when it started, she would try to get to her car before the onset of what came after the tingling: her heart rumbling around as though she had switched on a blender in her chest. Then came heat and sweats and a light-headedness that she always felt would surely end in unconsciousness if she could not get to a quiet place where she could calm down. Tilda figured it was anxiety and reasoned that knowing this, she could better control it, but the chain reaction of trembling to light-headedness continued just the same.

She had abruptly left Laura on several occasions. She knew her daughter was alarmed by Tilda's sudden departures because she'd call within the hour, pleading with her mother to "see someone," or at least to see her rabbi, who she said was very sensitive and who had been wonderful at her father's small service.

"Laura, surely you realize that a woman my age would find it ludicrous to talk to someone . . . how old? Twenty-five?"

"He's thirty, Mom, with a wife and a child. How about Rabbi Ross, then? Daddy liked him, and you did, too. He's the emeritus rabbi now, but he still talks to congregants."

Tilda had dismissed the whole conversation. She wasn't about to talk to anyone. Once again she reminded Laura of their oath of one year, to which Laura acknowledged their agreement but also said, "On the other hand, I can't sit doing nothing if I think you need . . . if I think you're having health problems, and I do."

Tilda had changed the subject, and Laura had let it go.

But the first night of Hanukkah changed everything. Tilda had turned down every invitation for remaining holidays from Barbara, Bev, George, and even Darren, who in a strange turn of events had invited her to Christmas dinner with his mother in White Plains—to which Tilda had replied simply, "You're kidding." Darren had laughed, and that had been the end of it. And now Tilda could not deny that her place was with Laura, Tilly, and Mark. Laura had decided a small, quiet family dinner on the first night of Hanukkah would be in keeping with her commitment to twelve months of mourning.

And so Tilda went as she said she would. Laura opened the door and gave her mother a big hug and then took her coat and told her Mark and Tilly were in the living room waiting to light the candles.

Tilda went in and kissed Tilly and Mark, noticing that Tilly once again was in jeans and her blue flannel shirt, decidedly underdressed, in her grandmother's estimation. Laura walked in behind her and took her place, standing with the others at the table. She placed the first candle in the far right on the menorah. Standing in the very spot where she had stood for so many first nights of Hanukkah while next to Harold, Tilda was keenly aware of the warmth the softly dimmed lights in the dining room cast, of the aroma of roasted chicken filling the house, encircling her with an odd mix of sweet sadness. Here were the remaining people on earth she loved beyond measure, and here also was the absence of Harold, an absence so strong it was a presence. She closed her eyes and listened as Laura recited, "*Barukh atah Adonai, Eloheinu, melekh ha'olam.*"

And then Tilda, Tilly, and Mark read from the copies Laura had printed out for them, "Blessed are you, Lord, our God, sovereign of the universe."

And Laura said, *"Asher kidishanu b'mitz'votav v'tzivanu."*

And Tilda, Tilly, and Mark read, "Who has sanctified us with his commandments and commanded us."

And they continued, *"L'had'lik neir shel Chanukah. Amein."*

"To light the lights of Hanukkah. Amen."

And soon they came to the last blessing, said on the first night only, *"Barukh atah Adonai, Eloheinu, melekh ha'olam."*

"Blessed are you, Lord, our God, sovereign of the universe."

"Shehecheyanu v'kiyimanu v'higi'anu laz'man hazeh. Amein."

"Who has kept us alive, sustained us, and enabled us to reach this season. Amen."

But we didn't reach this season, not together. This was Tilda's thought when the floor gave way.

It was the end of this prayer that kept Laura from lighting the shamash and then the first candle of Hanukkah, let alone singing "Hanerot Halalu," as they had always done. As soon as they recited "this season," Tilda "went out like a light," as Mark described it, or "fell into a heap on the floor," in Laura's words. "I thought you died, Grandma!" Tilly told her later that evening.

Of course, Tilda came to right away and was able to get up the stairs with Laura and Mark's help, where she lay down on their bed for a few minutes while Laura went for water and a cool compress. Tilly, who had come up, too, stood behind her father in the doorway. Tilda, with a flick of her wrist, shooed them away. "I'm all right, honestly. Go on now, I'll be down in a minute."

As soon as they left, she lay back down, one arm flung over her eyes.

"Maybe we should take you to the ER," said Laura, putting the wet cloth on her mother's head.

Tilda objected in the strongest terms and assured her daughter it was just a fainting spell.

"I'm mortified—and embarrassed by all the attention. It's nothing," she said, beginning to get up.

"Oh, Mom, please. You don't have to be embarrassed. We're concerned, that's all. Lie back down, just for a minute, okay?"

Reluctantly, she then told Laura about the anxiety attacks. To her surprise, Laura had already become suspicious.

"I knew something was up, when you kept disappearing on me, but I didn't know what it was. I'm relieved, actually, and glad you told me, thank you. I would've been after you about it at some point," she said, readjusting the damp cloth on her mother's head.

"But, Mom," she continued, "you can't just self-diagnose like this. It could be something serious. You need a full medical workup, a stay in the hospital . . ."

Tilda had to think fast. She had visions of an ambulance pulling into the driveway to escort her into the Medical Hell the practice of medicine had become.

She immediately sat up and assured Laura she was okay. "Look, I'm completely revived. No need to call anyone, really."

Laura stared at her mother.

"Okay, I'll tell you what, I promise I'll call Dr. Willis first thing in the morning to make an appointment."

Laura relented. "Do you think you can go downstairs? You don't have to sit at the table. We can eat buffet-style, around the fireplace. You might like that."

"I think I would," replied Tilda, starting to rise. But instead she reached for her daughter's hand.

"That night, Laura, the night your father died. It was the first night in a long time I had fallen into a deep sleep. I never heard him. I wasn't awake to help him."

"Oh my God, Mom. Is this what you've been carrying around? Surely you know it wasn't your fault."

"I guess in fact I don't." And then Tilda cried.

Laura stayed with her mother, her arm around her quaking shoulders.

When Tilda had exhausted herself with tears, she pulled a tissue from the box on the night table and wiped her eyes. She let out a deep sigh and patted Laura's hand.

"I need to freshen up," she said, rising and heading toward the bathroom.

Before opening the door, she turned to her daughter.

"Laura, thank you," she said. "I think that cry did me some good. I guess I know in my heart it wasn't my fault, but I'll probably never forgive myself for not waking up."

"Mom . . ."

"No," said Tilda, holding up her hand. "You don't need to say anything. You've done more than you know, just being patient, letting me cry, talk, whatever I needed to do. I'm relieved to have finally admitted it to you . . . to myself.

When they went downstairs, Mark and Tilly were waiting for them. Tilda was all right, but Laura had exacted a promise. Tilda would not only make an appointment with Dr. Willis; she'd also promised to see Rabbi Ross.

⌒ ৩৩

"I'm fine. It's vasovagal syncope. Simply put, fainting," Tilda told Bev in the afternoon after her appointment with Dr. Willis. "Of course he wants me to follow up with some tests, but that's the bottom line."

When Bev asked what had caused the episodes, Tilda told her it was triggered, in her case, by strong emotions and that Dr. Willis believed it was all part of what she was going through after Harold's death. "So, just as I told Laura, anxiety or panic attack."

"Isn't that a little simplistic? Look, I don't mean to be callous, but not all widows go around keeling over at their daughters' houses."

"I can always count on you to delicately get to the point. You think there's more to it, some underlying, as yet undetected, cause?"

"Couldn't have said it better myself. You're the one who brought up the whole guilt thing to Laura that night. Don't you see the connection?"

Tilda knew she didn't have to respond, that Bev would simply go on to answer her own question—and she wanted to hear it.

"So that night you slept soundly, and, ever since, you've been blaming yourself. Then the dodgeball dream, where you dream about the random nature of our mortal lives, leading to the obvious reality that our notions of control are illusory. What else can't you control? Everything, except maybe you could've saved Harold. Except you couldn't have. Crap, I might pass out myself just thinking about it. I haven't figured out the Kent State part, though."

"We were young then. We thought our good intentions would save us, could save the world," said Tilda.

"Yes, save the world. We were cocky, weren't we? But we did make a difference, I think, for the better, but people forget. Oh, don't get me started, please. When I see what is going on today, what is passing for reasonable . . . whatever, anyway . . ." Bev trailed off, as she often did, these days, thinking no doubt about her attempts to still make a difference. "What else did the doctor say?"

"He prescribed antidepressants, but I'm not taking them."

"Maybe you should."

"Maybe I should," Tilda responded.

Before hanging up, Bev had some advice. "Try to avoid guilt trips. There are better ones to take. So choose one, okay? While you're still here."

"My God, Bev. You certainly have become the dispenser of Zen-like wisdom these days. Too many fortune cookies and too much Chinese takeout, I think."

"Now you're being mean, and don't scoff. You'll see I'm right."

❧

Tilda had been mentally crossing off dates until the end of the year when she realized she hadn't paid her supplemental health insurance. Harold had always paid their premiums, and Tilda had yet to set up automatic payments for herself after Harold's had been canceled. Her payment was two weeks overdue when she dialed the customer service number listed on her last unpaid statement.

"Your call will be answered in the order it was received," a recorded voice told her.

This was enough to set her off. *Whatever happened to the preposition followed by the relative pronoun?* "*In which* it was received!" she screamed into the phone. After five minutes of repetitive announcements about how important her call was and an inane orchestral version of "Love Me Do," she hung up.

"Christ," she said, and she went to sit at the kitchen table with a cup of coffee and the paper, as she had begun to do again regularly now. Tilda knew her tirade over grammar was inconsequential, but what was happening in the news was serious. She read the articles and editorials about ongoing demonstrations against police brutality and looked closely at the photos of protesters holding up signs saying, "I can't breathe." Who could breathe after reading and seeing such barbarism? What happened to Eric Garner that day, the chokehold, the restraint by five officers, led to outrage and the rallying cry, "I can't breathe," the words Garner uttered before he died. No matter how you looked at it, there was no denying the horror of that video she had seen on her laptop.

She thought of Bev and knew she would be writing letters now that her days of protesting in the streets were over. *Good for her.*

Then out of nowhere she began to tremble. Tilda knew by now what to do, so she grabbed a glass of water and went to lie down on the sofa until the symptoms subsided. This time she had caught it before the heart palpitations had begun.

She picked up the phone again and called the temple number Laura had given her.

While the congregation had never built its own synagogue, the new Rabbi, a secretary, and Rabbi Ross had offices in a corporate park on the border of Connecticut and New York that had been donated by a congregant who was the CEO of a company headquartered there. Rabbi Ross, or Don, the name he'd asked Tilda to call him when they had spoken on the phone, greeted her warmly when she knocked on his door, welcoming her in. It was a small but pleasant space, with large windows on one side that looked out on woods with trees, now bare, allowing the sun to cast comforting light on the book-lined shelves. There were two upholstered chairs in front of the large dark-stained wood desk. It smelled of bergamot and pipe tobacco.

Rabbi Ross nodded and pointed to one of the chairs, indicating it for her while taking his seat in the other. He looked the part, Tilda thought, a full head of white hair neatly trimmed, giving him a distinguished look. A look of cheerfulness around his eyes made her hopeful.

"Harold wasn't very active in our little congregation, but he was very attentive to Laura and supportive of her Judaism," the rabbi said. His smile was so endearing that Tilda did what she always did when someone spoke kindly of Harold. She cried.

"I'm sorry," she said, reaching to catch an errant tear from the corner of her eye.

"Please, no apologies. I know. You can't really control when it hits. It comes in waves—and suddenly," he said, sliding the tissue box on his desk in her direction.

Tilda looked at him, waiting for an explanation—that someone close had just died, his wife or a relative. It wasn't what he said, neither profound nor unexpected, but how he had said it, as though from personal experience.

"Oh, no," he said, shifting in his seat, realizing what she was inferring. "It's just that I have a lot of experience with death, as part of my work." He cleared his throat and asked Tilda to tell him what was on her mind.

She basically told him the same thing she had told Bev, but with a decidedly lower level of comfort. It wasn't like her to reveal her feelings to strangers, and Rabbi Ross seemed like a stranger at the moment. She didn't know what she was doing there, revealing herself, her grief, her fears, guilt, anger—all of it—in this way. The words, which she regretted instantly, came just the same, yet the whole conversation felt forced. When she finally stopped in a bit of a stupor, Rabbi Ross began a long response. She could see his mouth moving, but she wasn't catching his words.

"I'm sure your doctor is right," he said, and yet she wasn't sure what he was referring to as he said this.

"You mentioned that you haven't filled the prescription for the antidepressants, but let me tell you what I know. The people I've talked to about the subject, many with their own qualms at first, like yours, have found some level of comfort taking them, so I wouldn't be so reluctant. It may help you get through this difficult time."

Tilda nodded in agreement, but she was still sure she wouldn't. She clung to the belief it was her portion in life, her lot to grieve and not to dull her feelings. Harold couldn't change his outcome; why should she? In her heart she knew this stance was extreme. Death of a loved one was the greatest pain to bear. Why would anyone refuse the relief? She didn't have a good answer, but she did remember her fainting spell at Laura's—and admitting to her guilt. She still believed it. She never should have slept through Harold's death. How could she forgive it?

"Is there anything more you can tell me, Rabbi? Don?"

"No matter what I say, it will sound trite. Look, Tilda, in truth there's no magic pill to clear our hearts—not like our computers, where we can hit 'clear all history.' Your history is your life, with loves, regrets, and losses. You can't hit delete."

While Tilda thought this was a tidy metaphor the rabbi had probably used before, at least now she was listening.

"It's only time that makes it possible to cope, to heal. I know that's the old line, but it's a cliché because it's true."

Tilda put her bag on her shoulder, shifted, and made a movement to stand, the universal signal of the end of a conversation, but Rabbi Ross ignored her.

"So time will help you to learn to live with the 'presence of absence,' as you so nicely put it, but your loss and the pain will always be there. That we don't forget. No, you've joined a new level of attainment in what it means to be human. It's an elite group we all join at some point."

It was a simple thought, but it registered. She took a deep breath and let it go. Then Rabbi Ross leaned over and put his hand on her knee. She smelled the bergamot again, this time realizing it was his cologne.

She rose instantly. Commingling emotions—comfort giving way to growing uneasiness—did not stop her from marveling that her head seemed to be floating above her shoulders like an overinflated balloon. She could marvel at this surreal feeling, or she could do something. She glanced at the door and, before leaving, managed to say, "Well, you've given me a lot to think about." It was lame, she was sure, but there was an insinuation there she hoped had registered. But no, that was too vague. A man who feels he has the right to touch a grieving woman's knee does not see his error or apologize when she rises abruptly to leave. He probably thinks he'll follow up with a phone call and an invitation to more "counseling." In the end, though, all she did was thank him, in a chilly tone (she thought), turn on her heels, and leave his office before he had a chance to say much of anything except "you're welcome."

She did not tremble or feel any of the other now-familiar symptoms leading to vasovagal. But she was having a physical reaction. *Was Rabbi Don hitting on me?* Whatever it was, the leaning in and the hand on her knee were not acceptable. Maybe she was overreacting, but nevertheless, she was angry that she hadn't said more.

"You have to call him and tell him it was inappropriate; otherwise you're left with your anger," said Bev, whom Tilda had called as soon as she got home. "Maybe he's just a touchy-feely guy, but you need to assert yourself."

"It was so strange. I mean, nothing he said was profound, but I was beginning to actually relax and to see some value, and then the hand on the knee, and the cologne. I didn't think men our age wore cologne anymore. It seemed oddly out of place to me."

"Call him."

And so she did, but not until she rehearsed what she would say, and not until her palms stopped feeling clammy every time she thought about actually tapping in his number on her phone. The call, when she made it, went as she had planned. She expressed her anger and her bewilderment. And Rabbi Don said all the right things: "I guess I can be too familiar, but I didn't mean to suggest anything inappropriate, I promise you. I honestly was trying to comfort you, and I thought you were beginning to come around."

"Well, I guess I was," allowed Tilda. She sensed that the call was coming to an end, and yet she still was not satisfied. What was missing? His words, she determined, were designed to make him look like the good guy. He was just friendly and misunderstood. But that wasn't the way Tilda saw it.

"Apologize," she said calmly.

"What?"

There was silence on the other end of the phone.

"Are you there?"

"Yes, but I . . ."

"I'm waiting."

"I'm sorry?" he said. At first Tilda thought he was asking her if he had said it right, but then she realized he hadn't understood her—or couldn't believe what she was asking.

"Apologize. I asked you to please apologize. I'll feel better if you do that."

"I see," he said. "But you know I didn't mean anything by it?"

Was he actually not going to do it? There was another, longer pause. Tilda held her ground, not replying.

He took a deep breath and said, finally, "I'm sorry, Tilda. I apologize."

"Thank you," said Tilda. And she gently hit the off button.

"It's better to clear the air than to cloud it with anger," Bev had said, when Tilda recounted the events of the trying circumstances to her. "I know, fortune-cookie sounding, but still, if you don't, you're the victim, even if it's of your own misconceptions. Besides, men have to know where the boundaries are. Rabbis, too. They shouldn't touch. Or wear cologne, apparently."

Exactly, thought Tilda, thinking back on her conversation with her friend.

Tilda chose not to mention the incident to Laura, though, telling her instead the part about having attained a new level of what it meant to be human. "I'm not sure why, but that made some sense to me," she said.

Two days after the rabbi encounter, George called. He belonged to a group of retired librarians who were taking a holiday trip to Cuba. The timing was perfect, he said. They would be celebrating President Obama's recent new policy on the island by going to Havana. They would leave on a flight to Miami the day after Christmas and be back in Connecticut before New Year's Eve.

"Sounds exciting—and historic," said Tilda. She'd seen George several times for tea, coffee, and once for dinner. She enjoyed his company, and that was that, as far as she was concerned, so she was shocked when he made a proposal: "So I was wondering if you would like to go. I think it will be interesting and get us out of Dodge for a chunk of the dreaded holidays. I still have a hard time with them, too, as you know."

"No," she said, barely letting him finish his sentence. "I would not like to go. I hardly know you, George." Even to her, this sounded harsh. But she had said it. Too late to take it back.

George seemed to be stumped, but only for a second, and then he laughed. "Tilda, I hardly know most of the people on the trip. That's why I'm going to have my own room. Is that what's bothering you?"

Now Tilda was embarrassed. "Oh, I don't know. I just don't think I'd have any fun. But I'm sure it will be great. And I have always wanted to go to Cuba. Just not now, I guess. Okay, well, thank you."

"Wait, Tilda. You're not going to hang up on me, are you?"

Tilda thought about this and realized she was about to do just that. The whole concept of going away with George was making her exceedingly uncomfortable. She wasn't usually one to follow the flight option in the fight-or-flight reaction. She was perfectly capable of taking care of herself, but why did she suddenly have to fight men off, two in one week?

"First the rabbi, now George. You're hot," said Bev on hearing the news during lunch the next day at the diner on Waterton. "Honestly, I think it would be a good idea. If a woman had asked, would you have had the same reaction? You say you think of him as a friend. He obviously wasn't suggesting anything too intimate. Maybe you should reconsider."

"I don't know. It's probably too late. There must be paperwork. You don't just go to Cuba."

"Nothing ventured, nothing gained."

But the subject was closed as far as Tilda was concerned. And yet in the back of her mind she considered that she could change her mind, if there were still spaces available. Her passport was up to date. No, the subject was closed. And yet if that were true, why did she choose then to phone Laura? Of course she spoke to Laura most days, but today she started the conversation with a pertinent question. "Guess who asked me to go away with him?"

This was a loaded question, to be sure, and it got Laura's attention.

"I can't imagine," she replied. "The only person you see is George, and you've said repeatedly he's just a friend."

"Well, yes. He is, and this would be just as friends, nothing romantic, for heaven's sake."

Tilda relayed the details and was surprised when Laura said, "Well, why not?"

"You mean, you think I should go?"

"Mom, he's a nice guy, you enjoy his company, and it's Cuba. It's an opportunity to see the place before it becomes just another tourist trap. I'd go in a heartbeat—if a friend asked me."

"Well, of course you're right, about seeing it now and all, but . . . no. I'm not going."

Laura sighed. "It's your decision, but I wish you'd at least consider it. You must be thinking about it, or you wouldn't have told me. Maybe you really want to go, but you're afraid. Are you afraid of letting yourself have some fun?"

Tilda wouldn't hear of it. "Don't be silly; I'm not afraid. And I told you about it because I thought it was amusing. But thanks, honey. And, yes, okay, I'll think about it."

Tilda did think about it, but she wasn't about to change her mind.

⟡

In the intervening days, Tilda had several more eventful encounters, none as unsettling as with the rabbi, but each with its own emotional weight.

One morning when Tilda braved the cold to retrieve the newspaper, she saw Darren approaching. She wrapped her coat around her and said hello. He wanted to talk but saw that she was cold and asked if she wanted to go inside.

"Come, Darren, come inside with me," she said.

He sat in the living room while Tilda put on some coffee. She joined him with a mug for each of them and with a banana bran muffin for him. "Once Harold and I thought of starting a coffee business and calling it Mug 'n' Muffin. Sounds pretty silly, but that was long before Dunkin' Donuts became so popular. So now I think it was quite a good name. Could've done well," she said, handing him the coffee and muffin.

But Darren only faintly smiled back.

She sat down across from him.

"Did you want to talk to me about something, Darren?"

"I've heard from Amanda."

Tilda was certain of what was coming, the moment she had dreaded: Darren now knew that she, Tilda, had betrayed him and Lizzie by not betraying Amanda's confidence. But he moved along to tell her things that had nothing to do with her. Instead, though, he said Amanda wanted to come home for Christmas. Tilda was elated with the news. She put her coffee down and smiled broadly, but Darren put up his hand to stop her, as if to forestall any momentary excitement.

"I'm sorry. I'm not explaining this right. What I meant is she wants to come home—for the day—to see Lizzie. She hasn't changed her mind about the rest. The truth is that I don't even want to see her."

He looked drawn, all the good humor drained from his face. It pained her to see him like this.

"How are you and Lizzie doing? I haven't seen you in a while."

"We went to see my sister in Rhode Island to get away for a few days. I thought it would do Lizzie some good to see her cousins. But honestly, she's better at this than I am, patient and understanding. I really don't understand how she does it."

"She is pretty remarkable," said Tilda. "I know I may be butting in, so just tell me to back off if you want to, but for Lizzie's sake—and probably for yours, too—maybe you should just enact a truce for the day, like the World War I soldiers, you know, who enjoyed Christmas together before getting back to fighting. At least you two won't go back to killing each other again when it's over. You wouldn't have to get into any of it, no arguments, just being together for the day."

Darren managed a little nod.

"You don't have to do anything you don't want to do, Darren. If somehow this is a prelude to her wanting to reconcile, you don't have to agree. You're not losing any control by letting her come for Christmas, for Lizzie."

"I don't know, maybe. I'll think about it."

He took the requisite few bites of his muffin and stood up to leave. Tilda walked him to the door. She wanted to give him a hug, but she wasn't sure how he would react. Instead, they just nodded and said good-bye. When Tilda closed the door, she thought she had dispensed some pretty good advice—without touching or hugging.

Later in the week she had a surprise visit from Tilly, whose mother had dropped her off unannounced.

"Where's your mother?" asked Tilda, craning her neck to look out the door as Tilly ducked under her arm to enter.

"She'll be back in an hour. She has some shopping to do, so I asked her to drop me off. It's okay, isn't it, Grandma?" Tilly ducked again when she saw her grandmother getting ready to fold her arms around her. "Okay, don't get carried away. It's just a little visit." She took her familiar seat on the sofa with Tilda sitting next to her. Tilda smiled at Tilly, for no reason, aside from one simple fact: Tilly was there.

"Okay, okay, I won't subject you to my utter joy at seeing you. And of course it's okay with me that you're here, if you haven't guessed that already. What's up, kiddo?"

"Nothing. Can't a kid see her grandmother without an ulterior motive?"

"Ulterior motive? What do you know about ulterior motives?" Tilda loved this banter with Tilly. It made her feel normal, not among the elite group of the grief-stricken. She reveled in how Tilly's character was developing, revealing her to be caring, bright, and witty, with a little edge and a pleasant strain of sarcasm, like her grandfather. But then she ached thinking of all Harold was missing, all he would miss, and all she would experience without him—both gratifying and troubling, no doubt. It would do her no good to romanticize too much.

"I watch a lot of CSI reruns. There are always hidden motives to be figured out."

"You seem in a good mood," said Tilda, wondering if this would be a good time to push for a deeper conversation.

"I'm good, really," said Tilly, nodding enthusiastically, which Tilda took to be a cover-up, not of the CSI variety, but rather her way of putting an end to further grandmotherly probing. Tilly looked at the fireplace and said, "Where are the lights and the stockings? And the decorations?" Tilda knew she was changing the subject, but she went with it.

"That's right, you haven't been here all month. Well, honey, I just didn't feel like it this year."

"Oh," said Tilly. "Yeah, I guess I understand, but Mom says you're not doing anything or going anywhere for Christmas. Won't you even come over to our house?"

Tilda didn't want to disappoint her granddaughter but decided to simply tell her the truth. "Sometimes it's better for me to be alone. Even when I can be with the people I love most in the world, like you and your mom and dad. Everybody's different, honey. This is just who I am."

"Mom says you had a chance to go to Cuba. I would love to go to Cuba. They have all those old cars there. I think that would be great—to see that. I know there's other neat stuff, too, like Cuban food and music. I also like the old buildings I've seen pictures of, kind of creepy but neat-looking, too. And it's only ninety miles away from Miami, where you grew up, Grandma. Don't you want to go?"

"Were you sent here to entice me to go to Cuba?"

"Grandma, I don't believe this is who you are, wanting to be lonely. I know you miss Grandpa. I do too, so much, but he would want us to be happy. You know that. You don't have to be sad all the time. Don't we have to follow our bliss?"

Tilda wasn't sure a trip to Cuba with George would constitute following her bliss, and wasn't that what Lizzie said was Amanda's mantra? Tilly was not exactly the "Follow your bliss" type, but Tilda understood what she was getting at.

"What do you have to lose, Grandma?"

"So you do have an ulterior motive. You little stinker." Tilly leaned in toward her grandmother, allowing herself to be hugged.

After Tilly left, Tilda remembered how her father used to gather the family into their 1953 Chevrolet and drive from Miami across the seven-mile bridge to Key West, where they would walk the streets and see the signs advertising short flights and cruises to Havana. "It's only ninety miles away," he would say. "Someday we'll go." But of course they never did. When she was a teenager, during the Cuban Missile Crisis, she wondered if she would even live to get married and have kids. Her life seemed to be teetering on the edge of nuclear annihilation. And now here she was, alone, wondering why her granddaughter was trying to convince her to go to Cuba with a retired librarian. *What a world.*

That evening, she googled the librarians' tour, paying special attention to the itinerary and the documents she would need.

It's too late, anyway, she said to herself as she closed the lid. She heated some leftovers for dinner and turned on the news. There was a segment on all the old American cars still running in Cuba. Since spare parts are very hard to come by, she learned, a trunk lock might be opened with a screwdriver, and a leak in a radiator might be stopped with a banana peel expertly placed. Still, the old cars gleamed like new.

First Tilly's unexpected visit and now this. Tilda didn't believe in signs, but maybe the fates were conspiring.

She picked up the phone and called George.

Chapter Eight

"YOU WANT TO TAKE ME TO
DINNER IN HAVANA, CUBA?"

As it turned out, there was one space available in the Librarians Tour of Havana, Cuba, when Tilda called to tell George that she'd changed her mind. Fortunately, Jaime, the tour organizer, was able to expedite the many documents and agreements needing to be signed, not the least of which were the application and affidavit for the charter flight from Miami to Havana.

"It is possible to scan the documents, yes," Jaime assured George when he'd called to add Tilda to the group. "Yes, even the passport, it is possible. And she must make payment today if she is to be included."

Tilda scrambled to get everything completed, and George came over to help with the scanning. Finally, it was done. "It was most unusual, to break the red tape in this way," Jaime told George, "but we have success. She will come with us."

When Tilda relayed the news over the phone to Laura that she had been cleared to join the tour, Laura was brought to tears—of joy. And Tilda could hear Tilly screaming, "Yes!"

in the background. Her next call to Bev was similarly joyful. "You are going to have a great time, and I think this will be the beginning, not only of the new year, but of a new you. Life goes on, my friend."

But Tilda stuck to her decision to be alone on Christmas. At least now she could say she had to pack. In truth, though, the packing was done. And while she also stuck to her resolve not to decorate the house for the season, she did haul out the Christmas box and extract one string of lights to hang over the fireplace. She poured herself a glass of wine as soon as it grew dark and plugged the end of the string into the socket. She sat on the sofa watching the lights flicker, noting the colors—red, green, gold, and white—watching the way she and Harold had always done.

Her family may have allowed her to miss Christmas, but they would not miss the morning of her departure. She was closing her suitcase for the last time when the doorbell rang and there on the doorstep were Laura and Tilly and Mark with coffee and doughnuts. "We thought you might need a little last-minute help."

"Well, no," said Tilda. "I'm all set, and I'm a little early, too, so please, come on in," she said, with a sweep of her arm ushering them over the threshold. She was touched that they had come, and happy to see them—and to see Tilly with a smile on her face. Tilda was beginning to think she could trust that Tilly was finding her way, the best Christmas gift she could hope for.

George picked Tilda up for their flight to Miami just as her visitors were leaving. There was time for quick introductions and handshakes, Laura beaming with tears in her eyes. As soon as Tilly could get her grandmother's attention, she gave her a thumbs-up, then quickly put her hands in her pockets when George looked her way. Tilda turned away to laugh to herself.

In the car, after the good-byes, she began to feel an unsettling mix of sadness and excitement. This would be her first trip without Harold, and yet her realization that she was still here caused her to catch her breath in gratitude.

On the plane to Miami, Tilda must have released a muscle or two along her spine, because as soon as she felt herself let go, George looked over and put his hand on hers, resting on the armrest between them. She waited a moment before pulling away, as if to remind him—and her—of the deal: *we're just friends.*

It was late afternoon before they checked into the Sofitel near the airport. Their rooms were next to one another, but not adjoining, Tilda noted. That evening they met the group and the tour organizers for a reception and talk about the trip. George and Tilda had dinner in the bar and said good night at the door to Tilda's room. "See you bright and early," he said, giving her hand a squeeze before leaning in for a quick kiss on the cheek.

The flight from Miami to José Martí International Airport departed early the following morning, leaving hardly time for a quick gulp of coffee and a bite from the soggy pastelito George secured for them at the hurried breakfast the tour organizers had provided. Tilda sat next to the window observing the thick white clouds, which made any view of the sea impossible until they slowly began to attenuate, showing a glistening Caribbean farther down. Soon she saw the outline of a large island come into view, ocean waves moving toward a white-sand shoreline, farmland and green hills in the background. As the charter plane glided above the coastline, Tilda could see gentle waves grow stronger as they began to splash against what appeared to be an old sea wall. She was surprised to see large buildings huddled together, an urban landscape rising from the sea. "We are passing over Havana," the flight attendant announced, "and will be landing shortly." Another green expanse of land appeared below as they began their descent. She instinctively grabbed George's arm, the same gesture she had used on countless trips with Harold. She quickly withdrew her hand and began to gather her things.

Getting through immigration and customs was effortless compared to the painfully slow process of retrieving their bags. Tilda fanned herself at the carousel as she watched an endless array of flat-screen TVs, household tools, kitchen appliances, and unidentifiable large objects wrapped in plastic go by before their luggage finally appeared. It was hard to believe that all this "stuff" was coming in as personal luggage, but then she remembered that the embargo meant these things available in any big-box store in the States were not available here.

She looked at George and frowned. "It could be worse. They can only bring in two flat-screen TVs per family," he said as several more rolled by.

On the bus Tilda felt as if she had boarded a time machine into the past as countless 1950s American cars sped by with an occasional Russian Lada ambling along. Tilda counted at least two cars similar to the dark gray 1953 Chevy her family had owned and several more similar to their later model, a 1956 two-tone blue Bel Air, Tilda's personal favorite.

There was a lot to cover that first afternoon, with no time to stop at the hotel first. At the tour's first stop, Plaza de la Revolución, Tilda turned her camera away from the image of Che Guevara on the wall of the Ministry of the Interior building to snap yet more photos of old cars, coupes, sedans, and convertibles. She could almost hear Bev chastising her for not paying more attention to the heroes of the revolution, *those who paved the way for the island's largely misunderstood experiment in pure socialism. Didn't the government of Fidel Castro provide health care, education, food, and housing for all? And wasn't that more than our country could say?* Tilda knew this was true, but she also knew there was another side to the story. She wasn't sure why she was so fixated on cars instead of the finer points of socialism on the island, except that they reminded her of long ago in Miami, her mother and father and her sister and their many weekend car trips. Then she thought of Anthony, and a little sadness descended as it always did when his image—as she imagined him—came into her mental line of sight.

Tilda wasn't sure what was next on the itinerary, but at least for now she was able to shake off any malaise and to be thankful for the conniving granddaughter who had in her way convinced Tilda to make the trip. *What do you have to lose, Grandma?* Indeed. Except, for a brief time, the constant reminder of the inevitability of death.

George and Tilda checked into their separate rooms at the Meliá Cohiba, dropped off their bags, and quickly joined the group in the lobby for a celebratory mojito. George stood at the bar talking to several members of the Connecticut contingent, while Tilda sat at a small table sipping her drink through a straw. She kept her eyes on George in an attempt to avoid eye contact with anyone else. George, like Harold, had an easy way with people, although he was more outgoing than Harold had been. She observed at least several slaps on the back and one hand lifted to clutch a shoulder attached to someone who had to have been an old acquaintance.

She slowly allowed that George was more attractive than she had originally thought, admitting to herself that his straight posture and good teeth, more than simply signs of good health, were physically appealing. (Yes, appealing.) And his brown eyes, though not (definitely not) comparable to Harold's, were deep and warm like his.

While Tilda wasn't in the mood for socializing with librarians, she was enjoying the sweet drink, so she soon ordered another.

"I'm sorry I left you here by yourself," George said when he returned to the table.

"No problem. I'm suddenly feeling very relaxed."

George laughed and said, "Well, those little mint juleps will do that to you. How many have you had?"

"They're not mint juleps. They're mojitos. Two. Just two, and they go down very nicely."

"Okay, well, I'm thinking of going up for a little rest. How about you?"

Tilda gave him a quizzical look while continuing to drink through her straw.

"I mean, would you like to go to your room for a little siesta before dinner?"

"I guess I could use a little quiet time," she replied.

Upstairs, Tilda looked out the window of her tenth-floor hotel room to see the waves crashing over the walls of the Malecón. The sun was setting, and there was a pink glow hovering above the blue water. On the sidewalk, lovers walked arm in arm. Couples, embracing, were leaning against the wall. Others danced along to music Tilda could not hear. She quickly drew the curtains and lay down on the expansive bed for a little rest. *I didn't expect life here to look so normal— under Castro, that big, bad socialist.* She giggled to herself, still feeling the effects of her two drinks. Her little rest turned into an unanticipated nap.

At seven, she waited for the elevator, hoping she wouldn't be too late. Fortunately, George had called her room to be sure she was up. "You seemed a little, well, very relaxed when I left you, and I wanted to be sure you still wanted to go to dinner," he had said.

Everyone stared at her and then at their watches as she approached the group, who had obviously been waiting for the latecomer.

"You were the one who just made the trip, the last one registered, weren't you?" one of the women commented as she boarded the bus that would take them to dinner.

"Yes, and I seem to have established a pattern of such behavior, haven't I?" she responded, owning up to her tardiness, just a bit annoyed for having been called on it.

George then introduced her to Helen, who had been a colleague of George's at the branch in Longview.

"She must be sorry I made it. I think she has designs on you, George," Tilda said after they sat down.

George smiled but didn't deny it. Tilda laughed and said, "How old are we? And here we are on what might as well be a school bus talking like kids about who has a crush on whom."

"I think what I like most about you is that you still say *whom*."

"Now why would you like that? And what you like most? That seems overstated, don't you think?"

George laughed, "A little, I guess. And yes, there are things about you I like more."

Tilda didn't respond.

The Bodeguita del Medio was cramped, crowded, hot, and full of life. The walls, covered in signatures, drew the curious searching for signs of the famous. George and Tilda, seated against a heavily autographed wall, had to shift and duck as the tourists came by for a closer look. Jaime, seated near them, told of the many writers and poets who'd supposedly been frequent customers—Cortázar, Neruda, Márquez. And of course Hemingway, who was, as far as Tilda could tell, the George Washington of Havana, having slept, drunk, and left his mark everywhere in the city. Everyone knew of his famous inscription on the wall: *My mojito in La Bodeguita, My daiquiri in El Floridita.* "But it is probably not true that Hemingway wrote it," said Jaime. "The true story is some friends of his wrote it—to be a joke—and now all the tourists come to see it."

The Bodeguita was also supposedly the birthplace of the mojito, so of course there were pitchers on every table. Tilda, growing attached to the taste, drank at least two more with her beans and rice, pork, and fried plantains.

By the time they arrived at the nightspot to see the Buena Vista Social Club, Tilda's vision was a little blurry, which put a needed soft filter on the scene, a rather rundown courtyard with droopy palms, a weary band and bandleader, and a cast of faded singers and dancers, who on occasion displayed signs of former glory, hitting the high note, taking and succeeding at a daring spin, surprising themselves for a moment before drifting back into the gloomy present. This Buena Vista Social Club was not related to the original group of that name, but was rather one of many similar bands and performers who came out at night and put on a show for the tourists in an attempt to revive the romance of a bygone era. It was Helen who had provided this explanation, which made Tilda sad and angry, sad for the performers and angry that Helen knew so much.

"C'mon, George, let's dance," she said as the bandleader was trying hopelessly to arouse some audience response.

George, it turned out, was a credible salsa dancer. Tilda was not, but she put up a passable front. "You're not bad," he said, as he spun her around.

"I'm dizzy," said Tilda.

They continued dancing even though Tilda would have appreciated it if Helen had left their table and if the room had stopped spinning. She needed to sit down, but Helen was waiting for her turn to dance with George, and Tilda wasn't about to give it to her. Helen finally gave up waiting and joined one of the two young dancers brought out to get the audience on its feet, kind of like the dancers at bar and bat mitzvahs. This seemed to placate Helen, but Tilda noticed her looking in their direction just the same.

What happened after that was not at all clear. There was the bus waiting outside to take them back. Then there was the adorable shiny yellow 1950s Chevy convertible, which in its new life in Cuba had been transformed into a taxi. Tilda had insisted they take it instead of the bus for the ride home. She remembered standing up with her arms outstretched, letting the wind whip through her hair as they drove along the Malecón, then losing her balance and falling back into George's lap.

She woke up the next morning in her bed with her nightgown on backward and over her bra and undies.

"Oh, this isn't good," she said, her head pounding, mouth dry, tongue thick. She sat on the side of the bed, the room spinning, as it had at the nightclub the night before. She reached for her watch, but her eyes wouldn't focus. Then she looked at the clock radio. The time, 10:15 a.m., slowly came into focus, and then she realized that she had missed the bus to the National Library.

She flung herself back on the bed, a move she instantly regretted because it made it all the more difficult to rise and to make it to the bathroom in time to throw up.

By noon she was feeling revived and had read George's note: *Dear Sarah Brown, Nothing happened. See you this afternoon. Sky*

He had been in her room. He had put her to bed. *Nothing happened.* Then she got it, *Guys and Dolls.* He was referring to the storyline of *Guys and Dolls.*

She was having quite an array of mixed emotions. She was getting over a hangover—that was good. Having a hangover at all—that was bad. Nothing had happened between her and "Sky"—that was good. She was happy when she thought of George—that was strange, and probably wrong. She was happy when she thought of George and guilty when she thought of Harold. She fell back to sleep.

Dinner was mercifully on their own. Jaime had provided a list of paladares from which to choose, and George and Tilda decided on a rooftop restaurant overlooking the water. They arrived before dark and were the only ones from their group. Tilda caught the briny scent of the sea. This and the light breeze brushing her bare shoulders brought back childhood nights on the single small balcony off her parents' bedroom in their Miami Beach apartment. No one in the family used it much, but Tilda liked sitting down on the concrete floor next to the wrought-iron railing and looking up to the stars, the warm breeze from the ocean a welcome counterpoint to the hot night air.

"Would you like a drink?" asked the waiter.

"How about a mojito, Tilda?" asked George.

Tilda cringed and then laughed. "No, gracias," she said to the waiter.

"I suppose you have to see the humor in it," she said to George after the waiter had left.

"You were actually all right, for the most part."

"And when did the 'most part' end?" Tilda asked. "The dancing like a woman possessed? Refusing to take the bus? Or blanking out on the rest of the evening? I think blanking out. What about you?"

George gave her one of his endearing looks. "Well, yes, the blanking-out part, I guess, because in the lobby you announced your solidarity with the Castro regime, apparently. At least that's what I think it means when you say rather loudly, *Viva la revolución!*"

"I did not."

"Yes, you did."

"What else don't I remember? How did you get me to bed?"

"I would rephrase that. In common parlance, that would mean I bedded you."

"You did not."

"No, I didn't. I did manage to get you out of your dress—sorry, but I thought it was the right thing to do—and to find your nightgown, which I tried several times to slip over your head, but I had a hard time with your arms. Finally, though, I managed. I got you to take a couple of aspirins I found in the bathroom. Then I put you to bed and left the note. End of story."

"Oh, God, I'll never be able to face the group after all this." She took her head out of her hands, looked up, and said, "Thank you, by the way. You were a gentleman, and I'm surprised you still want to be seen with me."

"Don't be silly. You've added a lot of color to what would have been a lonely time for me, except for Helen, of course, who would've kept me company in your absence."

Tilda wasn't sure how to take this.

"Oh, and thank you, by the way, for saving me from her," he added.

Tilda smiled and took a bite of the newly arrived ham-and-potatoes *croquetas.*

"Heavenly," she said.

For the rest of the trip, Tilda kept a low profile, smiling back good-naturedly when mojito comments were made in her presence, and obviously for her benefit. She also swore off mojitos or any other alcoholic beverage for the remainder of her time with the librarians.

⌒∿⌒

"She's missing, Mom. We've called the police," said Laura. That voice message and several others from Laura were there waiting to be retrieved the second Tilda turned on her phone upon arriving at Miami International late Tuesday morning, the day before New Year's Eve. Taken together, the frantic messages told the barest essentials of the story. The first call came early in the morning before the plane touched down. "Call me right away, as soon as you get in." The next one was garbled, but Laura had apparently been talking to Mark when the recording began. "She still doesn't have her phone on," she heard Laura say before hanging up. And then the last one left minutes before they landed.

Tilly was missing, but for how long, Tilda did not know. George dropped her off at Laura's and asked if she wanted him to come in, to stay with her. No, she had said, but she promised to call as soon as she knew something.

He carried her bag to the door, and, before she could go in, he grabbed her hand. "I hope you know how much you mean to me. I won't rest until I know everything is okay."

"Thank you, George. I promise I'll let you know." She turned, picked up her bag, and let herself in, leaving him standing there.

Laura was with Mark in the living room, talking to two

policemen who were just leaving. Tilda put down her bag and ran to Laura, who nearly collapsed in her arms before they both sat on the sofa, still holding each other. Mark walked the officers to the door, and Laura, gaining some composure, pulled gently away from her mother and began to tell her everything that had transpired since Tilly had gone missing the day before. Tilly had seemed fine and had asked for a ride to Andrea's. They were going to the mall, she said. Laura dropped her off, but later in the afternoon, when Tilly didn't call for a ride home, Laura began calling and texting. Tilly didn't answer, so Laura called Andrea's and spoke to Kelly, Andrea's mother, who said Tilly hadn't been there all day.

"I just dropped her off. She told me to drop her off, and I did." Laura's sobs were beginning to mount. "I didn't wait. I always wait, but yesterday I had left a cake in the oven, and I guess I was in a hurry to get home," she said before giving in to her tears. "She must've waited till I was gone and then went . . . wherever she was going."

She took a tissue from her pocket. "When she still wasn't home by dark, we called the police. They came right over and took all the information we had, which wasn't much, but they said they had to wait till morning to do a missing persons bulletin. Mark spent the night combing the neighborhood and driving the streets wherever he thought she could be. I kept calling her and texting, but nothing, no response. I called her friends, including Andrea again, after Kelly had talked to her again, too. Finally Kelly said she knew Andrea was telling the truth and didn't know where Tilly was. She politely said it was fruitless to keep calling. That's the word she used, 'fruitless,' but today the police talked to her again—and to all Tilly's friends. They were here to be sure we hadn't left anything out. They wanted to know if Tilly had been depressed lately." Laura rounded her shoulders, covered her face with her hands, and leaned into Tilda, who immediately wrapped her in her arms.

Tilda swallowed hard, hoping to keep the knot in her chest from rising. She cleared her throat and said, "So now she's officially missing. That's good, Laura. Now they will do a full search. A full investigation. That's good." She wanted to comfort her daughter, but at the same time, she felt her anxiety response begin. *Not now. Breathe, Tilda, Breathe.*

"Yes, but so far the police have nothing to go on. None of her friends know anything, or else no one's talking. I don't know which."

Tilda felt a tumble in her stomach, a small adrenaline kick. "Do you know exactly who the police have talked to?"

"Yes. We gave them the list. It's here on the table by the phone." Laura reached for it and handed it to Tilda, who looked over the names.

Laura shook her head. "I told the police something must be terribly wrong. She seemed fine. She wouldn't do this. The police said they don't think anything has happened to her. They think she's run away. At least that will be the story for at least forty-eight hours, until tomorrow."

Laura, as though in shock, kept saying, "She seemed fine. Hasn't she been fine? No more incidents since the, you know, those scratches on her arm." Tilda, handing the list back to Laura, answered that yes, she had seemed fine. Tilda, for a reason she could not yet articulate, felt the panic begin to subside. She suddenly did not think any harm had come to her granddaughter, but things obviously were not fine.

"She may seem fine to us, Laura, but the truth is that Tilly has been hiding in plain sight for a while. Maybe she just needs some time—away from us right now."

"I don't know what that means," said Laura. "Do you know what's happened to her?"

"No, I don't, but I believe she's okay. We'll find her. Don't worry." Tilda wasn't sure herself if she fully believed what she was saying. Maybe it was just wishful thinking, but she did know her first duty at that moment was to her daughter.

Laura searched her mother's face looking for more, for answers Tilda could not give her. Tilda hadn't seen that look since Laura was ten.

She'll be okay, right, Mommy? she had asked through her tears after her dog had been hit by a car. Jules, the sweet Yorkie, had been Laura's love since the day she and Harold had brought her home from the Humane Society after she had been abandoned.

Laura had seen the accident and had run to the maimed dog. Tilda, hearing screeching brakes, saw what was happening from the living room window. She saw that it was Jules who had been hit and not Laura, thank God. And then, instead of running immediately to her daughter, she ran to the closet to grab a sheet, wishing only that she had been able to get it there sooner. By the time she reached her, Laura was screaming, putting her hand into the red mass of fur, flesh, and bone exposed on Jules's side. Tilda tried to remove her hand but in the end had to pry her away in order to put the sheet over Jules's wound, where it immediately turned a deep red. Tilda stroked Jules's head. "There, there, baby, just be still. Everything is okay," she said as Jules's panting began to subside. Laura, seeing this, began to pet her dog, too, telling her how much she loved her and that soon they would be playing again, as soon as she got better. *Right, Mommy?* she asked, looking up at Tilda. That same look, the one she had now.

But of course Jules was not okay, and Laura took it hard, comforted only by the funeral in the backyard under the large oak tree that Laura liked to climb. After they had placed Jules's ashes in the small grave, Harold said a prayer. "May there be abundant peace from heaven, and life, for us. May the one who creates harmony bring peace to us—and to dear Jules—to which we say, amen," and Tilda and Laura repeated, "Amen."

"I think God will forgive that I've taken liberties with the Kaddish for a dog, don't you, Tilda?" he had said to her that night after they had put Laura to bed.

Tilda spent the next few hours assuring Laura that Tilly would be home soon. "It will be all right, I promise," she had said. Laura had wanted Tilda to stay, but she said she needed to get home to unpack and to get some rest if she could. She let Mark call her a cab but would not hear of him leaving the house. "Your place is here, Mark," she told him emphatically when he tried to object. She assured Laura she would be back early in the morning. "Don't worry," she said as she left Laura and Mark standing in the doorway, clutching each other as though they might drown if they let go. After the driver had put her luggage in the trunk, Tilda looked through the rear window to see them still standing there as the cab pulled away. She wanted to stay, to help in any way she could, but that was the very reason she had to leave.

As soon as she got home, even though it was late, she called Darren. He was happy to hear her voice and eager to share his news: "Amanda came here for Christmas, Tilda. And it was a good visit. It was just like you said. It was good for Lizzie."

Tilda took in this news with some puzzlement. She had forgotten all about her advice to Darren in the excitement of the Cuba trip. She was surprised that Amanda had been with Darren and Lizzie for Christmas, but in a way it fit in with the hunch she was about to act on. Surely the police had talked to Lizzie, but if they did, Darren was unaware of it—as well as of the fact that Tilly was missing.

"She and I didn't get into anything about what's going on with her, but that was okay, a truce, or a day without war, just like you said. I don't know what comes next, but . . ."

If her call hadn't been for a completely different reason, Tilda would have pursued Darren's thoughts on the problem of Amanda, but she had more urgent matters to attend to. She apologized for interrupting but the matter at hand, Tilly's absence, made Darren immediately empathetic.

In the middle of his reaction, expressing his shock and concern, she interrupted him again.

"I'm sorry, Darren, but can I speak to Lizzie? Just to see if she knows anything, if she can remember any little detail that may help."

"Yes, of course," said Darren as he called for Lizzie.

As soon as Lizzie got on the phone, Tilda was firm. "Did you talk to the police, Lizzie?" she asked straight away. Lizzie was silent, but Tilda heard her catch her breath.

"It's okay, Lizzie. Please let me know."

She didn't answer. Then Tilda thought she heard a door close. In a near whisper, Lizzie said, "Just for a second, I talked to them, when Dad wasn't here. But . . . I didn't tell them anything. I mean, I didn't have anything to . . ."

"Stop, Lizzie. You don't have to give up any confidences, or anything. In fact, please don't. Just say you'll let me know if you find out anything at all that you can tell me. But just do this one thing. Please tell her to call her mother. That's all she has to do, just call."

Lizzie said, "I'm not sure what to say—or to do."

"It will be okay, Lizzie. Just do as I asked, okay?"

Lizzie agreed, and they hung up.

Tilda felt as though she were walking on a high wire. Afraid to look down, she decided to keep going. She did not take any of this lightly. She realized she was taking a risk—assuming Lizzie knew where Tilly was, keeping Mark and Laura in the dark, possibly even interfering with a police investigation—but she kept going. *One step at a time, until this is over.* Then she settled down for a sleepless night.

The next morning, New Year's Eve, the phone by the bed rang.

"She called, Mom, she called," Laura, breathless with excitement and relief, said when Tilda picked up. "She's okay. She's clearly okay, but she wouldn't tell me where she is. She just said that I should tell the police that she was okay, that she's staying with a friend. I don't know what to think," Laura continued. "I asked her when she was coming home. And why she was doing this."

"What did she say?" asked Tilda, her beating heart pounding in her head.

"She said she knew school was starting next week, but that she didn't know when she was coming home. But I'm relieved. She's okay, thank God. I can't tell you how worried I was that something dreadful had happened. I don't know how you could've been so sure, but then so were the police. Apparently this happens a lot. Kids run away, mostly just temporarily for one reason or another. This has to be temporary. But she sounded so distant. I know she's okay, but I'm scared. Why would she do this?"

Tilda said she didn't know, but then she tried to bring Laura around again to the good news. "Try not to worry, Laura. I'm sure she'll be home soon."

"But now I'm frantic about who she's with. Not any of her friends that I know. I told her I would tell the police she's okay, but I really can't because who are these people? They may not be friends at all, just people who have lured her somehow. Now I'm beside myself again, just thinking about it."

"Of course you are. Yes, you have to tell the police about this," Tilda said, her stomach churning. "Laura, if you don't mind, now that we know Tilly is okay, I think I'll wait to come over."

"I don't know she's okay," she snapped. "That's what I'm telling you."

"It will be all right, I promise, and I'll be there as soon as I can," she said as she hung up the phone.

Tilda, who was still in bed, put her hands to her head and took a deep breath. Morning light was just coming through the corners of the night shades. She knew she had to move quickly, but she had learned by experience that she could avoid annoying her stiff morning muscles simply by moving methodically. *The indignities of growing older*, she thought, repeating to herself a comment she and Harold had often made to each other, laughing and taking comfort in growing old together. Now she was left having to be grateful that she was still here, alone. Not grateful she was dealing with her fears and uncertainties without him.

Sitting on the side of the bed for a moment before getting up, she knew what she had to do today: get to Brooklyn, where she was sure she would find Tilly in the throes of being young, trying to discover who she was. This was her hunch, which explained why she had needed to talk to Lizzie and why her pending trip was more important than being with Laura, who was beside herself with worry.

But it would all come to this one day, with Tilda, sitting on the side of the bed not moving too quickly, about to launch herself back to where her family had begun, only now—skipping a generation—on a mission to retrieve her granddaughter. She was about to launch herself completely out of her quiet life of semi-solitude, creaking bones and all. She knew Tilly was in her own kind of pain, even as she was creating pain for others. *The indignities of the young.* She was being philosophical, but in truth she had her sights on Amanda.

Although she hadn't talked to Lizzie beyond last night's call, Tilda was certain she was putting the pieces together accurately. The image in her head she kept coming back to was on Thanksgiving when she had seen Tilly and Lizzie talking together in the kitchen. *Thick as thieves.* What had Lizzie been telling her?

Chapter Nine

TO LIVE IN THIS WORLD

❧

*U*r gram called. May know where u r. Call ur mom.

Harper wondered how her grandma knew to call Lizzie. The text didn't really explain anything, so Harper called Lizzie, who told her in a whisper that she couldn't talk. "My dad might be listening. So look, your grandma might know you're with my mom. I don't know how, I didn't tell, but she knew to call me. Why, I don't know. She said you have to call your mom. I guess 'cause she's worried, but your gram isn't telling anyone what she knows, I'm pretty sure. She was real secretive."

"But how could she know where I am?" asked Harper.

"I don't know. Maybe she just figured it out. She's intuitive."

"I guess."

Harper promised she'd call her mom and put her phone on the nightstand. She decided not to call right away. She wanted to think about it. Maybe her mom was sleeping—and she probably wasn't sleeping much. This thought made Harper's nose tingle the way it always did before she cried. She wiggled her nose to make it stop and lay down on the squeaky cot and stared at the ceiling of the small office space that Amanda had made into a bedroom for her. *I'll wait till morning to call*, she thought, and then she drifted back to sleep.

But at two in the morning, she looked at her phone, on sleep mode, and saw that her mom was still texting her. She deleted what would have been like the two hundredth text she had received and determined to call at six. *I know she'll be up and making coffee by then.* She went limp thinking of her kitchen at home with her mom in it. She could smell the deep-roast coffee brewing, reminding her of the taste, both sweet and bitter until she put in sugar and cream, lots of cream. Her mom let her drink coffee. A lot of moms didn't. Her mom was strict, but she could be cool, too, thought Harper. She turned over and buried her head in the musty pillow.

At six, still in bed, she called. Her mom was hysterical, crying and laughing, making a sound in her throat like a cat, not a purr exactly. She was too upset for that, but it was close. It was nice, happy.

"I know I'm making you worry, Mom, and I'm sorry. But I promise I'm okay. I'm with friends."

"But who? The police have talked to your friends. Who are you with, Tilly?"

"You don't know them. I promise they're good."

"No, no, no. Tell me where you are."

Her mother was crying into the phone when Harper started crying, too.

"Mom, just, please, please, try not to worry. Try to understand. I'm really, really okay. I just have some things to work out."

"What do you have to work out?" her mother asked, pleaded to know. "You can tell me anything. Your dad and me. You know that, don't you?"

Harper didn't answer. *Tell you anything? No, I don't think I can tell you anything. You don't even get that I'm Harper now.* But she didn't say that. She didn't know when she would be able to tell them, didn't think she could bear their looks of disappointment. Their perfect Tilly, now Harper? No, she couldn't imagine it.

Instead she asked her mother if she had called the police and told her to tell them she was okay.

"When are you coming home?" her mother asked.

Harper said she didn't know and hung up.

She thought about getting out of bed, but she suddenly felt too heavy to move, so she lay there, staring at the ceiling. It was covered with white plastic stars someone had glued up there once. Maybe they were fluorescent, but they didn't glow in the dark anymore—or if they did, Harper hadn't noticed. The thought of someone on a ladder gluing stars to the ceiling made her sad, and tears streamed from the corners of her eyes and rolled down the sides of her face into her hair. She didn't brush them away, though. She just let them roll while she continued to look at the stars.

Outside the small window in this attic space she heard a few stray winter birds calling to one another. She thought back to how she had come to be here, in Amanda's new home. Lizzie told her at Thanksgiving that she knew where her mother was and made Tilly promise not to tell. She had promised. But she kept thinking about Amanda and how she was making a new life for herself. She wanted that, to start over—as someone else maybe. She called Lizzie, who said it would be okay, and here she was. It was all so strange, she could hardly believe it.

She thought about her grandmother and about what she knew and wondered how she knew.

I told her I wanted to be Harper. She was supposed to help me tell Mom and Dad, but she didn't—because she got so upset by the cuts. They wouldn't listen anyway. They don't listen to anything I try to tell them. Just make good grades and dance and say nice things and always, always be good. Well, I'm tired of being good. And even Grandma, at the mall, when I got so mad, all she did was freak about the cuts.

Maybe I'll just stay here.

One summer afternoon when she was ten and visiting her grandparents, she went out in the backyard to be alone, as she often did. She climbed her favorite tree, going higher than she had ever gone before. The tree, a large oak, was heavy with midsummer leaves. She leaned forward on a high sturdy branch until she was hugging it with her arms and legs and shimmied as far out as she could to see better her yard and house below, when suddenly she realized how high she had come. She didn't know how she could get back to the ground below without falling. So she stayed awhile longer, but she still didn't think she could make it safely down from her little perch. She thought about just staying there. That wasn't as scary as the thought of climbing down.

Eventually, her grandmother came out the door and began calling for her. She called back. "I'm up here," she said. Her grandmother told her to come down and she said no.

Soon her grandfather called to her. He told her to come down, and she answered, "I can't."

Her grandfather came and stood under the tree. He asked her how she got there.

"I climbed—and then I scooted out here on this branch," she told him.

"Well then," he said, "scoot back down."

"How?" she asked. "I can't turn around."

"Backward, then."

"Backward?"

"You can do it."

So she did, backward off the branch, and then hugging the tree, all the way down.

❦

Emile's address had been easy to find in the white pages online. With that information, Tilda had tapped the Williamsburg house number into Zillow to see that Emile Baptiste was the last person to have bought the house, and that was a little more than fifteen years ago. Driving east now on the Brooklyn–Queens Expressway, Tilda began going over the pieces of the puzzle she had put together in preparation for the moment at hand, when she would knock on Emile's door and Amanda would answer.

First puzzle piece: Lizzie.

Why had she been so understanding of her mother's abandonment? What if, Tilda speculated, she had known all along where her mother was? Tilda thought back to that first night when Lizzie had come over, when Darren was trying to find Amanda. She had said something about her mother needing to follow her bliss. (Funny that Tilly had used that phrase too, trying to convince her grandmother to go to Cuba.) Tilda had wondered how Lizzie knew such things and how she could think about her missing mother with such serenity. It made more sense to think that Amanda and Lizzie had a strong bond, one that enabled the mother, perhaps an emotionally adolescent mother, to confide in her daughter about her own needs. She wondered how much Lizzie might know about Emile. Surely Amanda hadn't involved her daughter in her betrayal of Darren. Before indulging in any self-righteousness, though, Tilda, felt the tug of her own duplicity where Darren was concerned—and Lizzie, too—if it turned out she was wrong about her suspicions.

And then there was Tilly.

Why did she run away, if that indeed was what she'd done? Tilda believed that her granddaughter had given her parents and her reason to see that she was troubled—the cutting, her grief, her meltdown at Thanksgiving—these were all signs of her unhappiness. And yet, had they really paid attention to the flares Tilly was sending up? Didn't they agree on some unspoken level that her arm had "scratches," not cuts? Hadn't they put Thanksgiving behind them? Where was the reckoning, the admission that all was not right? Here Tilda had to stop. Why was she including Laura and Mark? Was she so reluctant to face her own negligence? After all, Tilly had confided in her from the beginning that she wanted to be Harper, and Tilda had said nothing. At Thanksgiving, Tilly said she wasn't sure who she was—and Tilda had let it go. Really, she had. Why? It was all too much. That was it. She could scarcely help herself since Harold had died.

As Tilda thought about Thanksgiving, she remembered Tilly and Lizzie engaged in conversation. *Thick as thieves, indeed.*

And now nagging Tilda was the way in which Tilly had questioned all aspects of her life, including her name and her desire to be called Harper. And Tilda had forgotten all of it, swept it all away so that she could continue to adore her perfect granddaughter, who was helping her slide out from under her grief.

Hadn't Tilda been charmed by their last conversation, their bantering, Tilly's admonition to Tilda to follow her bliss? Where had that advice come from—from Lizzie, explaining to Tilly her mother's motives for leaving? She hadn't been paying attention, but that would change, she vowed.

Among the many unanswered questions (if her suspicions so far were correct) were these two: What had Tilly told Lizzie that made Lizzie offer her mother's new residence as a hideout for her friend? And, most perplexing, why had Tilly found her unhappiness so compelling that she had left home to find refuge with Amanda and Emile?

These questions might have given Tilda reason to take it slowly, to be more cautious, and yet on a hunch, she was embarking on what might prove to be an ill-conceived mission. Or worse, she might be hiding from Laura and Mark what could be valuable information—and at the same time potentially disrupting an ongoing police investigation. These things might have given her pause, if it hadn't been for one thing: she was in pursuit of her missing granddaughter, and for that she gave herself permission to be very wrong.

Let the chips fall where they may, she thought as she turned onto Metropolitan Avenue and then onto the street where she would find Emile.

Tilda found a parking space nearby. Emile's home was one of two in a humble red brick duplex. The two single-family homes were side by side, each with two floors. The building was surrounded by expensive rehabbed artists' lofts, no doubt inhabited by well-off non-artists.

She rapped Emile's doorknocker, a cast-iron depiction of a spider catching a fly, and felt a sudden seizing in her chest. *That's creepy*, she thought, and rapped again.

A very slim, very pale young man in sweatpants, a navy sweatshirt with the sleeves cut above the elbow, and a gray wool cap answered the door. Tilda noticed the single but very prominent tattoo running along the inside of his left arm, quite visible when he opened the door. In bold capital gothic letters, it read, 𝔓𝔈ℜ 𝔄𝔪𝔒ℜ𝔈.

"Can I help you?" he asked.

Tilda, though on a clearly defined mission, found herself stammering in response. She was searching the room behind him for signs of Tilly.

"Emile Baptiste?" she managed to say.

"Emile? Oh, no, I'm Gregory. I work with him, but he's not here now. I can show you his studio out back and what he has available, if you want, though."

"What he has available?"

"Yeah, his paintings. Isn't that why you're here?"

At that moment she saw Amanda walk by and stop at the foot of the stairs. She saw Tilda and came toward her.

"It's okay, Gregory. Let me," she said, taking his place at the entrance.

"I'll be out back if you need me," he said.

"Are you going to let me in, Amanda?"

"What are you doing here?"

"I think you know why I'm here."

And with that, Amanda stepped aside and gave Tilda her answer.

"Where is she?" Tilda asked, wishing she didn't sound so breathy and therefore nervous. She needed to be strong in her self-cast role as granddaughter rescuer.

"I'll get her in a minute, but first we should talk."

Tilda was relieved, knowing that Tilly was actually close by but also anxious to see her. Amanda was standing between her and her granddaughter. "You have some explaining to do, it's true, but no, no talking." And yet . . . she was curious to hear what Amanda would say to excuse herself somehow for harboring a missing child, but no, she was more eager to get her granddaughter and leave.

"Tilda, please, just for a minute, and then I promise I will get her for you."

Amanda's calm response gave Tilda little room for further resistance, and so, reluctantly, she gave in, following her into a small, dimly lit living room.

Sitting on two old sofas, facing each other and draped in colorful fabric helping to soften their obvious state of dilapidation—the whole room was a manifesto against anything fashionable—she and Amanda looked at each other across a steamer trunk functioning as a coffee table.

"Can I get you anything, coffee?" asked Amanda.

Tilda chose to skip the amenities. "What is it you have to say to me?"

Amanda leaned forward, her elbows on her knees. "First, I want you to know, I didn't say she could come here. She showed up on our doorstep, so what was I supposed to do? Turn her away? I figured she'd be safer here with us than out on the street."

"Fair enough, but why didn't you let Laura and Mark know? You must have known they'd be sick with worry. She's been missing since Monday."

Amanda sat up, a slight frown drawing her dark eyebrows closer. "I don't know how much of this you want to know."

Tilda, trembling, felt a chill in her stomach. She took a deep breath and asked for a drink of water. "No ice, just water." She needed a minute to gain control over the fainting symptoms she hadn't felt since she had agreed to go away with George. She took several steady, slow breaths and thought if she began to feel better, she could just bolt upstairs, grab Tilly, and make a run for it. But she knew she needed to hear Amanda out. By the time Amanda came back with the water, Tilda felt in control.

"So Harper and Lizzie have become pretty close," Amanda offered.

Harper! She was Harper now—to Amanda? It was all Tilda could do to hold her glass of water steady. She had entered a new reality here in this house in Brooklyn, and she wasn't sure she could contain herself, but somehow she did and nodded, and she refrained from saying that she'd had no idea their friendship could be described as close.

"So of course they tell each other things." Amanda suddenly stopped. "Look, I think some of this you need to hear from Harper and not from me. I just wanted to let you know I—Emile and I—didn't ask for this."

"And I want to know why you didn't tell her parents their daughter was with you." She set the glass down on the trunk between them, its surface lumpy with peeling leather. "I don't know what kind of relationship you have with your daughter, but this is all a little strange. I've been beating myself up over not telling Darren what I know—because that's what you asked—and feeling pretty bad about Lizzie. And now I see that Lizzie is in on it, Emile and the whole thing. How do you do it, Amanda? Go back home to be with Darren and Lizzie on Christmas, and all the while Darren hasn't a clue about what's really going on?"

Amanda took a deep breath, clenched and unclenched her jaw, then slowly let the words come.

"Harper came here because she thought she could be herself without judgment, that she wouldn't have to live up to everyone else's idea about who she should be. So maybe my less-than-perfect situation isn't so bad in that regard. And Lizzie? She's fine. And Darren will be fine, too."

Tilda nodded, but not in agreement. "I'm glad you have this all worked out. But you still haven't answered my question, and now I just want my granddaughter."

Tilda stood, and Amanda rose, too. "Tilda, wait. I'll get Harper, of course, but please don't rush off with her. I think that would be very upsetting."

"I can't stay here and go along with this. I have to call Laura and let her know her daughter is okay."

Amanda didn't move, standing her ground, giving Tilda a minute to think.

She swallowed and said, "You should let Tilly know I'm here—and, please, make sure she knows the only reason Lizzie said anything is that I figured out where she was."

"It's okay, Tilda. Lizzie told her already, and Harper figured you'd be coming for her."

Tilda could take it no more. "Please, stop calling her Harper to me. None of that has been settled yet. Don't you think you may be intervening in a family matter—the child's birth name, for God's sake?"

Amanda stood facing Tilda, not backing down. "Really, Tilda?" she replied.

Tilda took a breath, exhaling forcefully, deflated by what she knew to be true. Who was she to call out anyone for intervening?

"I'll wait and talk to her here, but just the two of us."

"No, Tilda. You've raised the subject—and I said I didn't know how much of this you wanted to get into. So now I think we should talk." She pointed to the sofas. Tilda took her seat once again.

"Do you know *why* Harper chose a new name?" asked Amanda.

"Of course I do. She's confused and mixed-up right now. She misses her grandfather and, frankly, I think, she's afraid of growing up."

Amanda continued to stare at Tilda. "You honestly think that's all that's going on?"

Tilda could no longer stifle her anger, knowing where this conversation was headed—and that Amanda was setting herself up to be the teller of the truth everyone close to Tilly had been avoiding, including Tilda.

"If you have something to say to me, just say it. Do you honestly think I'm so naive that I don't know she's questioning her sexuality?"

"I'm not the enemy, Tilda. I'm honestly trying to help."

There was that word, *irony*, again popping up in Tilda's head, in Amanda's stance as the concerned surrogate parent even though she had just recently abandoned her own child.

"I'm glad you realize this is deeper than some free-floating confusion, but it isn't her sexuality she's questioning. It's her gender."

Being schooled in these distinctions rankled, and in spite of her opinion of Amanda, Tilda knew she had to hear her out.

"Harper trusts you, Tilda, and she wants to talk to you. She knows on some level that you will understand. And right now, she doesn't have that confidence in her parents. That's all I wanted to say. She will tell you the rest. Let me get her for you." She turned to go but then stopped and faced Tilda once again. "I'm sorry about the name business. I know it must be hurtful to you. She's named after you, isn't she? But I'm afraid she's Harper now." And then she left to get her.

Alone, Tilda smoothed her skirt and looked down at her hands, her mother's hands. She wondered what her mother would think if she were suddenly thrust back into the world. What would she think of her beautiful great-granddaughter, named after her grandmother, wanting to be Harper?

Just then, Gregory walked in, holding two bare canvases. "Have you seen Amanda?" he asked.

"She went upstairs," said Tilda.

Gregory set the canvases down and sat across from her. "So you're Harper's grandma," he said.

Harper to everyone, it seemed. Tilda shifted. "Um."

"She's a great kid."

"Yes. She should be down any minute, so . . ."

"Oh, don't worry, I'm just leaving. Have to get these in the studio for Emile," he said, gesturing toward the canvases leaning against the wall.

Gregory was younger than Tilda had first thought— maybe early twenties. "Have you worked here long?"

"Oh, yeah. I was . . . friends . . . with Franklin," he said, "Emile's son. Died. Motorcycle."

"Oh, I'm sorry," said Tilda. Her thoughts immediately gravitated to Harold, a reaction that occurred at any mention of death.

"Yeah, he was a great guy. I knew him since we were kids, when they first got here from Saint Lucia—Franklin and Emile. His Mom, well, she left them when he was just a kid. So they came here. Emile was already pretty well-known as an artist there. Portia, she had her own gallery then, said she would rep him. She got him started."

Gregory must have seen Tilda looking at his arm. "This is for Franklin," he said, turning the inside of his arm up so Tilda could see more clearly. "*Per amore*, it's what I believe. Everything should be about love. That's how I think about it. I've tried a lot of things, even hate, but love is better. It makes me happy, so that's what I choose now."

"Good, Gregory. Good for you. I'm glad that works for you," said Tilda, not knowing what else to say.

"Well. Gotta go. Nice talking to you." He left with the canvases, one under each arm, unfazed, if he had taken any note at all of Tilda's less-than-sincere response to his philosophy.

Tilda thought about how often these days she seemed to be confronted with poster-like sayings. Was everyone cranking this stuff out? *Choose love: it makes you happy.* Just as she was about to congratulate herself on her discriminating taste, she realized Gregory was a member of the same "elite group" to which she now belonged—the one Rabbi Ross had told her about. Franklin died; Harold died. Gregory and Tilda mourned. And Emile, she realized. It also did not escape her that his wife had left him—and now he was harboring Amanda. There was more wonderment. It seemed odd to her that Gregory had a tattoo on his arm, and Tilly may have "scratched"—no, tried to cut a word—into hers. The ironies abounded.

Tilda began to grow impatient. It was taking a long time for Tilly to come down. When finally she did appear, Tilda had to hold back from folding her into her arms and heading for the door. Still in that plaid shirt, her hair obviously uncombed and hastily pulled back into a stingy ponytail, it did not appear that Tilly was thriving under Amanda's unjudgmental care.

"Hi, Grandma," she said softly. She hesitated, and then she rushed into Tilda's waiting arms. Amanda was nowhere to be seen. She must have stayed upstairs, and Tilda was grateful for her discretion. They sat on the sofa where Tilda had been waiting, and, still holding on to each other, Tilda rocked her and told her everything was okay, relieved that Tilly was apparently not mad at her for coming.

"Have you called Mom yet?" Tilly asked.

"No, sweetheart. I wanted to talk to you first."

"I don't know what to say. I don't know if you want to hear it, about why I ran away."

She pushed Tilly away just enough so that she could hold her by her shoulders. "You know how much your mother and father and I love you. You could tell us anything, and as long as you were all right, we would still love you. You couldn't make us stop loving you, no matter what."

Tilly looked at her grandmother. What she was thinking, Tilda couldn't know. What must it be like, she wondered, to be so confused and unsure of your place in your once-familiar and comfortable world that you take off from everything you know, not understanding exactly why you're running or where you hope to end up? *Maybe her world was never that comfortable*, thought Tilda.

Looking into Tilly's eyes, Tilda saw something soften, a subtle shift in her expression. She began to talk.

"Weren't you curious about why I wanted to be Harper?" she began. "It's because if my name is Harper, no one knows if I'm a boy or a girl. And honestly I don't know, and maybe I don't want to be either one. All I know is I don't want my body to change. I don't want breasts, and I don't want to bleed. I know something's wrong with me because when my friends talk about getting married and having babies I want to puke."

Facing each other now on the sofa, Tilly grabbed for the fabric to wrap it around her, as if to shield herself from what her grandmother might have to say.

But Tilda thought it best to keep listening. "It's okay, Tilly."

"And I don't like boys. But I don't like girls, in that way, either, I don't think. I don't know. I don't like anybody in that way. What's wrong with me?"

Tilda slowly shook her head. "Nothing, Tilly. Nothing is wrong with you. It's like we talked about at Thanksgiving. You don't have to have all the answers now. No matter what, you're okay."

"How can I tell Mom and Dad? I'm not even sure I should be talking to you about it," she said, pulling back and pointing an accusing finger at Tilda. "You almost saw at the mall, but all you cared about were the cuts."

"Almost saw what?" asked Tilda.

"They were cuts," Tilly said, pounding her fists into her lap. "Kinda deep, too, and definitely not just scratches. Mom didn't know because by the time I showed her, it had stopped bleeding. I used a razor blade and *then* a safety pin to make it clear, but it wasn't."

Tilda remembered grabbing Tilly's arm at the mall and then thinking she had seen something there. But she wasn't sure, and the whole fucking mall day had gone so badly.

"Tilly, I did care about your arm, about the cuts, and I also wanted to know more about what I thought I saw there, but you shut me out, remember? We hardly spoke, for a long time."

Tilly's eyes brimmed with tears. Tilda wanted to reach for her again, but she waited.

Then, lips trembling, Tilly continued, "But you didn't even try. And Mom was sure it was just scratches. Even though you saw it was something more. I needed you. Why didn't you try harder?"

Tilda, now on the verge of tears herself, would not put her own grief on Tilly, would not say she didn't have the strength for something so deep as cuts.

"You're right," she said, her voice soft with regret. "I think your mom and I . . . I danced around how much you were hurting. I think I was afraid, maybe, to admit that my perfect Tilly was having problems I might not have been up to handling. I'm so sorry." Tilly, whose chin was jutted out in defiance, pulled back into herself and looked down at the fabric she had let drop.

"It's not just you, Grandma. I wanted you to know how I was feeling; I wanted Mom and Dad to know, but also I didn't. I was scared, too. That's why I got so mad at you."

"If we could go back, instead of getting so upset at the mall, I would've asked if you had written a word. I would've asked calmly, not the way I did. I thought maybe I saw a word, but I didn't know for sure, honestly."

"I tried to write *Truth is beauty*, but it was too long, so I quit after *truth*, but I couldn't really make it clear. Mom couldn't even tell what it was. She thought I just scratched myself with the pin."

"*Truth is beauty*? Is that what you believe. Do you know where it's from?"

"It's Keats. We studied it in school, and I liked the ending because I think it's true that truth is beautiful, but truth is also scary sometimes, and people hide from it. Did you know he died when he was only twenty-five? I wonder what I'll be like when I get to be that old."

"You'll be as extraordinary as you are this very minute," said Tilda. "You know, Tilly, nothing you've told me is so terrible you had to run away, so it troubles me that you thought you couldn't talk to us about it."

"Even if I want to be Harper?"

"We will love you just the same, Harper."

Tilda watched as Tilly's expression changed. The sadness, while not entirely gone, was eclipsed by the brightness, missing for so long, that now shone in her eyes.

"I guess we should call Mom."

Tilda and Harper turned when they heard the front door open. Amanda came down the stairs and met Emile as he walked in. He looked in the living room and saw Tilda and Harper looking back at him.

Emile was tall and muscular with blue eyes that complemented, in an unexpected way, his brown skin. Tilda met his extended hand with hers.

"So, you have come to reclaim our houseguest," he said with a warm smile, charm being an easy option for him, Tilda sensed.

"Yes. As soon as I call her mother, we'll be on our way," she said, not yet giving in to her relief to be so near the end of this whole episode.

But then Amanda broke in. "Tilda, please, stay for lunch. It would mean a lot to us. And Harper should eat something before she leaves.

Tilda wasn't sure why Tilly—why *Harper*—would need anything more than to get into the car and go home, but she agreed when she saw Harper smile at Amanda.

"I'll call Harper's mother and let her know we'll be home soon," she said, trying to hide her anxiety. "Harper, why don't you go in and help with lunch. I'll be in in a minute."

Once alone in the living room to make her call, she focused on Harper's smile, needing some encouragement. She dreaded letting Laura know where her daughter had found refuge.

The call to Laura did not go well. She was confused and angry that so much had transpired without her knowledge, wanting to know how and why Tilly had turned up in Brooklyn with Amanda, how Tilda had known where she was, and, for that matter, how she had known where Amanda was, wanting to know if Darren knew. It was true she was relieved that Tilly was safe and would be home soon, but it was clear that she was also more than a little irritated at her mother's role in the rescue, especially since she had chosen not to let Laura in on it. "I don't know how you managed to get in the middle of this, but I guess you've thought it through, like how and when you're going to talk to Darren, who apparently is in the dark as much as we were. This is really, really sad, Mom."

And I haven't even told her about the rather definite name change or about the now out-in-the-open gender issues. "Yes, I know you're upset with me, Laura," she managed to say to her daughter.

That aside, Laura had gone right to the heart of Tilda's remaining troubles. She hoped that Laura would forgive her for the secrecy of the rescue operation once she explained she had been acting on a hunch. She had to be right before getting Laura's hopes up. And she knew that Laura and Mark would know how to help Tilly—*Harper; I'll never get it right*—get through her doubts and obvious fears. But Darren was different. He would have to deal not only with Tilda's involvement in his family's problems, but also, and more importantly, with what was sure to be his disappointment with Lizzie. Tilda had her own share of guilt to contend with, but in addition to that, she was troubled, still, by Amanda, who had drawn Lizzie into her domestic drama. This was unforgivable, as Tilda saw it. She was not looking forward to lunch.

❦

Soon the smell of onion and unidentifiable but slightly familiar things frying filled the downstairs room, where Harper and Tilda were waiting. Before long Emile walked into the living room and told them lunch was ready. Tilda and Harper followed him to the large wooden table in the dining area. As he walked into the kitchen, Tilda looked through the archway to see a bay window, outside of which was a small garden and a large shed, Emile's studio no doubt.

Amanda, wearing a chef's apron, came in from the kitchen and placed a large green ceramic platter in the center of the table. Emile and Gregory followed her out. The hosts and guests sat on long benches on each side of the table. Emile stood between Amanda and Gregory on the side opposite Tilda and her granddaughter and began to serve as plates were handed to him.

"It's green fig and saltfish, in case you're wondering. And

there's also coconut milk and spices in the mix," he said of the colorful arrangement on the platter. "It's a Saint Lucia specialty," he added, passing Tilda her plate.

"My mother used to make it when I was a boy. A little taste of home," said Emile, smiling at Amanda.

"This is the first time I've made it myself," she said. "Usually it's Emile who does the cooking."

Tilda took this in, noting the affection that passed between them.

"Bacalhau," said Tilda. "Well, it's not the same thing, but it's a cod dish. Portuguese. Harold's mother used to make it. I tried, but not very successfully."

"It's ancient, using salt to preserve fish. And then it becomes a favorite dish."

"Yes, as long as there are other things added, like fig? It looks like banana," said Tilda, allowing the pleasure of the sweet yet spicy smell rising from her plate to momentarily distract her from her discomfit at having agreed to stay for lunch.

Emile laughed. "You are right. It is banana, green bananas—not fig, just called fig."

"Well, it's wonderful," said Tilda to Emile but not to Amanda. "Do you like it, Harper?" she asked, rolling the name around in her mind, trying to see if she could ever make it stick.

Tilly . . . *Harper*, who had been peeking at her phone, looked up.

"Yes, Grandma, I do like it," she said brightly.

And so it was: sitting around the table and talking of food began to repair Tilda's ragged emotions. After lunch, she helped Gregory clear the table while Harper went upstairs to get her few belongings. *If I think of her as Harper it will stick*, she thought, as the new name continued to plague her.

"Tilda, sit with me a minute, please?" asked Amanda, seeing Tilda about to leave the dining area. They sat opposite each other at the table. Amanda said, "I'm sorry. I just don't seem to get things right. I thought I was helping. She seemed so lost. I didn't know what to do."

"I'm not going to say it's okay, Amanda, because it's not. You've put me in a bad spot. Now I have to face Darren—and Lizzie, too. But more important, what are you going to do?"

Amanda looked agonized. "I don't know. When I met Emile, Franklin, his son, had just died—killed on his motorcycle on this very street. Emile was shattered. Gregory, who was Franklin's lover, tried to commit suicide. And in his grief, with his life in ruins, Emile took Gregory in, and he's lived here ever since. I was so touched by his sweetness and his grief that I knew my place, maybe not forever but someday, would be with him. And over the next year or so we became very close, and before long, I knew I was in love with him. You think what I'm doing is some sort of irresponsible fling, but I truly have deep feelings for him."

Tilda listened to Amanda's story with sorrow. Her empathy for Emile and Gregory was palpable—they were in her elite group, and she knew something of what they had suffered and would continue to endure—but her empathy did not extend to Amanda. Her compassion was admirable, but not the rest.

"It doesn't matter what I think. What are you going to do about Darren?" she asked again, emphasizing each word.

"If you'll give me a minute, I'll try to explain. I love Darren. I do. I was happy being home at Christmas. I miss my family. I feel that in consoling and being with Emile I've lost Lizzie, and I can't bear that. I know something has to change. I just don't know what to do or how to do it yet. At first I was blindly following my heart. I'll admit, I wasn't thinking about what I was doing. Not all of it. Not what maybe could never be repaired."

"But how did you bring Lizzie into it?"

"I know you'll find it hard to understand, but Lizzie knows me. She knew I wasn't happy. I was able to talk to her about things in a way maybe a mother shouldn't. But our relationship is different. In some ways, I'm not proud of it. Look, she's wiser than I am. I think she wanted me to, I don't know, just see if somehow I could be happy. And she was willing to take that chance. I know it's unusual—but then, so is she."

Yes, she is that, unusual. "So she agreed to this?" Tilda asked.

Amanda looked pained. "I'm not proud of what I've done. I know I put her in a terrible position. She was willing to take the brunt of it, for me. She said she would look after her father—and that I should go."

Tilda was astonished that this could ever have seemed tenable to Amanda. She listened but could not accept what she was hearing. Her place was not to judge, but she was judging, she knew. And yet, Amanda did appear to be having her doubts now, certainly some regrets, romantic notions at odds with the pain of her actions, like a prism refracting light at different angles.

Tilda put a hand on the table, as though she were about to lay out a plan, but there was no plan beyond the small step she knew she had to take.

"Well, Amanda, you know that I'm going back to explain what I can to Darren and to ask him to forgive me. And I want to talk to Lizzie and help her, too, but I'm not her mother. You are."

"I will deal with it."

"When? You told me the same thing back in October."

"I don't know what more I can say." Amanda put her hands in her lap, looking down at them.

Tilda was suddenly weary. "You can *say* that you will tell Darren before I do, that you'll pick up the phone and tell him soon, right away, as soon as I leave." She paused to see if her words were having any effect. Amanda seemed pained but said nothing.

"Look, Amanda, I can't force you into anything. But I will tell you this: At some point in your life, if you're lucky enough to get old, you may be left alone to grieve for someone. And the best you can hope for in life is that you are overcome with grief at that time, because you would've lived your life with the person you loved."

She knew she was talking about herself now, but so what. It was true, and maybe it could help.

They both stood. Amanda stepped forward, holding out her arms. Tilda allowed the embrace as Harper walked into the room and quietly tiptoed back out.

Chapter Ten

TO THE NEW YEAR

～✍～

The afternoon sun was growing weak as Tilda and her granddaughter began their drive home to Connecticut.

"Grandma, I know you're mad at Amanda . . ."

Tilda was on alert for anything Harper might say that could cast a favorable light on Amanda. She knew she was still harboring some resentment there and wasn't ready to hear anything about how wonderful Amanda might be. "Why do you think so? Is it something she said?"

"No, it isn't that. It's just that, you know, I could just tell. The way you looked at her and how you talked to her."

"Really? I wasn't aware . . ."

"Well, anyway, I just wanted to let you know, when she came to get me, to tell me you were there, she said some really nice things."

Eager as she was to hear more, Tilda wasn't falling for it. "Like what?" she asked.

"Okay, well, don't take this the wrong way or anything, but I . . . well . . . I wasn't sure what to do. I wasn't sure I wanted to go home with you. Can you understand, Grandma? It wasn't anything against you. It was just . . ."

"It's okay. I understand. You ran away, well, you went to Amanda, because you felt you couldn't talk to us, so I understand if you weren't sure you were ready to come home, but I'm so glad you talked to me, honey."

"Well, that's just it. It was Amanda. She told me you wouldn't be there if you didn't love me, and that Mom and Dad love me, too, and that they're worried, and it's not fair to them. She said she was going to have to tell them where I was and that it was time to go home."

"She told you all that?" Tilda asked, genuinely surprised. Seeing an opportunity, given her granddaughter's openness, she asked another question she'd wanted to know the answer to: "So you haven't told me how it was that you went to her and Emile in the first place. I mean, I know you talked to Lizzie, but why Amanda?"

After an awkward moment during which Tilda was certain Harper was searching for the right words, she began:

"At Thanksgiving, you remember—it was hard—you know? And so I was talking to Lizzie and thinking she was easy to talk to, understanding, and that was good because it was hard for me to figure things out. I told her I didn't know what was wrong with me, but I just didn't want to be me anymore. I felt like I was someone else in my own body."

Harper paused and glanced at Tilda before continuing.

"Maybe a boy, I didn't know. I didn't feel like a girl or a boy, really. I just felt all mixed-up. I told her I wanted to be called Harper so people would stop asking if I had a boyfriend, and my friends might leave me alone and stop asking when I was going to start kissing boys. Maybe they wouldn't see me as just a girl. I could be a boy . . . or a girl, just a different kind of one."

Tilda nodded, and Harper seemed comforted by her grandmother's willingness to hear her out.

"She was cool and laughed and said she felt the same way sometimes and was glad to know she wasn't the only one. That made me feel a little better, but I knew it wasn't the same for her as it was for me. I mean, I couldn't stand it anymore, how I felt. Then I told her I wanted to run away, and she asked where I would go. I told her I didn't know. And that's when she told me her mom was gone, and not to tell anyone, but that she knew where she was."

"Lizzie told you that . . . then, at Thanksgiving?"

"Yes," answered Tilly.

Tilda had been right from the start, when she first suspected where Harper might be. She felt like a detective who had put the puzzle pieces in the right places. She was embarrassed by her satisfaction, but mostly she was gratified.

"She said her mom was different and that she understood things that other people didn't. 'She doesn't judge,' she said. 'And she lets you be you, so if you need someplace to go, you could go there.' That's what she told me. I said I'd think about it, and then things got worse. When I didn't feel any better, I decided to do it. So Lizzie talked to her mom, and she said it was okay, but just for a day or two, so I could try to figure out what I wanted to do."

"And do you know," asked Tilda, "what you want to do?"

"Lizzie asked me that same question today at lunch. We were texting."

Harper paused and Tilda wondered why at first, but then a great sadness overcame her. She thought her hands would fall from the steering wheel. It was as though she could climb inside Harper's skin and feel her great confusion. How awful for her to feel so out of herself. To be so confused, not knowing what to do next, not knowing who to be. Literally not knowing who she was. And then to be so alone in her confusion, like stumbling in some great fog, with no one to guide her. Tilda wanted to pull over and explain that she finally and truly understood, but before she could, Harper spoke.

"I want to go home," she said. "That's what I told Lizzie. And I do, Grandma. I want to talk to Mom and Dad. Do you really think they'll understand?"

"Yes, I do. And I'm so very proud of you, because I know

this is hard, and yet you're willing to face it and try to sort things out. So if it took a few days away from home to figure that out, then I think it must've been worth it."

Tilda took her eyes off the road just long enough to look at Harper and to see the corners of her lips turn up ever so slightly into a smile.

⁓

Laura and Mark were at the door, appearing to Tilda as though they hadn't left that spot since she'd last seen them. They opened the door and their arms wide, embracing their errant daughter. After Harper went upstairs and Mark had quietly left Tilda and Laura alone over coffee in the kitchen, Tilda waited nervously for Laura to voice her anger. But Laura, more thankful than angry, welcomed her mother to stay awhile before heading home.

Tilda, taking comfort, began to fill Laura in on some of the missing details and to let her know that Harper was ready to talk to them, to take them into her confidence about all she was struggling with. They both agreed it was time to listen, to really listen. Tilda offered that it may be time to broach the subject of outside help again, to see how Harper might react to the suggestion of counseling. Laura, who had raised the subject at the beginning but who had let it drop when Harper balked, agreed. Tilda, happy that Laura was once again in charge—making plans for her daughter's future—nodded in agreement and soon went home.

She had ignored George's texts and calls to her cell phone, and now her home phone was twinkling like a Christmas tree. He had left no fewer than seven messages, the last one reminding her that she had promised to call as soon as she knew something, which reminded her that she hadn't. His voice was not angry or nagging. Maybe worried with a dash of hurt feelings. "It's New Year's," he said, for no particular reason, and yet there was an implication, and it stung. She had left him in the dark without explanation. He wanted to know everything was okay, maybe to see her on New Year's Eve. Tilda felt terrible, but more tired than anything. She thought she might lie down for a minute, a little power nap, and then call.

When the doorbell sounded, she fumbled in the dark for her phone to check the time; it was 11:30 p.m. Could she have slept for nearly six hours? It was George, of course. She backed away from the peephole, smoothed her hair, and opened the door.

She hadn't expected to spend New Year's Eve with George, but as they listened to the countdown and watched the ball in Times Square drop, she did indeed usher in the New Year with him. And now, in the morning, there was what remained of his gift to her: a bottle of champagne, empty, on the side table by the sofa.

She tiptoed into the living room from her bedroom, and there he was still, sleeping. Once again there had been the intimacy of a night between them without sex. She wasn't ready yet, she had told him so. But then after the glass of champagne and their quiet celebration, as he was moving toward the door to leave, she asked him to stay. "I guess I don't want to be alone," she had said. They decided on a fire. Tilda watched as George opened the flue and put on the firewood. She was thinking of Harold and having misgivings and doubts, but also knowing she wanted George with her on this, the beginning of a new year. They sat quietly together drinking the rest of the champagne and watching the fire. When the flames began to turn to embers, Tilda made a bed for him on the sofa and said goodnight.

Now he turned toward her, squinting a little as he opened his eyes to the morning light.

"Breakfast?" she asked.

"Well, I never expected to start the New Year like this," he said, pushing the blanket aside and sitting up. "But don't get me wrong, I'm happy to see you first thing in the morning, especially today. Happy New Year. And yes, breakfast would be great. Can I help?"

"You just get yourself together and meet me in the kitchen."

They sat at the kitchen table, ate their scrambled eggs and toast, drank their fresh-squeezed orange juice and their coffee, and talked again about the "Tilly Rescue," as they began to call it, Tilda's siege on Brooklyn to reclaim her granddaughter. By the end of the conversation, the venture had become the "Harper Rescue," George raising his glass of orange juice to acknowledge her new name and her courage in facing her doubts.

The sun was streaming in the window, casting a soft light on the table, glasses gleaming, plates shining. It was the kind of morning that had always filled Tilda with hope—a whole day lay ahead, with possibility, even if there was nothing more to look forward to than a winter walk on the beach, the kind of thing she and Harold had done most New Year's Day mornings. Now she sat in her sunny kitchen with George— and it was okay, more than okay—but the conflict between hope and sadness competing for space in her heart continued, as it would, Tilda surmised.

"It's not a happy ending yet," said Tilda, getting back to the topic at hand. "So I'm not getting too excited. She still has a long way to go to find out what's going on with her. I'm hoping counseling is the next step, and I'm sure it will be. Laura and Mark will see to it."

Tilda looked away, staring intently, as though peering through the kitchen wall to the house next door.

"And I still have some unfinished business I have to take care of."

"Ah, there's still Darren, isn't there?" said George. Tilda nodded, answering his question and suddenly realizing how much she had shared with George the night before. Had it been the champagne, or was he slowly finding his way into her heart?

After George left, after the sweet parting kiss on the cheek had turned into an embrace and a proper kiss on the lips, Tilda was left sorting out her feelings. There was no doubt the kiss had opened up a desire to pull George back inside, to take comfort in his arms. But she resisted, and he had left. She wasn't sure if she put him off because of the "unfinished business" next door, or because of her resolve that she was not ready for George or for anyone, now or ever. She soon put her personal dilemma aside to face the more easily managed dilemma of Darren and Lizzie.

Tilda looked through her cupboard to see what ingredients she had on hand, decided on brownies, baked a dozen, and was soon standing on the Esmond doorstep, ringing the bell.

She heard steps inside. No one came to the door. She rang again and waited. When the door eventually opened, it was Lizzie who asked her in.

"Thank you. These look delicious," she said, taking the tin from Tilda's hands. "It's lunchtime, though, Mrs. Carr. So before we eat the brownies, want some salad? I made one. There's enough to share."

"Thank you, Lizzie, but I was wondering if your dad was home," said Tilda.

Lizzie leaned in to speak quietly. "He's here, but he doesn't want to talk right now."

Tilda paused a moment, lifting a hand to press a finger on the spot between her eyebrows. *It's done*, she thought. *Amanda has told him.* She patted the spot and put her hand down.

"I think I'd better go. Maybe later."

Continuing in a soft voice, Lizzie said, "Don't go. C'mon. Let's go in the kitchen."

There, Lizzie put the brownies on the table and began to set out two placemats, bowls, and the rest of the setting for a lunch of salad and lemonade.

And so, against her better judgment, soon the two were eating. Tilda decided not to mention Amanda, but soon it was Lizzie who did.

"Mrs. Carr, I don't know what to say to you except that I'm sorry. I think it was a mistake to tell Tilly, *Harper*, she could go stay with my mom."

Tilda didn't know where to begin. She did not want to be

in the kitchen with Lizzie apologizing for what Tilda thought was not her fault. And yet she didn't think she should be telling Lizzie her mother was the one to blame.

As though reading her mind, Lizzie continued, "My mom. I know you think she's wrong, and my dad, he's super mad at her, but I know my mom. She's doing what she has to do. It isn't all selfish on her part. She couldn't stand to see the way Emile was suffering after Franklin died."

"You don't have to apologize or explain to me, Lizzie. But I am worried about how you're doing, how you're handling all this, and I hope your dad isn't *super mad* at you."

The light in Lizzie's eyes shone less brightly when she talked about Darren. "He's having a hard time with it, with me, about me knowing and not telling. I'm sorry about that, too, but I didn't know what else to do."

"Have you tried to talk to him? Can I help?" Tilda offered, knowing there was little she could do, since Darren wouldn't, apparently, even be in the same room with her.

"Thanks, Mrs. Carr, but there's nothing to do, I don't think. And I have tried to talk to him, to explain that Mom's different and needs time to do this. I think she'll come back, but Dad, I don't know. He may be too hurt to even want that. But I think he understands about me. He's coming around."

Just as Tilda was rising to leave, Lizzie said, "Oh, I want to tell you, I have a great new Scrabble word for you. I hope we can play again soon, maybe you, me, and Harper."

"I'd like that, Lizzie. Yes, soon. You, me, and . . . Harper."

Tilda went home, comforted somehow by Lizzie's calm in the middle of the domestic storm around her. Her parents seemed to recognize how remarkable she was and maybe relied on her strength a little too much. At any rate, so far at least, Lizzie could handle it—and them.

Since Darren wouldn't see Tilda—and who could blame him?—she decided to write him a letter, which she did and which she slipped under his front door the next morning. Her concluding words were:

I think now it was a mistake from the beginning to involve myself the way I did. I thought I could help, but I wound up only making things worse— the law of unintended consequences, maybe. All I can do now is say I'm sorry. I wish the very best for you and Lizzie.

She wanted to add how fond she was of Lizzie, how special she was, but decided it best to be brief. She wanted to say she hoped he would be able to forgive Amanda, but decided against it. Who was she to preach forgiveness? She still saw Amanda as the root of her family's problems, of Darren's despair, and of Lizzie's fledgling forbearance.

❦

On a brutally cold day in January, Tilda was regretting her decision to meet Bev in the city for lunch. As she walked to the train, the cold Connecticut wind found every inch of exposed skin around her nose and eyes, causing a torrent of tears that Tilda began to fear might actually freeze on her face.

Lunch was at an East Side restaurant they could both reach without having to venture far from the subway. By the time Bev arrived, Tilda had already shed her coat and had ordered a glass of wine.

"Why do we do this to ourselves?" asked Bev, removing the rings of fabric she had wrapped round her neck for extra warmth. "Where do I put this thing, now that it's off?" she asked, before deciding to wad it up and stuff it in the sleeve of the coat she had hung over the back of her chair.

Finally settled, she wiped her eyes and let out a lingering sigh. "I feel like Nanook of the North," she said. "And what's up with all this tearing? Dry eye, the doctor calls it. Counterintuitive, isn't it, dry eye, and all your eyes do is run like you've sprung a leak? I tell you, I've had it with getting old, and this is only the beginning, I'm told."

Tilda looked on patiently as Bev vented her dissatisfaction with the weather and the aging process, winter's double threat to one's comfort and safety, as Bev saw it. "Next the snow will come by the truckloads and then ice, and then living every day with the dread of the false step, the broken bones. Or worse, brain injury, if you smack the back of your head on the pavement when your feet fly out from under you."

Bev had become more and more sensitive to the perils of falling since her arthritis and added weight had made her less steady on her feet. Tilda had tried to get her to consider joining a gym, but Bev had countered that if she felt better she'd join. When Tilda pointed out the circularity of the argument, they just laughed, but Bev never truly considered exercise. "I was never much for it," she explained. "Remember Kennedy's Physical Fitness Program? We had to do all sorts of things—run, jump, do pull-ups, sit-ups, remember? All the while in those silly white gym suits? I think those sit-ups were the beginning of my back problems. Anyway, winter, yes, it's going to do me in one of these days. I have three words for you: *Flor-I-Da*. Do you see our waiter?" asked Bev, turning to look.

Tilda and Harold had talked about getting a place in Florida for the winter but had never reached a decision. *Never had the time to make a decision*, Tilda thought. But not now, anyway. Not now. She would never leave Laura and her family behind. They were her only comfort, they and Bev, of course.

They decided on chili, two steamy, meaty bowls of it. That and the two glasses apiece of red wine had taken their minds off the cold and their own vulnerability to it. Hesitant to leave, they decided on two cappuccinos. "You know the Italians never drink cappuccino in the afternoon—and never after a meal," said Bev, wiping the foam away from her upper lip with her napkin.

Tilda nodded at this bit of trivia and took a sip, holding the large cup with both hands. It was good, this afternoon with Bev, this time to be with a friend whose faults and foibles were comforting, Tilda having learned to accept and to take them in stride years ago. And comforting, knowing that the same was true for Bev as well, Bev, who knew every angle of Tilda's personality, better than she knew herself, most likely.

Bev put her cup down and said, "So we've talked about George and your New Year's platonic sleepover. You've told me about the continuing Esmond family domestic drama, but we haven't talked about Tilly. What's going on?"

Tilda hadn't been avoiding the topic of her granddaughter exactly, but she also hadn't brought it up. Why, she wondered, before determining that she was enjoying an afternoon away from worries—and Tilly was a still a source of worry.

"Harper," said Tilda. "She's Harper now. We all call her that. Laura and Mark, her friends, even her teachers, at the behest of her friends, so I'm told." Tilda knew a note of disapproval had slipped into her tone, but she didn't intend it. She wanted to be fully supportive.

"Wow. Things have moved rather quickly, haven't they? You sound unsure of the Harper business. What's the deal?" asked Bev, taking another sip.

Tilda paused for a moment. "The deal, hmm. I don't know. I'm just a little worried about where all this is headed. Is it just a phase? Is it for real? Laura and Mark have gotten Tilly into therapy sessions with someone they really like, who Tilly is responding to very well, they tell me." Tilda paused to clear her throat before continuing. "They're talking about hormone therapy. Well, hormone blockers, to put off puberty. Tilly . . . Harper . . . isn't fully pubescent; she hasn't started her period yet, late for her age, but she's starting to develop, and apparently, she should be at the earlier stages of puberty anyway to be on blockers, so depending on how her sessions go, she may start on them, but it's early yet. The therapist has gone over the options with Mark and Laura, but no one knows what exactly is going on with Harper, including Harper, I think."

"So is she identifying herself as male, then? You know, the way she dresses, no makeup or whatever?"

Tilda noticed the young couple just in from the cold, hanging up their jackets and waiting for a seat. For a minute they held hands before hugging themselves against the cold as the front door swung open again. They looked like any other boy and girl out together, grabbing a bite, but who could know for sure anything about them?

"Harper . . . oh, look. I'm just going to call her Tilly with you. I'm still finding it hard . . ." Bev reached a hand across the table toward Tilda, but she pulled away. "No, it's okay, really. I'm fine, mostly, but I am finding it difficult to deal with in some ways, when you start talking about medicating against puberty. I have to wonder . . .

"Anyway, she's never been a frilly girl, ever since she was small. She's always been more comfortable in jeans and a T-shirt, and she's never been all that interested in makeup. She wears none now. Now that her friends are all behind her on the Harper business, it's applying some pressure, I think, to stick with it. Or maybe that's just my interpretation. I don't know. I really don't know. I don't know if she's identifying as male or just doesn't want to be either. That's what she told me anyway, when we last talked bout it."

"Well, there must be something, some indication, one way or the other, no?"

"When I think back, I guess there were some hints . . . that she wasn't your ordinary girl. She never liked dolls, for instance. And she loved tinkering around with Harold in the garage, with his old tools and his collections. She loved his old stereo system and all his 45s. She'd rather be with him and all his old stuff than with the neighborhood kids any day. Oh, whatever," she added glumly. "I know none of this means anything, putting my gender labels on things."

Then as an afterthought, providing some hope, Tilda added, "But she has always and still loves to dance. She's on the team—and she's really good."

She turned her gaze directly to Bev, who looked back at her, her eyebrows raised a millimeter higher than usual.

Tilda knew the look. Bev wasn't buying it; she was just letting her friend talk. Tilda lowered her shoulders and bent over her bowl. "Oh, I don't know, none of this really means anything, does it?"

"It sounds to me that you're not so okay with it, that maybe you just really want her to be your Tilly again. Look, it's understandable. This is pretty heavy stuff. In our day, we just went with the gender we were born with. There were no options. Kids today have choices we never dreamed of. Thank God her parents are behind her on this. And you should be happy about that. You played a big part in making that happen. Before you went after her, she was alone. How scary for her, no?"

"Yes. Everything you're saying is right. And yes, I am worried about what comes next. Very."

Chapter Eleven

THE UNCHARTED WORLD

O n a Saturday morning in January, Harper poked out from under the covers and flipped over onto her back. She immediately ran her hands over her breasts, as she did most mornings. They hadn't changed since the day before, still small, but she was not flat, and her nipples were a little sore— maybe a little more than they had been lately. Then she ran her hands over her stomach. There was a new feeling there, too, low in her belly, a little like the time she had eaten too many soft, chewy caramels. She had a stomachache, then that didn't get better until she finally went to the bathroom. But there was something stranger yet. Behind the pain was a feeling like the butterflies she got in her stomach when something scared her. She didn't know what was happening, but she would ask her mom, just it case it was something having to do with getting her period. She knew it had to be coming soon. She had been lucky so far.

She would definitely ask her mom about it, and Dr. Miriam, too. Harper liked Dr. Miriam and found her easy to talk to. She was older than her mom. She had gray in her curly hair and wore her wire glasses low on her nose. She wore long skirts and big boots, not very stylish, but she seemed to really understand, like the time Harper told her she didn't want to be Tilly anymore:

"I know you want to be Harper, so tell me also how it feels when you think of your friends calling you Harper?" she'd asked.

"Well, it feels good to think about that," Harper had said. "I mean, a lot of kids at school already know, like my friend, Andrea, and another friend who even says she understands how I feel, like she wants to be someone else sometimes, too. It's nice to know I'm not that weird or something."

Dr. Miriam had made some notes in her book and asked, "So all your friends are okay with it, with you being Harper?"

"Well, yeah, and my teachers, too. Most of them call me Harper. I mean, if they're not okay with it, nobody's saying anything. Right after the holiday break, Mom wrote a note, and all my teachers were asked to go along with the name change. The way Mom put it was that they were being asked to 'respect my decision.' I guess it's no big deal, really."

"Okay, now can you tell me a little more about why you like being known as Harper—by everyone, right, not just your friends at school?"

Harper thought she had already said a lot, but if Dr. Miriam wanted more, she would think about it, and when she did, she knew the answer.

"Yes, by everybody, my friends, teachers, my family, of course. Because if people call me Harper, then it's me, like they really know I'm me."

Dr. Miriam had nodded, and they'd talked about something else.

Another time Dr. Miriam had asked that Harper close her eyes and think about herself as Harper. "Who do you see?" she asked.

"I see me."

"Do you look different?"

"Not really."

"Okay, now with your eyes still closed, imagine you are Harper, say, a few years from now, a little more in the future. Do you still look the same?"

Harper had paused, trying to imagine herself then, but she couldn't really see that far. "Not clearly," she had answered. "I guess I don't really know."

⟨⟩

After the lunch date with Bev, Tilda kept coming back to their conversation about Tilly—and about where her therapy may be headed. She felt like she used to follow the first rule of grandparenting—"Stay out of it"—but lately she was falling far from the mark on that one. That may have been the rule she and Harold followed, but things had certainly changed. And she couldn't help but congratulate herself. Tilly was, after all, safe and sound at home, thanks to her grandmother's meddling. Rather than letting her doubts continue to grow while maintaining her silence, Tilda decided to call Laura, which she did on a Monday morning when Tilly would be at school and Mark would be at work. She sat down at her desk, straightened out a few papers, and made the call.

After a brief conversation on the weather (it was cold) and the state of world affairs (worse than ever), Tilda brought up Tilly.

"I don't know if you can tell me more about what's going on, if there's some policy of keeping the information among the three of you, but I'd like to know about Tilly's—Harper's—therapy. You told me that she may be transgender and that you may be considering puberty blockers. But that's all I know. Can we talk about it?"

"Sure, it's okay. But don't jump to conclusions. We don't know anything yet, and I don't want you to worry about her. I'm sure Harper is okay with talking about what's going on, too. She's been very open. After all, you're the one she went to first. You need to talk to her yourself, Mom."

"I will, but things are moving pretty quickly, and I'm concerned about the blockers. Is it safe, you know, to put off the natural course of things?"

"We're still discussing it, but you don't have to worry about safety, and nothing is moving so quickly. Dr. Bernstein is very thorough and is doing a full medical workup. Harper's on the late side, not getting her period yet—as you know—and Dr. Bernstein wants to be sure everything's okay. But I don't think she's absolutely sure yet, about Harper being transgender, I mean. And until she's absolutely sure, there won't be any blockers."

"What does that mean?" asked Tilda, rising from her chair to look out the window, her free hand rubbing the small of her back where the tension usually began to build. It looked like it might snow. "If she isn't transgender, what is it, then? And can't we just call her Tilly, just between the two of us?"

Tilda heard Laura sigh into the phone. "Mom, this isn't easy for me, either, you know. I'm trying to get used to the idea. It matters to her that I, that we—Mark and you—get it right."

Tilda let her free hand drop to her side. "I'm sorry, Laura. Of course this is hard for you. I don't want you to have to worry about me, either. You have enough on your mind. Do you still want to talk about it?"

"Yes, yes, it's okay. You have a right to be concerned about your granddaughter. You can ask me anything."

"Okay, then. So—is she transgender or not?"

Laura sighed into the phone. "Mom, I just told you, we don't know yet. That's what her therapy is all about. It's a huge step, and you have to be sure you're dealing with a trans-gender child—that it isn't something else. It's a process, and it takes time."

"But what happens then, after she has her period, when she's fully into puberty?"

Tilda knew she was wearing on Laura's patience, but she pressed on.

"Well, at that point, if her doctor was absolutely certain, Tilly would begin to get testosterone."

Tilda noted, thankfully, that Laura was allowing the lapse back to *Tilly*. But testosterone. That sounded so drastic—and so final. "But what about her dancing? She's an elegant, feminine dancer. Doesn't that mean something? She's never been overly girlish, but she's not exactly a tomboy, either."

"I know. Don't you think I've been over these same questions a million times? But I guess I've come to understand, to put it simply, that there are no right answers. We think in such stereotypes, even now, when we're supposed to be beyond 'gender roles.' Isn't that what your generation taught us?"

Tilda wondered if all that bra-burning years ago had led to this, to her granddaughter struggling to be not a liberated woman, but maybe a liberated man.

"So," said Laura, "a transgender male—that's someone who was born a girl but who identifies as a male—can still be a dancer and still be interested in fashion."

Tilda noted her daughter's clinical tone. So like her—to grab on to any issue and deal with it, especially when the "issue" was her daughter's welfare and future.

"In fact, some kids don't identify as one gender or the other. They're called 'non-binary,' or 'genderqueer,' one word."

"This is all a bit much," said Tilda, who had been pacing around the room and who now reached for her office chair and sat down again. "I'm sorry. I'm trying, like you, Laura, but what makes a girl want to be a boy?" she asked.

"Is that a serious question, or are you just overwhelmed?"

"A little of both, I think."

"I feel like I'm lecturing you, Mom. I'm not. Mark and I are confused and worried, too, a lot. I mean, sometimes we're very adult and accepting and other times we can't believe what's happening, but Dr. Bernstein keeps us grounded. She's very practical and evenhanded. She helps us to understand—for Harper's sake."

"But why Tilly, and why now? She's never shown any signs of being anything but a darling little girl."

"Mom. Please. Try harder to understand. And try to use

Harper. I need to also, we have to, it's important." Tilda knew her daughter was right, and she was struck by Laura's new-found strength. Tilda was no longer the one handing out tissues. Now it was Laura bolstering her.

"I am trying, believe me. But just when I think I've got it—she's definitely Harper, and this time it will stick—I waiver, and I want Tilly back."

She waited for Laura to soften and to admit to those same feelings, but Laura ignored her plea for more understanding.

"One thing is very clear," Laura continued. "These kids are vulnerable. They need a lot of support—and love."

And that was the bottom line. Laura would be as strong as she needed to be to not lose her child.

"She'll always have that," Tilda answered. *Always, no matter what.*

☙

Winter wore on. Tilda, who hadn't been to the Y in months, since Harold had died, began going again regularly, in hopes of staving off the continuing toll taken by the mounting years.

As for the other, less serious, almost-not-worth-worrying-about indignities, she added to the list dryness—of nails, hair, and skin. Everything was dry, especially in winter, as if instead of being put out on an ice floe, nature was seeing to it that she would simply dry up and blow away. At least her hearing was still good, as were her teeth—yes, they were still her own.

So she went back to the Y, hoping that would help. She worked out with weights, having read a long article recently extolling the benefits of lifting for bone health, strength, and other things she couldn't remember. She swam for the benefits to her body and mind, having read that aerobic exercise helped the brain. She'd never been much for aerobics (a joke to a former gymnast) or Zumba (an even worse, newer model). And she'd never had the patience for yoga, but swimming was almost spiritual. Once she eased into the water and began taking long, leisurely strokes, the world fell away. There were only the awareness of her breath, the sensation of the water against her skin, and the near silence—the only sounds were the ones her heart and her body made with each stroke and as she flipped with each turn. *Like flying . . . this is what meditation must be like*, she thought. Then came a quiet joy, gratitude for the privilege of growing old. *I'm still here.* The thought engendered a surge of energy in her strokes. But then she felt the accompanying quiet sadness that Harold could not share in the privilege or the joy.

Once back at home, after showering and lathering her body in lotion at the Y, she used her time to catch up on emails, bills, and the minutia of daily life. She made sure she kept up with Barbara. Although there were no visits imminent on either side, they stayed in touch at least once a week, by phone or by texting, and sometimes by Skyping. Looking at one another on the screen, they denied the reality of their mutual aging. When Tilda remarked, "I look terrible," her sister would counter, "It's the angle or the light or something." They would then laugh, ignoring the inevitable march of time. Tilda would ask about Mike and Jake and Nate and be satisfied that all were fine. Barbara would ask earnestly how Tilda was doing, and when she responded in the affirmative, Barbara would ask her to please come visit. Tilda would say yes, soon, and the conversation would end until the next week. It was all that was required of their relationship now attenuated by time and distance.

Closer to home, she was in touch with Bev almost daily. And George, too, although since their New Year's kiss, she had been keeping her distance. There were lunches, dinners, and the occasional movie, but aside from some friendly hand-holding, there had been no more kissing. George seemed to be resigned to Tilda's ambivalence, patiently giving her the time she needed. When she boldly asked if he was growing tired of her reluctant-lover routine, he had simply replied, "You're more than worth the wait, my dear." This had sounded to her like something Rhett Butler might say, and the thought had pleased her.

And she had been in touch with Tilly, or Harper, as she was trying hard to always say out loud and to get right. But in her mind, her granddaughter was *Tilly*. Their most recent outing had been to the Wayne Museum of Art and History in Water Haven, the pride of the town, a cultural jewel larger than most of the regional museums outside New York. Tilda thought Tilly would enjoy the interactive celestial navigation exhibit. It was supposed to simulate the heavens of the fifteenth and sixteenth centuries through the use of virtual reality headsets. She had read about it in the local weekly. The exhibit was in conjunction with the main attraction, the display of ancient maps and sea charts from the Age of Discovery.

Tilly was waiting at her school's entrance when Tilda picked her up. They would have a good two hours at the museum, Tilda thought.

In the car, Tilly took off her down jacket, under which she wore a loose dark gray sweater vest over a long white shirt, no budding breasts visible. She was wearing zero makeup. Tilda noted the requisite jeans, but also saw that they were not the skinny ones the girls all wore. They were baggy, but not as drastic as hip-hop jeans. It was quite a get-up, Tilda concluded. Tilly pulled off her wool cap and ran her fingers through her hair. It was short. No more long ponytail.

"When did you cut your hair?" Tilda asked, aware and sorry for the breathy sound of disappointment in her voice.

"Don't you like it, Grandma?" Tilly asked.

Before pulling out of the school's driveway, Tilda looked in the rearview mirror and said, "I think the traffic monitor is going to chase me if I don't hurry up and get out of here."

As Tilda drove, Tilly pursued the topic of her hair. "It's so much easier this way, but Mrs. Watson is furious. We're all supposed to be bunheads on the dance team."

Tilly waited for Tilda's reaction, and when Tilda didn't say anything, she continued. "She wants me to grow it back out right away, but that's crazy. Hair doesn't grow that fast. But do you like it, Grandma?"

Tilda finally said, "Yes, of course I do, Harper. It's cute. You look great no matter what. But what about your coach? Can you still dance on the team?"

"Yes. But she actually wants me to get extensions for performances, so I can wear my hair however she decides we should all look. It's getting a little silly, if you ask me."

"But you'll do it, right?" Tilda was aware that she was sounding a little too invested in Tilly's dance career, but she guessed she was. Tilda held on to the hope that Tilly's love of dance would help see her through a difficult time. She worried what would happen if she didn't have dance any longer.

"Oh, I guess. But she's the only teacher who won't call me Harper."

ᕦ～ᣞ

As fine as the maps and sea charts exhibit promised to be, Tilda was sure Tilly would want to go directly to the virtual reality display in the adjacent exhibit hall and be fitted with a headset. Much to her surprise, her granddaughter seemed to be intrigued by the prospect of the maps. As soon as they entered the dim room, separate spotlights gently illuminating each one, Tilly appeared to be enchanted, taken by the idea that explorers had actually used these mistaken versions of unknown lands to find their way. The maps, though wildly inaccurate, were works of art in themselves. Some were woodcuts, some metal-plate engravings, many still with their original, hand-painted brilliant colors. Tilda imagined them hanging in dark, wood-paneled libraries of long ago.

"Did you see the sea monsters painted on the map?" Tilly asked, delighted by her discovery. "Look, you can see one there at the tip of Africa." She was pointing to a green-and-red sea dragon of sorts, large and out of perspective with the depiction of nearby land. "I think that's supposed to be Africa. Can you imagine, Grandma, going out to sea with these maps?"

Tilda didn't know how to respond, this sort of adventure being something she had never contemplated. But before she could say anything, an elderly man who had overheard Tilly commented, "Oh, the explorers didn't use these maps."

Tilly turned to see who was answering her question.

"Sorry to disturb you," he said, "but you seemed so interested, I had to say something."

In his woolen flat cap, vest, and corduroy trousers, Tilda thought he looked rather old-world and wondered if he were a docent with a historic bent.

"These maps are the product of early cartographers . . . do you know that term, young lady?"

Tilly's back stiffened as she pulled on the shirttails hanging out under her vest. "Yes, sir, I know they're mapmakers."

"Good for you. I'm glad to see they're still teaching about maps in school, now that you kids all have a GPS device in your pockets."

"Oh, I didn't learn it in school. Well, I mean, I learned it a long time ago. My grandfather taught me. He told me about the Age of Discovery because his family was from there—Portugal, I mean. That's why I wanted to see the maps."

This was news to Tilda. And she wondered why Tilly hadn't told her.

The elderly man explained that the maps were made from explorers' tales of their travels. The mapmakers made them to sell to their rich clients, he said. "Getting these maps was like being first with the latest iPhone, very impressive," he added, grinning and obviously proud of his analogy.

"If the explorers didn't use maps, what did they use?" asked Tilly.

"Are you going to the virtual reality exhibit? That may answer some questions for you. And when you get home, look up Abraham Zacuto."

After the exhibits, Tilda and Tilly went to the cafeteria for some hot chocolate and pastries. They found a small table by a large window overlooking the park, its trees now bare, the ground mottled with patches of gray snow, lingering from the latest storm. Tilda looked at her granddaughter, who was gazing into her cup and then taking a sip. Intent on her chocolate, she reminded Tilda of days gone by, not that long ago, when she was a little girl, even then capable of great concentration. And now with her boyish short hair brushed over to one side, she looked a little like a stranger.

Tilda had been surprised by several things on this day, the haircut the least of it. She'd known that was coming. No, it was Tilly's interest in the maps, her desire to see them because of Harold, a wish she had not shared with Tilda. *Sometimes I don't know who she is.* And this feeling of estrangement was the hardest. Did anyone really know what this child meant to her? From the day Tilly was born, Tilda had felt a love she didn't know existed. All she knew about the experience of having grandchildren before Tilly was that people who had them were incessantly showing pictures of average-looking babies to people who didn't really want to see them.

But Tilly changed everything, for her and for Harold. He too was smitten. The new grandparents eagerly anticipated each visit, looked forward to babysitting. Once the young parents were gone, after what seemed like hours of instructions, the new grandparents were content to hover over the crib for hours it seemed, doing little but staring at this miracle, this sleeping baby.

"I've figured it out," said Harold one day after a long afternoon with Tilly when she was two and a handful by any measure. "It's from some vestigial part of our brains, when the old people looked after the babies while the young ones went out hunting and gathering. They took care of the babies because their brains made a chemical that made them do it."

"Whatever are you talking about?" Tilda had asked.

"How else do you explain it? I've been on my knees picking up Cheerios all afternoon. Why?"

"I don't know, Harold, but I'm glad you're here."

"Maybe it took generations for the love potion to work, to ensure the survival of the species."

"It's a love potion now."

"I think so."

"Okay."

Some time later they laughed when Tilda came across an article online entitled, "Grandparents and the Love Hormone."

"You were right," Tilda told Harold. "Your love potion is a hormone the brain makes when you're in love. Apparently, it works for grandparents, too. It says, 'The role of oxytocin is particularly important to ensure that grandparents bond with their grandchildren.' How did you know? You're an accountant, not a psychologist."

Harold joined her at the computer, the blue light shining in his eyes, and said, "Huh. Look at that. I just figured there was something going on, so the love potion theory."

"Well, I'm impressed," she had said.

Tilly was still drinking her hot chocolate in silence.

"Til . . . Harper," she said. "I didn't know you and Grandpa talked about the Age of Discovery—and that was the reason you wanted to see the maps. Why didn't you tell me?"

"I didn't think about telling you, but I didn't mean not to tell you?"

Tilda noticed the question that was not a question, the inflection most kids her age used but that Tilly did not, usually.

"Does that make sense?" Tilly said, fidgeting a little in her seat.

"Well, sure, I guess. I mean, it must've been a very personal memory for you, then."

"Yes, exactly," said Tilly.

Tilly seemed relieved to have had an explanation handed to her, and Tilda let it go. "How did you like the virtual reality?" Tilly asked.

"I liked it, but it made me dizzy."

Tilly laughed. "I know, I don't get dizzy, but it was weird

when it moved around a lot. I loved it," she said, her eyes wide. "I mean, it's so big." She paused to clear a catch in her throat. "It's almost scary—the whole sky with so many stars, and you have to figure out where you are—and where you want to go. It seems so unreal."

Tilly's eyes narrowed. "But it was good, Grandma. I enjoyed it. Thanks." Then she went back to her hot chocolate, now nearly gone.

Tilda wondered what was going on behind those green eyes, whose shading seemed to go from light to dark with each new thought.

⌒⌒

That night, after the museum outing, Harper put her plate in the sink and asked if it would be all right if she went to her room.

"Everything okay?" asked Laura.

"Yes," she answered. "I have a project for school I should work on." Once in her room, she shut her door and kicked off her sneakers. She grabbed the laptop on her desk and sat down with it on the edge of her bed. She looked up the Age of Discovery and scrolled through a few sites, some showing maps like the ones at the museum and like the ones her grandfather had shown her. Without reading much, she closed the lid and lay back on a pillow, one arm crossed over her head, the other over her heart.

She was ten when he had pulled out an old cardboard box stored in her grandmother's office, way in the back of the closet. "These were mine when I was a kid, not much older than you, Tilly," he told her. "These are like Wikipedia, only books, I guess you could say." They were old encyclopedias, he told her. "These were what students used to do research back in my day."

She remembered going into the living room with him. He was carrying one book, "*P*, for Portugal," he told her, opening to that page when they sat down. She snuggled in under one arm and nestled against his chest as he began to read to her. She felt warm and safe and happy as he read to her, his voice deep yet soft, she remembered.

⌒⤳

"'Portugal, under Prince Henry the Navigator, dominated the high seas and ushered in the Age of Discovery. Desirous of discovering new trade routes, the prince was determined to reach the Indies by sea, although no explorer had yet proved such a route existed.'

"Was it possible? If it could be done, there would be riches beyond your wildest dreams, all from spices. Nutmeg, worth its weight in gold. Pepper, cinnamon, cloves—they all were valuable, like rubies, emeralds, and pearls," he said, nudging Tilly, as though asking her to imagine it. "Bet you didn't know that once upon a time pepper was as valuable as jewels," he said before continuing to read to her.

"'The prince encouraged exploration along the western coast of Africa, longing to know what lay to the east, around the Cape of Good Hope. . . . Prince Henry died in 1460, the trade route to India not yet found.'

"And who would finally discover the open-water route to India? Do you know, Tilly?" She put a finger to her closed lips and thought hard before shaking her head no.

"It was Vasco da Gama," he said.

"Oh, I remember. We studied him and Christopher Columbus," she said.

"But he was the first to get beyond Africa, to get into open water off Africa's east coast. See, look," he said, tracing the map in the book with his finger down the west coast of Africa, around the cape, and out into the Indian Ocean. He stopped tracing the route near the southwestern edge of India. "That's where he landed, somewhere around here, not far from the place where he would meet with the Indian king about the spices. It was an amazing discovery. But Prince Henry didn't live to see it. He sure was ahead of his time, though."

"How did he do it, when nobody else could?" Tilly had asked.

"Da Gama? He had new tools to guide him, better maps, and new ways to navigate by the stars," her grandfather had replied.

Of course. She was jolted from her dreamlike state and sat up with a start. It was celestial navigation, but there was something new, new ways to do it. She remembered the man in the library and the name he had given her.

She reached for her laptop and looked up Abraham Zacuto.

Chapter Twelve

THE AGE OF DISCOVERY

The pool at the women's Y in Water Haven was a thing of beauty. It was glass enclosed, full of light, and warm as summer on this January day. Swimming there in the winter reminded Tilda of her days at the beach in Miami. As she was emerging from the pool after a satisfying morning swim, she had a thought: instead of stopping for tea at the Y's café as she usually did, she would rush home to look at the calendar she had marked in the kitchen, which had the dates for Tilly's winter break.

As soon as she got home, she checked the dates and called her daughter. "Laura," she said, breathless with enthusiasm, "Harper's February break is coming up. What do you think she would say to taking a trip with her grandmother, to Portugal?"

There was absolute silence on the other side of the phone, after an initial gasp.

First came some redundant questioning: "To where? Portugal? When? Her winter break?" Then Laura asked an essential question: "Why?" To which Tilda replied with what she was certain were the essential reasons: "Because she was so interested in the museum's exhibit on the Age of Discovery. Because I think it would be educational."

When Laura's "uh-huh" let it be known she was not convinced, Tilda realized she wasn't convinced by her answers,
either.

"And because I think it would be good for her to explore
her roots . . . because she's interested in Portugal . . . because
of her grandfather."

With this, Laura's questioning became more practical, if
not less full of doubt.

"She doesn't even have a passport."

"It can be expedited."

"She has schoolwork during the break."

"She can work on the plane."

"She can't miss her therapy sessions."

"It's just one week and two weekends."

"Maybe she won't want to go."

"Let's ask her at Friday night dinner."

6 ～ꝺꝺ

"Well, what do you think, Harper? Would you like to go?"
asked Laura at Shabbat dinner that Friday, looking first at
Tilly and then at Tilda, who had arrived an hour earlier with
a warm challah from the local bakery. They had just finished
the blessing and had begun to eat when Laura could wait no
longer and blurted out her question.

"Me, go to Portugal with Grandma over the break?" asked
Tilly, eyes wide.

Her eyes filled with tears. "I can't believe it. Yes! I'd love
it. Thank you, Grandma," she said, rushing to Tilda and
throwing her arms around her.

So it was decided. Tilda's heart swelled every time she
relived her granddaughter's joy when she heard the news
about Portugal. Tilda went into high gear to make the trip a
reality. The Friday night of the dinner, Tilda had gone to bed
renewed with hope for the future. She dreamed that she had
presented her granddaughter with a passport with the name

Harper Jordan written next to her picture. When Tilda woke up, she knew she could not make the dream a reality—that would take a legal name change—but there was one thing she could do. She could set the name Tilly aside as a memory of the past and from that day forward know in her heart that her granddaughter was Harper.

Tilda was able to arrange for an expedited passport. She made the flight and hotel arrangements, but it was George who had researched tour guides and had found Paulo Mendez. Tilda became convinced he would be the right guide for her granddaughter after reading the reviews on TripAdvisor. He received high marks for his "sensitivity and ability to relate to teens." After several attempts, she was able to reach him by phone. He listened intently and told her he had a trip coming up that would fit in with her dates. "I think I can make this trip special for your granddaughter, Harper," he had said. That had sealed the deal as far as Tilda was concerned.

Tilda didn't mention anything about their history, the death of Harold, or about Harper's recent change in identity, but she liked Paulo and felt she could trust him to be as sensitive as his reviews had indicated.

They would be on a trip with five others, an older couple and another couple traveling with their adult daughter. The itinerary would take them from Lisbon to Sintra, then north to Porto, then south again to Évora, before heading back to Lisbon.

"Since she is interested in history, I'm sure she will enjoy this trip," Paulo had emailed Tilda, as follow-up to their phone conversation.

Tilda wrote back, "We will be there."

The passport arrived. Packing decisions were made. If they were lucky, the temperature would be in the fifties and sixties, the sky sunny. If not, it would rain and be cloudy, with temperatures in the forties. "Pack rain gear, a jacket, and several sweaters," Tilda had told Harper.

The tearful Laura of her childhood returned at JFK's international departures terminal. It was a cold Friday night, threatening to snow, but there were no travel alerts from Delta, so it looked as though there would be no delays.

"Don't worry," said Tilda, reaching into her coat pocket for a tissue to hand to Laura.

Mark put his arm around Laura, now blowing her nose into the tissue, and gave her a tight reassuring hug. He seemed to be stifling some tears himself.

"Harper, say good-bye to your mom and dad before they dissolve into a puddle," Tilda said, hoping to lighten the moment.

"I'll text you every day," Harper said, hugging them before reaching for her bag and backpack.

"We'll be fine," said Tilda as she and Harper walked toward the departures entrance.

On the plane, Harper sat near the window, although it was too dark to see anything. After takeoff, she began digging into her backpack.

Seeing a textbook among her things, Tilda asked, "Are you really going to do homework?"

Harper looked at her. "It's not really homework, Grandma. It's my reading from the AP list. Mom made me pack it."

She handed the book to Tilda, who began to leaf through it.

It's pretty big, isn't it? But *Moby Dick* is a great book. I didn't think they read the classics much these days," she said, handing it back.

"It's not required. It's for extra credit, but you know Mom."

They both laughed, and Harper put the book away. "Maybe on the way back, but not now. I'm too excited."

"Oh, that's good. You had me worried there for a minute. What teenager does extra-credit reading at the beginning of her first trip to Europe?"

Harper laughed again and took her iPad out of her bag. "I downloaded a bunch of movies," she said, putting her earphones in.

"Good idea," said Tilda. *And a good idea, this trip,* Tilda said to herself, hopeful, as she closed her eyes and let her head fall back onto the headrest.

Almost nine hours later, in a daze and jet-lagged, the pair checked into the Hotel Santa Justa near the historic elevator that separated lower and upper Lisbon and that rose almost 150 feet in the air. The hotel was near Rossio Square, where the group would begin its tour in the morning. In spite of the convenient location, and though they had the rest of the day ahead of them, Tilda and Harper were in desperate need of some rest, which turned into a very long nap. They wandered around in the late afternoon and had a light dinner at the hotel before showering and going to bed, though neither of them slept very well.

"You snore, Grandma," complained Harper.

"I'm sorry, but can you stop pulling the covers off and hitting me every time you turn over?" asked Tilda.

They were a little cranky by the time they met Paulo and the group in the lobby in the morning, but the sun was shining and it promised to be a seasonably warm day in the sixties.

Maybe it was the pattern of waves in the black-and-white limestone pavement in the square (the "Largo Mar," or "wide sea," effect), or maybe it was lack of proper sleep, but by the time Tilda and Harper and the tour group sat down for lunch at several tables under the awning at the Café Nicola, Harper was looking a little peaked.

"Are you okay?" Tilda asked, pushing a glass of water in her direction after the waiter had taken their order.

"I'm okay. Really. I'm fine," she said.

Tilda put Harper's reticence off to her reluctance to talk in front of Paulo and the others. The elderly couple were from Chicago, John and Sandra, probably in their early eighties but already proving to be tireless walkers; the other couple were Mitch and Connie, traveling with their unmarried daughter, Louisa, who appeared to be about thirty and who was very quiet.

Paulo, the guide, probably in his mid-thirties, seemed a little worried that Harper wasn't looking too happy, but Tilda had hope that his ability as a tour guide would include his lauded skill in recognizing and handling the moodiness and sensitivities of teenagers. And he had already shown promise that morning, quickly noticing that Harper, with her short hair and wearing no makeup, baggy jeans, and a loose-fitting white shirt under a shapeless brown cardigan, was defying easy gender identification.

"And, Harper, tell us something about you and your interests," he had asked during the morning introductions. When she replied slowly and quietly, "I don't know. I'm a dancer. I guess that's all," he didn't jump to conclusions.

"Ah, dance. We have many famous dancers in Portugal, men and women. Did you know that, Harper?"

Harper shrugged her shoulders but also cracked what could be called a smile, and Paulo deftly moved on.

A part-time history professor at the university, he gave small, specialized history tours during school breaks, this latest having coincided with Harper's.

Harper took a sip of water from the glass Tilda had pushed her way, eyes downcast. She looked up and directed her gaze at the square in front of her. Suddenly she came to life and, pointing at the square, said loudly enough for the group to hear, and probably the next few tables, too, "Look at this. You can't tell anything about all the people who died right in front of us, right here, right, Paulo?" Paulo looked stunned. "And the droughts and famines and earthquake and the inquisition. I'm sort of not hungry." She folded her arms on the table and rested her head.

Apparently, the morning walk and Paulo's instruction had struck a chord, and Harper was responding with empathy and despair for the generations before her who had suffered unfathomable horror. It was true. The morning had been dedicated to calamity, a history of fire, drought, and famine. It was a tragic history, to be sure, with more to it than adventure on the high seas and the glorious age of the discoverers, but who could have predicted Harper's reaction? Tilda hadn't thought this historic tour might not be much fun for a teenager, and she wondered what was triggering this reaction. She was about to suggest they go back to the hotel for a rest when Paulo intervened.

"Okay, Harper. So the history so far is troubling you?" She nodded yes and slid down in her chair.

"I'm sorry, but actually, I think it's a good thing," said Paulo. "It means you are paying attention. And it's true, Portugal's history, like that of other countries, has many terrible things. You can't escape it, you know?"

Harper apologized and looked around as though she wanted to flag down a waiter, but actually it seemed to Tilda what she wanted was to deflect attention from herself.

"Drink some water, Harper. It will make you feel better," she said.

Harper grabbed the glass and began to drink earnestly. Everyone was looking at her and smiling, except Louisa, who was checking emails, apparently.

"I wish I could tell you the afternoon will be better, but there is more injustice ahead. Oh, but then tomorrow the river and the explorers and Portugal's Golden Age."

Harper smiled a little.

"Ah, that's better," said Paulo.

The afternoon city walking tour, though, included strolling down the memory lane of more drought and famine, adding plague and war. But Harper seemed to be adjusting as long as there were pastry and ice cream breaks along the way. Then they came to São Domingos Church in the Largo de São Domingos, and the group learned about the New Christians, or converted Jews, and about the 1506 massacre there, and they saw the monument. They listened to Paulo explain the history about how Jews had been forced to leave Spain in the late fourteenth century and how many had fled to Portugal, where under King Manuel they had been able to stay.

But Paulo's talk was about to take a particularly dark turn, and Tilda worried about the effect his words might have on Harper. On the other hand, she couldn't help but be moved by the passion with which he spoke and by the bleak picture he was painting.

Even as the climate for Jews in Portugal was far more favorable than in Spain, he explained, by 1497 they were forced to convert. And many did, but their conversion was viewed suspiciously, apparently, because on April 19, 1506, while the devout in São Domingos were praying for the end of the latest drought, famine, and plague, one assembled there—as the story goes—who was perhaps a little carried away in his worship, said he saw Christ on the altar. His fervor spread among the assembled as quickly as the fire following the earthquake that would ravage the city in 1755. But one who remained seated and calm on that fateful day was a New Christian, who said no, it was just a reflection of a candle shining on the crucifix. There was then an audible gasp. A disbeliever in our midst. A heretic. A Jew.

Here Paulo paused, as though to regain his composure, as though no matter how many times he told it, this story had the power to touch him anew.

The poor man was lifted out of his seat, dragged onto the street, and beaten to death. That not being enough, his body was dragged to the Rossio, where it was burned to ashes.

Tilda wished Paulo's telling weren't quite so dramatic, though, because Harper was listening intently and, from the look on her face, was becoming distraught.

But that was just the beginning. Paulo continued in his retelling of the massacre: more deaths in Rossio Square, a massacre of two thousand, maybe more, men, women, and children, brutally beaten and burned to death, newly converted Jews, all heretics to the frenzied mob. The killing continued through the following Tuesday, until word reached the king, who sent the Royal Guard to put an end to it.

Harper took her place by the stone monument that looked like half an egg balancing on a platform. It was massive yet vulnerable. Tilda stood behind her, a hand on her shoulder. On the face of the monument, a large blue Jewish star was set into the stone with an inscription:

1506–2006
In memory of the thousands of Jewish victims of
intolerance and of religious fanaticism murdered in the
massacre begun on 19 April 1506 in this square.

"Why did it take them so long?" Harper whispered to her grandmother. "Grandpa's ancestors may have been here. They may have died in this terrible way." Harper wrapped her arms around her.

So that's it, thought Tilda, as she realized what was at the heart of Harper's dismay. *It's about Harold, and his family.*

"Ask Paulo," said Tilda. "Go on, he can help you with your question." And she gave her granddaughter a little push.

"A good question, Harper," Paulo replied. "Nations apologizing, it's rare, you know. When did Germany apologize for the Holocaust? Some say it began without a word, when chancellor Willy Brandt fell to his knees at the Warsaw Ghetto, the *kniefall*, or genuflection, it is called. Officially, it came later, with reparations.

"Look," he continued. "Countries don't like to revisit their ugly pasts. Besides, it's expensive. A real apology comes at a price, but maybe true healing happens only then. It has taken us centuries for this monument, but it is a good thing, isn't it, Harper?"

"Yes," said Harper. "But still, it took too long. Too much suffering," she said, shaking her head.

"Well, yes, but tomorrow, the Age of Discovery. That will cheer you up."

Paulo smiled at Tilda, who was surprised at her granddaughter's newfound need for answers.

The following day would be devoted to Portugal's Golden Age, when the Portuguese had dominion over the seas. To learn about this glorious period in history, that had been the purpose of this trip, and Tilda was curious to see her granddaughter's reaction, given her persistent questioning on their first day of touring.

Back in their room after dinner, Harper, in the hotel's white bathrobe, sat on the bed rubbing a towel through her wet hair. She seemed renewed, adjusting to the time difference, but still keeping to herself, Tilda thought.

"Are you feeling better?" she asked.

Putting the towel aside, Harper shook her head vigorously. Tilda was afraid her granddaughter was about to launch into a tirade about the day, but no, Harper was simply shaking away any drops of water remaining from her shower and shampoo. She edged back on the bed, leaning against the pillows.

"Much," she answered.

"Good. I hope we sleep better tonight."

"You know you snore, Grandma."

"Yes, I know. Sorry. Maybe you should wear your earphones to bed. Fortunately, Grandpa was a sound sleeper."

No response.

"You had a lot of questions today. That was good, I thought."

"I guess."

Tilda, hoping to draw her out, decided on the direct approach. "Why?" she asked.

"Why?"

"Why did you ask so many questions?"

"I don't know."

Tilda was about to give up.

"I mean, I never thought much about it before, you know, history—and real people." She sat up and pulled one of the pillows out from behind her, hugging it to her.

"It's pretty awful, what happened," she said. "And to the Jews. Grandpa used to say, 'It's always the Jews.' I'm beginning to understand what he meant—and maybe why Mom converted, like she was doing it for Grandpa and his ancestors—who had to be Christian or die."

Harold's storytelling. He used to tell tales about the *conversos*, the Jews forced to convert, and he had always told it as though those ancient Jews had been recent relatives, grandparents, aunts and uncles.

The Carrs had traced their family going back centuries, to someplace near Lisbon, the exact location lost to history. How much of this was lore and how much was true was impossible to sort out, but in the retelling of events, the Carr family could be counted among the lucky, who, having survived after forced conversion years earlier, fled to Amsterdam just before the start of Portugal's inquisition.

Centuries later, Harold's father, Ben, met Harold's mother, Gladys, in New York. They were with their parents at a Sephardic temple on the Upper West Side, attending a memorial service for a friend of both families. Later, after the burial, the families discovered they shared a similar past. Both claimed their families had come to New York from Amsterdam by way of Portugal, and had, thank God, left Amsterdam long before the German occupation of World War II.

Harold often quoted the poet Marge Piercy: "We Jews are all born of wanderers, with shoes under our pillows." Once, when she was too young to understand, Harper had asked why, and Harold had responded with another question: "If you have to get dressed really fast and leave your home very quickly, don't you always want to know where your shoes are?"

Harold and his family never stopped considering themselves Portuguese, pointing proudly to the name *Carr* as proof of their heritage. It had been changed along the way, they said, from *Carvalho*, an old Portuguese name for a type of oak tree, one that does not bear fruit. That name was chosen when the family had been forced to convert. The name to them signified the curse of having to renounce their faith or die. They did not believe there would truly be a future for the family until the day they were free to reclaim their rightful name and their rightful heritage as Jews. The irony, of course, was that the family's once-true name was lost to history, and the future generations, all of whom remained Jewish, gratefully claimed the name *Carr.*

"Your grandpa and I used to laugh about our family names. Mine was Marrone . . ."

"I remember, Grandma, your nickname was Bony for 'Bony Moronie.'"

"Yes, but also interesting to note is that *Marrone* in Italian is *chestnut.* Both our names are types of trees."

When the lights were off and they settled into bed under the covers, Tilda heard the rhythmic pattern of Harper's breathing. Then she too drifted off to sleep.

⌐～ و

The little tour group looked fresher in the morning. John and Sandra were wearing matching safari-looking outfits with matching soft-brimmed sun hats substituting for pith helmets. They reminded Tilda of the ads she'd seen in the old J. Peterman catalogs. And they were wearing the same cushioned shoes that had enabled their tireless walking the day before. Both were short and lean, with severely cropped salt-and-pepper hair. They were remarkably fit. Yesterday's activities were not enough for them, and when the others had opted out, they had taken Paulo up on his offer of additional exploring, which began with a tour of several old and rare shops, including Bertrand Bookstore, "the oldest bookstore in the world," it is said. While this other tour was in progress, grandmother and granddaughter chose instead a café near the elevator for hot chocolate and yet another pastry, this time *pastel de nata,* a custard tart much to Harper's taste.

The add-on tour apparently ended with a ride to the top of the Santa Justa elevator and a quick look around the square, Largo do Carmo. "Charming," was their appraisal the next morning.

Even Mitch and Connie seemed brighter in the morning,

all smiles. Louisa, however, lingered over breakfast and her second cup of coffee and said she had some work to catch up on and would meet everyone later.

The group assembled in the lobby and waited for Paulo, who would lead them down the Rua da Prata to the Arco Triunfal da Rua Augusta. Passing through the tall stone arch, Harper tilted her head back to take it in.

"Wow," she said.

"It is impressive," said Tilda.

They stopped to take pictures while Paulo led the group farther on to the Praça do Comércio, the grand commercial square leading to the waterfront on the edge of the Tagus River.

They caught up as Paulo was wrapping up his description of the statue of King José I, the massive bronze standing in the middle of the square.

"Everything here is large in scale. The arch, the square, and the statue were all part of the rebuilding that took place after the earthquake and terrible fire. They pay homage to Lisbon's importance in the world of commerce."

Paulo directed the group back to the massive arch, explaining its history and pointing out the statues atop it, representing Glory, Valor, and Genius.

"The statues over the columns on the right," he said, "are the great general, Nuno Álvares Pereira, and the Marquis of Pombal, responsible for rebuilding Lisbon after the earthquake; his full name is Sebastião José de Carvalho e Melo."

At this, Harper turned sharply toward Paulo. "Did you say *Carvalho*?"

"Ah, Harper, yes. I wondered when we would hear from you. Yes, why do you ask?"

"Was he Jewish?"

Paulo shook his head at first, but then he added, "There is some speculation that he was. But even if he wasn't, one could say he was a friend of the Jews. People don't usually ask about the Marquis. You are proving to be a future historian, Harper."

Tilda grabbed Harper's hand and squeezed before letting

it drop. She, too, was eager to hear more about the Marquis with the old family name.

There were, according to Paulo, documents in the Marquis de Pompal archives, in his own writing, drawing up the laws that would end the carnage of the inquisition aimed at the *conversos*.

Harper, still not satisfied, asked, "Why did he do it, help so much, I mean, if he wasn't Jewish?"

Paulo shrugged. "Well, we don't know for sure if he was or wasn't, but the best answer, I think, is he was practical, and he knew the inquisition was bad for business. He was, you must remember, above all else interested in the future of Lisbon, its rebuilding and its strength in commerce. The Jews, he knew, could help. It may be as simple and as complicated as that."

Harper leaned over and whispered to Tilda, "I think he was Jewish. Do you think we might be related?"

Tilda laughed, a little too loudly. Paulo and the group looked on.

"Sorry," she said.

Then she whispered back to Harper, "You're going to get us in trouble."

In the afternoon, they took the number fifteen tram to Belém. The day, which had started sunny and warm, began to grow cloudy and windy. Leaving the tram, Tilda pulled Harper's windbreaker out of her backpack and helped her on with it before putting on her own. They both put on their hoods and zipped up before walking to the Monument to the Discoveries.

Approaching the monument from the large square on which it sat, Tilda could not imagine this massive simulated ship of concrete and stone ever doing anything but sinking quickly to the bottom of the sea, victim of its size and weight. But then her perspective and sense of it changed as she and Harper drew nearer. With its prow pointing over the Tagus River, framed by gathering clouds, its sails, she thought, might just catch the wind after all. The stone statues on the prow, more than a dozen on her side, seemed eager to follow the leader depicted at the top.

"Grandma, come look over here," said Harper, who had wandered off. "It's Henry the Navigator, and Paulo said the third one on this side—after that one behind Henry—is Vasco da Gama. This is right where he set sail, this very spot. Oh, I wish Grandpa could see this."

Tilda's heart took an extra beat. The wind picked up yet more, blowing her hood back. She stood watching as Harper disappeared to the other side before coming back, beaming. "I counted. There are thirty-three of them altogether, the statues. Isn't it amazing?"

Tilda smiled. "Yes it is." *Truly amazing,* she thought. *And yes, if only Harold were here to share in Harper's discoveries.*

And so, as their journey continued, Harper remained engaged and excited over each new fragment of history she learned. The group of seven, led by their increasingly esteemed guide, Paulo, forged on. First, they traveled northwest to Sintra for one day; then, continuing north, they headed to Porto for a visit of the old and historically rich harbor and city; and then, going south, they took a riverboat down the Douro. The vineyards they passed were dormant this time of year, but in the late afternoon sun, still it was the river of gold. Over these days, Harper continued asking questions, and Tilda continued admiring her granddaughter's curiosity and drive to learn all she could about the land of her grandfather's family.

And then on Friday they came to Évora, the last city they would visit before returning to Lisbon and their Sunday-morning flight home. Paulo explained that in the morning, another guide, Maria, would join them for the day and travel with them to see the ancient menhirs, or standing stones of the Almendres Cromlech. Tilda and Harper rose early to begin their journey to the small village of Guadalupe, where nearby the stones would be found. They climbed into the van before dawn and took their seats with the rest of their group, except for Louisa, who wanted to sleep in.

Harper, by the window, sat next to her grandmother. They looked at each other when they saw and passed the sign for the village, but not long after, Maria turned onto a narrow dusty road in the midst of a vast grove of olive and cork trees, which included occasional cows, searching for edibles, heads lowered.

There was a short walk to their destination, a hill with two rings of large and weathered granite stones, almost a hundred of them. Maria instructed the group to stand among the stones of the smaller ring, facing east. Harper sank down into her jacket, hands in her pockets, in an attempt to stay warm in the near darkness. Tilda cupped her hands to her mouth and blew into them. Then, beyond the hill, on the horizon, the sun began to rise. It rose quickly on this clear winter morning and began to shine through two of the stones, gleaming brightly for a moment before continuing its ascent into the sky above them.

Tilda heard Harper draw a deep breath and hold it before letting it go. "Wow," she said. "Did you see that?"

"Amazing," answered Tilda, happy they had made the effort on this early cold morning.

When were the stones placed in these circles, how long ago, why? These and more questions were raised and answered or partially answered, since, as with so much of the truly remarkable in history, definite answers were elusive or not possible at all. Were these stones, placed over seven thousand years ago, used to aid new farmers in some way after they gave up a more nomadic existence to settle in a rich land with the confluence of three rivers? Were the stones essential for religious ceremonies, for sacrifice? Or did they serve, in conjunction with other nearby monoliths, as early astronomical observatories? We would probably never have definitive answers, said Maria, but these ancients, she told the small, huddled group, were exploring the same constellations of emerging knowledge as the ancients of Stonehenge and all the other early wise ones of antiquity.

"They were all looking for something celestial, Grandma. That's what I think," Harper said softly to her grandmother on the ride back to Évora. "That's what makes them all the same—these ancient people with rocks or navigators and ships, they all wanted the stars and the sun and the moon to give them answers. That's what I think," she said again.

On their second and last day in Évora, they went to the Roman temple and to excavations in the public offices. There in the middle of the day, with city employees all around them, they walked onto the glass floors and looked down to see the ruins of an old Roman cemetery.

Outside the public offices, they clustered around Paulo, who told them about their next stop on the day's itinerary.

"Before we leave this remarkable city," said Paulo, "we will visit the Évora Public Library. There they have many relics of the past and tools of the navigators, but it is a rare book that will be the main attraction."

When they arrived, the librarian was waiting for them. She led them to the research room and mentioned that of all the fine manuscripts of antiquity housed within the library's walls, one in particular would be of interest to them, since they were learning about the days of the explorers. She left them for a moment to retrieve one of the library's rare books. She returned wearing white gloves and holding an original copy of the *Perpetual Almanac.*

"That's the book the man in the museum that day told me about. Remember, Grandma, by Abraham Zacuto?" Harper whispered to Tilda. "I looked him up. It's celestial navigation."

The librarian explained the significance of the worn leather volume in her gloved hands. "Zacuto was the mathematician to the royal court of Portugal. He had calculated the position of the stars on any day of the year. With this book, Zacuto gave to Vasco da Gama what he would need to navigate in the open waters of the Indian Ocean, to make his way to India—for the first time. This was a momentous a gift to the navigator."

Harper looked at her grandmother and smiled, as if to say, *I told you.*

The librarian offered gloves to those who would like to look at the book. John and Sandra preferred to take another stroll to the church, which should be open now, they said, declining the offer. Mitch and Connie said they would join them, and Louisa looked at the book as the librarian held it, said no, thank you, and walked outside.

"I want to hold it," said Harper.

Tilda looked on as the librarian helped Harper put on the white archival gloves.

She watched as Harper opened the book and began to carefully turn its pages. She closed it, looked at it front and back. Then she opened it again and began again to turn pages—this time as though she were waiting for it to reveal its secrets.

"I don't understand how this worked," she said, turning to Paulo.

"I know, Harper. It is hard for us to grasp. First, this copy is a translation into Portuguese, so if you understood the language, you could read it, but to make things even more difficult, Zacuto wrote the original in Hebrew, and no one in the court could understand it, so it had to be translated. But da Gama would know what these charts meant. He would use them together with the astrolabe. Here, come with me, I'll show you."

Harper took off the gloves and gingerly placed the book on the table, reluctant to leave her spot until she saw the librarian, who had left them when Harper began her examination of the pages, returning to collect it.

The only three of the group still in the library, they walked into the other room, where, under a glass globe and on a pedestal, stood an antique astrolabe, the instrument that together with the *Perpetual Almanac* had enabled da Gama to read the stars and to chart his course to India.

Paulo and Tilda stood back against the wall as Harper circled the globe several times, looking up now and then to smile at them.

Tilda, smiling back, took a mental snapshot of the moment.

That night in a special room off the main restaurant of their hotel, there was a group dinner and toasts to Paulo. Even Louisa joined in. Although no lasting friendships were to come out of the trip, the group proved to be amiable. Louisa would remain a mystery: Why had she come? Why was she so distracted? The only drawing back of the curtain occurred when Connie said, "She is just getting over a breakup. We thought the trip would do her good, but I'm not sure." Tilda felt a twinge in her chest, as she did these days when confronted with the sadness of others—usually it was because of death, but recently, any loss could trigger sympathy. "I'm sorry," she said. Connie's smile did not mitigate the sadness in her eyes.

While everyone was commenting on the trip, Tilda thought of going home, and after her brief conversation with Connie, her thoughts turned to Darren and Amanda. Would one or both of them be facing more heartbreak? She looked at Harper, who was smiling, and this brought her back to the moment, for which she was grateful.

"And I have an award for Harper," said Paulo. "It's a travel diary from Bertrands," he said as he handed it to her. "I don't find many fifteen-year-olds on these trips so interested in history. To Harper," he said, raising his glass.

The little book in her hand had a ribbon to mark pages and a black elastic band to hold its pages shut, until the owner chose to open them. The front cover had a drawing of the bookstore, with the date, 1732. "The oldest bookstore in the world," she read. "Thank you, Paulo."

Tilda watched her granddaughter as the conversation turned to packing and getting some sleep before the early morning wake-up call. First Harper turned the book over in her hands several times. Then she clutched it to her and looked at Paulo, who smiled.

Tilda had hoped to talk to Harper that night in their room, but both fell into bed in a stupor after they finished their packing.

"We have to put the bags outside the door by six," she said, reaching to turn out the light. Then she added, "Good night, future explorer."

"There's nothing left to explore, unless it's outer space," she replied.

Tilda thought about all there was for her granddaughter yet to explore about her known world—and about herself. And the latter, that was the adventure upon which she had already embarked.

Early in the morning, a shuttle drove Tilda and Harper back to Lisbon for their morning flight. Paulo, who would be leaving later with the rest of the group, rose early to say good-bye. Harper, Tilda noticed, waved to him and wiped a stray tear from her eye before turning to face forward for the ride to the airport and then home.

When Laura and Mark picked them up at international arrivals, the first thing Laura did was grab her daughter and hug her tightly, as though, it seemed to Tilda, Harper hardly had space in her rib cage to take a breath, but at least now Laura could exhale in relief. Her daughter was home safe.

Turning to Tilda, Laura said, "Well done, Mom. I can only imagine she had a wonderful time, and I can't wait to hear all about it. Now you get to return to the real world." Tilda must have made her mother face, the one Laura always said began when she drew her eyebrows together and ended with tightly closed lips, because Laura looked as though she had just said the wrong thing. The real world wasn't exactly what Tilda was looking forward to rejoining.

Returning to the real world would be a shock. Harold was still dead. She wondered if her anxiety attacks would return, but, in her favor, she had become so attuned to the warning signals that she could stop them at the first sign. This was a feat to be proud of. When she thought of Harper, she was renewed. The trip had been good, of that she was sure, and while Harper hadn't talked much on the flight back, Tilda thought she had sensed a change, as though Harper's own breathing had become more relaxed, her eyes clearer. She was more inclined to stay with you when she spoke, as though she could now endure a steady gaze, not needing to turn away as she so often did.

This was good, but there were two great burdens Tilda still carried, and they had become intertwined: her grief and her worry. The first she would carry forever, she was sure; the second could only be relieved when she knew Harper had found her true self.

Chapter Thirteen

TRUSTING THE HOURS

THAT CARRIED US

～∾～

In her room Harper sat at her desk and loaded her photos from the trip onto her laptop. As each thumbnail suddenly came into focus, she felt as though she were reliving her time in Portugal. There was the elevator, the hotel, the group, Paulo, the church of the massacre—each with its own special memory. She lingered on the Monument to the Discoveries, where da Gama first set sail, and she thought about how that journey had begun with questioning until, one at a time, the pieces fell into place. And then India.

Her grandmother had taken the last pictures in Évora, of Harper in white gloves, holding the almanac, and then another of her with Paulo next to the astrolabe. *They had the tools they needed.* Those had been Grandpa's words, and now she had been there, had seen the tools that had made celestial navigation possible.

Suddenly the sky and the stars didn't seem so big. It was possible to find your place. Harper's world began to return to the familiar, not more exciting—to be sure—but familiar was good, too, she thought. Her mother had let her miss school on Monday, but late Tuesday afternoon after school, she drove Harper to her therapy session. Harper, still a little jet-lagged, had wanted to skip it, but her mom reminded her of the deal they had made. "We agreed you could go with Grandma on this trip, but your schoolwork and your sessions with Dr. Bernstein couldn't fall behind. Remember? As it is, you've missed a session." Harper nodded. Yes, she had agreed, and now here she was.

She knocked on the door, and Dr. Miriam asked her to come in. Before taking her usual spot in the huge and soft upholstered chair, she said, "I have something for you. It's from Portugal."

"Harper, I'm so touched, thank you," she said, opening the neatly wrapped little package. "I love the paper."

"It's from the museum in Lisbon. I hope you like it."

"I love it," she said, holding up a mosaic tile.

"It's a replica of the huge rose compass in Belém."

"I'm honored, Harper. Thank you again. And this trip obviously meant a lot to you, seeing Portugal with your grandmother."

Harper nodded.

Dr. Miriam waited.

"It did mean a lot. My grandma and me, it was like we were there together, looking for grandpa. I don't know. I'm not sure I even know what I mean."

"I understand, Harper. It's not always easy to put our feelings into words."

"I was mad in Portugal," she quickly added. "Not at Grandma. Nothing like that."

"Why were you mad?"

"Horrible things happened there. Probably to my grandpa's ancestors. I know it was a long time ago, but Grandpa used to talk about it. And I saw and heard about how cruel and awful it was."

"Do you mean about the inquisition?"

"Yes, that and more, about living in fear, about not being

able to be who you are. Did you know that the Jews had to convert or die? They had to hide who they truly were."

"And knowing that made you mad."

"Yes, because it was so unfair."

"It was unfair, and cruel, and everything you say."

"But that isn't all about Portugal. I was happy there, and sad, too. I mean, I was happy because it was so cool to see everything from history, to be there. But I was sad because I couldn't be there with my grandpa, and I know he would've loved it. And I know my grandma felt the same way."

"So it was good being with your grandma, because she understood."

"Oh, yeah, we didn't even have to say anything. All we had to do was look at each other."

"It sounds like an amazing trip, Harper. It really does. What did you like the best?"

"At the library in Évora, we saw an old book that had charts in it that told the navigators how to get where they wanted to go—that and they had a thing on display called an astrolabe." Harper paused, remembering the copper disc with the coat of arms embossed on the top.

"And you thought that was most interesting? Why?"

Harper looked up, realizing she hadn't heard the question.

"Why was it interesting, Harper, the things at the library?"

"It's funny because I think, or I used to think, the sky and the stars are kind of scary. But so does everybody, I guess, even going back to the beginning. But what they did was try to figure it out, and then do amazing things, like go out on the ocean and find new countries. I guess that's what humans do, figure things out."

"Does that mean anything to you, personally, Harper?"

"No, not really," she answered, not sure what to say. Her mind was blank, but then she said, "Did I tell you that the kids at school always talk about sex?" It was an abrupt change of subject, she knew, but there it was. She was suddenly thinking of her friends and their constant boy talk.

Dr. M looked at her and smiled. "I think you may have said they talk about boys all the time, but I don't think you mentioned sex."

Harper noted that Dr. M didn't seem to mind the change in subject at all.

"Well, okay. But they don't just talk about it. One girl has already done it."

Harper stopped to see Dr. Miriam's reaction to this news. But she just looked at Harper, waiting for her to go on.

"And all the other kids, the girls I hang around with, think it's cool that Sage has had sex already."

"But you don't."

"I don't like boys."

"I know, Harper, but what do you think about Sage having sex?"

"I think it's gross."

"Having sex is gross?"

"At our age? Yeah, I think it's gross."

"What about later, when you're older and in love?"

Harper shook her head. "This is what I mean. I don't have feelings. And I think that's what's wrong with me. I don't want to kiss anyone or fall in love or get married or have kids. I don't care about it, any of it."

"I don't think that means there's anything wrong with you. Lots of people don't do any of those things, and they're still happy. Do you think you can be happy without any of those things?"

Harper didn't respond. She hoped Dr. Miriam might help her out, as she did sometimes, but she didn't say anything either.

"I don't think about it, about being happy, I mean. Mostly, I just try not to be too sad."

Dr. Miriam just turned her head a little, as though she were trying to hear words that hadn't yet been spoken.

"People die."

"Yes, they do, Harper."

"And when you love those people, it's horrible."

"Yes."

"It's the most horrible thing on earth, and I don't understand why God, if there even is one, put us here to love people so much and then to take them away. It's an awful thing to do. It's the most unfair thing I can think of, and I don't want to do it."

"I understand. I feel that way sometimes, too, that's it the most unfair thing in the world."

"Really? But you're married and you have kids."

"Well, yes, but people I love have died, my mother, my father. I still cry when I think about it."

"When did they die?"

Dr. M paused, as though she were thinking of something very important. "Harper," she began, "I don't usually talk about myself, but I'm going to make an exception because I think it may help."

Harper sat up straight to give Dr. M her full attention.

"My mother died when I was twelve."

"Twelve. Oh, that's . . . so sad."

"Yes, it was. It was a long, long time before I stopped being sad—and scared. Life seemed very scary to me then. Just as you said. It's the most horrible thing, when someone you love dies."

Harper didn't want to talk anymore. She drew her arms across her chest and scrunched back into the chair.

"Is that it, Harper? Enough for today? Our time's not up yet, and I don't think your mom is here."

"But I'm tired. Still on Portugal time, I guess." She put on her coat and then her backpack. Before she left, she said, "I'm sorry, about your mom. But thank you, Dr. M, for telling me."

"You're welcome, Harper. You can make yourself comfortable in the waiting room until your mom gets here."

"Okay, and thanks again."

"See you next week," said Dr. M.

"I'll be here." Just then Harper saw through the window that her mom was pulling into the entrance. *Better to be too early than to be even a little late,* one of her mother's favorite expressions. *That's Mom, all right,* thought Harper.

❧

There was no way of avoiding it. Tilda's six-month cleaning appointment had been put off for so long, it had now been eleven months. The last appointment was just before Harold died. Dr. Renu's last message had bordered on incredulous. "I don't know how you can think it's okay to go this long, Tilda. But really, it's time. Please call so Ruth can make an appointment for you." Then obviously aware of her tone, she added, "I know this is a difficult time, but you have to take care of yourself."

Tilda wanted to make the appointment, but every time she picked up the phone, she had an image of her teeth, in her gums, in her skull. And the image was terrifying, so she hung up each time.

Now, here she was sitting in the chair, Dr. Renu all but indiscernible with the exception of her lovely brown eyes, those perfect almond-shaped orbs, the ones Harold had always said relaxed him.

But there was nothing relaxing about this venture—though it was just a simple cleaning, Tilda was tense. Dr. Renu, who always did her own cleaning, asked if everything was all right. Tilda, mouth open, made a guttural sound and nodded yes, certain her hands firmly grasping each armrest would give her away.

Dr. Renu scraped while her assistant, Wilma, vacuumed. The scrapping reverberated in Tilda's head, and beyond that was the background music of the office: oldies. She heard the hauntingly lovely Hawaiian version of "Somewhere Over the Rainbow," the strains of the ukulele softly crying, saying to Tilda, isn't this the sad truth? That it's somewhere over some rainbow, perhaps, where all this wonder is possible, but not here, not now.

Maybe it was a combination of things: her anxiety, her first visit to the office since Harold, or the horrible morning news about the schoolgirls murdered by ISIS. But somewhere over the rainbow seemed so far away, so unreachable in this mutilated world. Without making a sound or moving a muscle, Tilda began to feel the tears streaming down the sides of her head, surely soaking the protective paper-wrapped pillow beneath her.

Dr. Renu stopped scraping. Wilma stopped vacuuming.

"Would you like a break, Tilda?"

Tilda nodded yes and took a few minutes to collect herself in the empty examining room. The music had stopped, turned off, Tilda guessed, maybe on purpose to relieve her suffering. It was true that songs on the whole were taking her back, which in itself was not always a bad thing. There were times when Harold's favorite songs, or theirs together, gave her the kind of pain that was comforting, but this one had for its own reasons been overwhelming. Over the rainbow was too far away, and without Harold, there was no real comfort in this world, just occasional reprieves from her grief.

At the reception desk, after the completion of her cleaning, when Ruth asked if she wanted to make her next appointment, Dr. Renu came to the front and said not to worry about it now. "I'll call soon, and we can make the appointment together."

"She must've thought I was too undone to put a date on my calendar. Oh God, I've become the stereotype of the bereaved widow, barely functioning," Tilda told Bev, whom she called as soon as she had retuned home. "You know, the whole thing, lying there in that chair, masked people over you—the whole setup is designed to promote patient vulnerability," she said. "And then there's me. A little on edge, I guess."

"I don't know. Ordinarily, I'd agree with you, the whole sad state of medical and dental care in this country today, none of it patient-oriented, but in this case, I probably would've cried too. A perfect storm for a meltdown, if you ask me. And the world isn't going to give us bluebirds singing and that land of lullabies anytime soon. It seems the savagery just keeps getting worse. Don't be so hard on yourself, but . . ."

"But? I was just taking some comfort, and now I feel a dark cloud about to descend."

"Nothing like that. But it's been almost a year now. How are you doing with those five stages?"

"Well, I'm not at acceptance, if that's what you mean, but I'm very familiar with the others, since I revisit them all the time."

"Meaning . . ."

"Okay, yesterday for example, I was sure I heard Harold in the kitchen making coffee. Was that denial or a visitation? I like to think he visits from time to time. Then there's anger. That happens every day. Sometimes I'm even mad at him for leaving me the way he did. That leads to guilt. I don't think that's one of the stages, but it should be. Ah, yes, those pesky, neatly packaged five stages."

"Hmm. I detect a little sarcasm. Not directed at me, I hope. I'm just a little concerned."

"No, not directed at you. I'm just tired of the whole five-stages thing. It's so much more complicated than that." Tilda cupped the phone closer to her ear, as though she were cupping a hand on her friend's cheek.

They were both silent. Then Tilda said, "Honestly, I don't know. Some days I'm actually happy. Other days, I think I can't get out of bed."

"Well, that sounds like depression. You still don't want to take anything?"

"If this goes on much longer, this roller coaster, I mean, I might. But mostly, I think I do okay. I stay busy, friends, family, you know."

"Meddling, yeah, I know."

"Meddling—mostly it's worked out okay."

"By the way, what's with Darren? Have you seen him since you've been back?"

"No, but I do think about him. I know Harper and Lizzie have been in touch."

"Wow. So it's Harper now?"

"Yes, ever since Portugal. I finally realized how much it means to her."

"How is she doing, then?"

"As far as I know, very well, and everyone seems to be adjusting."

"But to what? Besides the name change, I mean."

"I don't think anyone knows just yet. But there's nothing drastic going on; no puberty blockers or hormones or anything."

After she and Bev hung up, Tilda pulled the antidepressant prescription from Dr. Willis out of her file and stared at it for a moment. She thought about tearing it up, but then she put it back and closed the drawer. *Who knows? Maybe.*

❦

Harper went to see Dr. Miriam right after school for her regular Tuesday-afternoon appointment. She had news to share. She had just started her period.

"How do you feel about it?" asked Dr. M. Harper knew this would be her first question, and she was prepared for it.

"You know how I feel. I told you from the beginning of our sessions. I don't want anything to do with it."

"You sound angry, Harper. It's okay to be angry, but I'd like to know more about why."

Harper stopped to think about it. Yes, she was angry, at having her period, and maybe, yes, angry at Dr. M, too.

"We talked about stopping it. You said there were ways of doing that, and now it's too late. Isn't that right? It's too late?"

"I see. Okay, Harper, let's back up a bit. I understand that you may have wanted me to help you with stopping it if that were possible, but we also talked about the process, right? That it would take a long time, maybe years, before I could be sure what we should do. And that in the meantime, you more than likely would begin menstruation. Do you remember?"

It was true. Harper did remember, but somehow she had hoped that when she became Harper, she would be able to leave it all behind, the periods, the breasts, the boys, the sex and doing it, like Sage. She could go back to the way it was before.

It was the before part that Dr. M wanted to talk about today.

"What about before?" she asked.

Harper told her, "It's just like I said, before I had to do all the stuff I didn't want to do."

"What 'stuff,' Harper?"

"It's like when all the changes happen, you know, physically, everyone expects you to start thinking about things differently. Like all the makeup. What's that about, anyway? Okay, it's about boys, right? So you're supposed to like them and get them to like you, and to kiss them, and fall in love. I don't want to be in love."

Harper stopped and brushed away imaginary lint on her jeans.

"It's not like you don't love people now, though, right?" Dr. M said.

"That's totally different. It's easy to love your family. You have to love them, of course, but grown-up love, that's way different. It's weird and funny, even to think about it."

"Why 'funny'?" Dr. M asked.

Harper hesitated. She cast her eyes down and shut her lips tight.

Dr. M waited for a response.

"I don't know. With your family it's different," Harper said. "You're born loving them. You don't have a choice. You love them, even though you know it can hurt you, but you have to love them."

"Has loving your family hurt you, Harper?"

"Well, no, they haven't hurt me, not really."

"What about loving them has hurt you?"

Harper felt her eyes begin to burn and her nose tingle. She didn't want to answer.

Dr. M moved up in her chair and asked softly, "Does loving them hurt now?"

Harper felt a huge swell in her chest that went up to her head. She started crying so hard she couldn't stop.

"Grandpa. He died," she said. "We didn't even say goodbye. He was like a friend. He was my best friend." She couldn't talk anymore.

Dr. M rose from her chair to sit next to Harper. She patted her hand without saying a word. They stayed that way for a time, Harper crying.

When the tears began to dissipate, Dr. M handed her another tissue, and Harper wiped her face and blew her nose.

"Grandpa and I were 'pals,' that's what Grandma used to call us. And it was true. We hung out together. He told me everything. I learned more from Grandpa than my teachers, practically."

"Oh, Harper. That makes so much sense. You really miss him. You loved him and he left you and that hurt. And so maybe in the future you could make it hurt less somehow."

"I don't know how I could make it hurt less. I'm going to lose Grandma and then my parents. Everyone I still love is going to die. Just like your mother did. How can I make it hurt less?"

"What was it you were thinking about grown-up love when you said it was funny? It isn't really funny, is it?"

"Funny, like weird. I mean, all of sudden you love someone new?"

"Well, it's not that easy, it takes time to know someone, but maybe it has to do with . . . when you're grown, you have a choice. You decide to let someone into your life. You're not born loving anyone but your family. But grown-up love, as you said, is different."

"Right, so maybe I won't love someone new."

"Maybe the difference is you can make it hurt less by choosing not to love anyone new."

Harper pulled her knees into her chest.

The two sat quietly, and then Harper said, "I don't know. My head hurts, maybe from crying so much."

"It's okay, Harper. We can leave it here for now. We'll talk some more next week. But I want you to think about our conversation, about love and choosing to love. Okay? Will you do that?"

Harper blew her nose again and nodded yes.

Chapter Fourteen

THIS WHOLE EXPERIMENT IN GREEN

⧸⧹

Was it possible? Tilda wondered on her way home from Saturday grocery shopping. She had been angry with herself for going out on a busy Saturday instead of during the week when she noticed the forsythia bushes beginning to bloom along Old Church Road. It was March, and they did appear to be peeking out from behind the berm by the church. They were not in full bloom yet, but the flash of yellow caused her heart to leap. The first signs of spring had always shaken her out of the dull mood she fell into from the autumnal to the vernal equinox. She immediately thought to tell Harold as soon as she got home. Oh, how Harold loved the forsythia, especially in full flower when the sun shone on them, turning them into beacons of light. He would not be home when she arrived, but still she would share this moment with him. She spent a lot of time talking to Harold these days. And it was comforting, but was this denial or acceptance—or something worse? She wasn't sure it mattered.

Pulling into the driveway, Tilda spotted Darren and Lizzie getting out of their car. She lowered her window and waved, but Darren turned away. Not Lizzie, though. "Hi, Mrs. Carr!" she shouted, waving her arms. "Welcome home from Portugal."

She was a bit taken aback to realize that this was the first time she had seen them since she and Harper had returned from their trip. Tilda had been waiting patiently for some sign from Darren that a friendship between them was still possible, but he continued to avoid any contact with her—apparently even eye contact, Tilda thought as she gathered her bags and went into the house. At least there was Lizzie to keep the connection alive. And Tilda knew from Harper that she and Lizzie were spending more time together.

After putting the groceries away, she took a newly purchased box of crackers with her and wandered onto the porch. *Remarkable Flavor and Intelligent Snacking*, the package read. Tilda had always eaten rice crackers, even though the flavor wasn't all that "remarkable." And she supposed they now made for "intelligent snacking" because they were gluten free, also prominently featured on the label. Almost all food packaging these days, it seemed, included something about gluten, whether people seriously needed to avoid it or not. Faddish marketing had always annoyed Tilda, but she pulled out a cracker and began to munch, intelligently, nevertheless.

Mark would be calling before long about taking down the storm windows, she thought, looking outside. The crocuses were blooming in the backyard, although she had hardly noticed till now—white, purple, and her favorite variety, the silvery ones with the fine and bold lilac stripes, made all the more lovely because they would not last. Not only was their time fleeting; there were other perils to shorten their season. Even now she saw a fat gray squirrel holding an entire crocus, flower and bulb, in his tiny paws, more like little hands, nibbling furtively, as though he too knew it was sinful to be consuming such beauty, but survival was survival after all. And sometimes there was more to eat than dry grainy acorns. Sometimes, for a short time, there were succulent petals, stems, and roots to provide sustenance. Tilda wanted to shoo the squirrel away. They bordered on being a nuisance, but there was nothing to be gained from interfering with a squirrel being a squirrel. Maybe she had finally learned a thing or two as well about undue interfering, she thought. She was putting the box of crackers away when the doorbell rang.

It was Darren. After looking through the peephole, her hand floated up to her chest. She took a minute to collect herself before opening the door.

"Can I come in?" he asked.

Tilda opened the door wide and had to restrain herself from opening her arms as well. She didn't want to scare him away with too much emotion, but by God, it was good to see him.

She offered coffee, tea, soda, all to no avail. He couldn't stay long, he told her, as he sat on the edge of the sofa. He looked thinner, Tilda thought, his face more drawn than when she had last seem him in this room. She sat on the other side of the sofa, facing him.

"First, I want to say I'm sorry for . . ."

Tilda put up her hand as if to put an end to his forthcoming apology. "There's no need, Darren. I may have been well-meaning, which I hope you know I intended to be, but I . . ."

Now it was Darren's turn to interrupt.

"Mrs. Carr, Tilda, I came over to tell you I appreciate what you've tried to do for us. And I know you meant well." He looked down at his folded hands, his elbows resting on his knees. "I've been in my own world and not very nice to you, I know." He looked up and said, "That's why I owe you an apology."

"Not necessary, but thank you. And I know, I think I know, how hard this has been on you."

He nodded and said, "There's more. Amanda has been in touch with me. I know she talks to Lizzie, but after what happened with Tilly, I didn't want to talk to her anymore. And I haven't until recently."

Tilda looked into his blue eyes, ringed with worry.

"I don't know what to do. She wants to come home."

"Stay right here," she said. "I'll be right back."

Returning quickly, she handed him a glass of sparkling water and put a plate of cookies on the table in front of him.

He politely picked up a cookie and began to fill in the details. Although Amanda had been calling him and texting, asking for some time to talk, he had not responded, but in one of her texts she said she wanted to see him and that it was important. He thought she wanted a divorce, and if that was it, he would be ready to give it to her. So he had agreed to meet her at the diner in town.

As it turned out, she didn't want a divorce. She wanted to come home. He was furious and was about to tell her to go back to her lover, when she said plainly it was time to let him go.

"Did she think that would make me want her more?" Darren asked. "I got up to leave, but she pulled me back. 'I won't lie to you,' she said. 'I love him.' I swear I wanted to hit her, honestly. I know, terrible, right? But what did she think? That I would just take her back like nothing had happened? That she had done nothing? Then she said, 'But I love you and I love Lizzie, and I need to come home.' I said I didn't care what she needed. It wasn't going to be about what she needed."

Tilda remembered her conversation with Amanda, when Tilda told her this day would come, when she would have to decide, and apparently she had made her decision. Now it was up to Darren.

Amanda had told him about Franklin, about Emile's grief, and how all of it had played a part in her decision to be with Emile. None of her explanations had caused Darren to relent, but Tilda acknowledged to herself at least that Amanda had decided to be brutally honest, leaving herself open to almost-certain rejection. But she was taking that chance, apparently.

Darren didn't say anything else, but there were so many unanswered questions. Tilda knew it best not to overwhelm him, but she opted just the same to ask at least a few.

"Is that how you left it, then? That she wants to come home, and it's up to you to decide? Has she talked to Lizzie about any of this?"

"Lizzie knows. She's been leaving Post-it notes everywhere, all about forgiveness. Not very subtle, but I get the message. I know what she wants, and I have to say, Amanda doesn't want Lizzie to be the reason I would take her back. Not that I've hinted of that to Lizzie. But of course, I have to think about her. This whole thing is as much about Lizzie as it is about me."

"So what do you think?" she asked.

He shook his head and almost hissed. "A lot of nerve, that's what I think. She leaves, has an affair, says she loves him, but it's time to let him go. What does that even mean? What am I supposed to make of that?" He drew in his lips and continued to shake his head, in awe, it seemed, of his wife's . . . what . . . gall?

Tilda had to agree it sounded outrageous. By "following her bliss" Amanda had left a wake of despair. And yet . . . Tilda couldn't believe she was beginning to feel some sympathy for Amanda.

"She also said she loves you, Darren. I guess it's hard to think that counts for anything, but it is possible, you know, that she does love you . . . very much . . . and she does want to come home for that reason."

Darren was unmoved.

"And about letting Emile go. I don't know, maybe that means she knows that it isn't right to stay with him if it was his grief that drew her to him in the first place. Maybe it was a complicating set of circumstances, and it took her a long time to sort it out. I don't know if that makes any sense."

When Darren remained silent, she continued. "Maybe Lizzie is onto something with her messages of forgiveness. Look, Darren, this is what I think, if it's okay."

He looked at her, his eyes beginning to fill, Tilda thought. He nodded.

"If you find that under your hurt and your anger there is even a shred, a tiny shred, of love left, then forgiveness is possible. Possible. And maybe worth the chance."

Darren looked away and wiped his eyes before standing

to face her. "I've got to go," he said. "Thank you for listening. I shouldn't be putting this on you."

Tilda walked him to the door and once again restrained herself from offering a hug. He seemed withdrawn, and she was beginning to regret her advice. *Still a meddling old bitty*, she said to herself as she closed the door.

Then the phone rang. It was Laura wondering if her mother was up to a visit. Tilda hadn't had such an active Saturday in some time. "Of course I'm up to a visit. What does it take? I've already been out and done the shopping and had a guest."

She told Laura about Darren only to learn that Harper knew most of it and had already told Laura. "I don't think it's a secret," said Laura. "But I have news. Harper got her period."

"Really? When?" Tilda sounded so casual, even to herself, she thought. But her words belied her surprise.

"Last Thursday." Tilda was more than a little miffed that it had taken over a week for Laura to be sharing this news. She wished that Harper had called and told her, but she put her hurt feelings aside. Her primary reaction was actually relief. To her the news signified a reduced likelihood of hormone blockers, but this she kept to herself. "Oh, how wonderful," she said. "How is Harper taking it?"

"Okay, I think. But I'll tell you all about it when I see you. You haven't been to Shabbat dinner. How about tomorrow?"

Tilda immediately said yes without her usual first reaction: searching for a reason to decline the offer. It would be good to see Harper free of worries—at least, Tilda would be free of worries, but she wasn't sure about Harper.

Harper wasn't sure she wanted to go back to see Dr. Miriam. What had been easy, talking to her, was becoming hard and confusing. Besides, she was in it now. She'd had her period. It would be years before hormone therapy would change that truth, that she was changing from a girl to a woman. And then what? Even if finally Dr. M agreed to hormones, what then? Her period would stop, and she'd become a boy? She wasn't sure, not really, that that would be any better. She'd still have to be a something, and she didn't feel like being an anything. Why did she have to choose? Her head was hurting, her stomach turning. Some people weren't in their right minds, she thought, but she wasn't in her right body. She liked saying that to herself. It made sense, to think that she wasn't in her right body. Yes, that much she knew, but that wasn't all there was to it, because she wasn't sure what her right body was. Suddenly, she was tired and didn't want to think about it anymore, or talk to anyone about it anymore. Why couldn't she just drop out, not be a girl, not be a boy, just be Harper.

She closed her bedroom door behind her and pulled her phone out of her jeans to look at her calendar. One more visit, and that was it. She would stop going to see Dr. M after that.

Then she thought about Grandpa and what he would think of all of this. He would understand, she knew, and love her no matter what, and it was the worst thing possible that he was gone. She didn't know if she would ever stop being mad, sorry, and so sad that he was gone. When the reality hit her, as it did from time to time, it was like the top of her head was exploding. Everything went white. It was impossible that he was gone. Where did he go? Why couldn't he come back? But of course he couldn't. Then it happened again, the top of her head blowing up in raging disbelief. And she cried again, just as she had in Dr. M's office. She fell onto the bed and pushed her head into the pillow so no one would hear, or knock on the door, or try to comfort her. There was no comfort; she didn't want it, anyway.

᠊᠊᠊ᴄ∿ᴐᴐ᠊᠊᠊

Tilda hadn't been avoiding him, she told George when she finally answered the phone. It was just that there was so much to do after her trip, and she was just getting settled and back to normal. Yes, it was true, she hadn't called him back, and she knew he had been trying to reach her. These excuses sounded thin, even to Tilda. It was well into March, and she was back to normal, whatever that was, but she was surely over jet lag and any other lingering effects of her trip with Harper.

"So what is it, Tilda?" he asked. "I can't keep chasing after you. It's not good for my self-image." He was half joking, but Tilda knew there was a trace of truth in what he was saying. And she had to be honest: she had been avoiding him, though she wasn't sure why. Her life felt complicated, too complicated to add another person, to add George.

"I'd like to see you," he said. "A nice, quiet dinner. How about it?"

She listened and began thinking about the little place on the Sound she and Harold used to go to when they wanted some time to themselves when Laura was growing up, when they needed a break from parenting and working, the getting-and-spending time of their lives. That's when they would call the sitter and go to The Shack for oysters, beer, the sun setting, and the night surrounding them in a temporary respite. It had been good, and they had known it.

"I'd like to go someplace on the water," she told him, surprising them both.

◦～◦

On April 1, Tilda invited Bev to the beach.

"Are you serious?" she said. "I haven't been to the beach since I was twelve. I've been wearing black since then, and the beach is too cheerful for an old nihilist like me."

"Yes, I'm serious. This isn't an April Fools' Day joke, and you're not a nihilist. Nihilists don't spend most of their lives trying to save the world. So come. Anyway, it's still cold, so not all that cheerful, and maybe you'll get lucky and it will rain when we get there. Besides, I'm not talking about Maine. Just here by me, at the Point." Bev reluctantly agreed. Before hanging up, Tilda said, "And one more thing. We're going to talk about you this time. My invitation. My rules."

"How about we take turns? You have to fill me in on things. Say yes, or I'm not coming."

Water Haven's beach was on the grounds of an old estate that had been left to the town sometime after World War II. If Water Haven's shoreline looked like a hand, the beach was the thumb, and the Point, as it was called, was the nail. Tilda and Bev got there a few days after Tilda's invitation, in the early afternoon, and they took over a picnic table vacated by a family of four. The kids, about two and five, had left cereal and cookie crumbs scattered over their places, and a colony of seagulls had descended, screeching and trying to make off with as much as possible as quickly as possible. Tilda and Bev moved in and spread their tablecloth over the blotched and marred wood surface. No matter. The sun was high. Temperatures in the high sixties had mitigated the still-cold breeze off the water. The salt marshes just in front of them emitted the sweet briny smell of shoreline spring. Tilda breathed it in deeply. She took off her sun hat, letting the air blow through her hair. Even Bev was serene, despite a brief struggle to balance her ample buttocks on the narrow bench.

Taking out a chilled bottle of rosé, Bev asked, "What shall we toast to?" She placed two glasses on the table, unscrewed the top, and began to pour.

"To life," said Tilda, taking up her glass.

"To life," said Bev.

And they drank.

When the bottle was half-empty, Bev began to eye a bench nearby with a backrest. Tilda suggested they move. The sun went into shadows, but the wine had left a glow they both enjoyed as they gazed out over the water.

"It's almost a year," said Tilda, barely getting the words out.

"Yes, it is," said Bev, leaning a little closer to her friend, an offer of bodily as well as emotional support. "And it's been quite a year, hasn't it? Let's start with you."

Tilda nodded in agreement. "Quite." Her dinner with George was uppermost on her mind this afternoon, and she was eager to talk to Bev about it, even though this beach trip wasn't supposed to be about her.

She'd known George wanted to talk about their "relationship," a term he had used on the phone. It struck her at the time as the sort of term George wouldn't use, too "Dr. Phil." To her relief, he was not in a Dr. Phil frame of mind at dinner. He was open and direct and his words were from the heart.

He had called her back the same afternoon she'd agreed to go to dinner to ask if she liked the Loading Dock, a restaurant on the water by the yacht club. Tilda thought about it, searching her memory for any previous associations, and had come up blank. She and Harold had passed there many times, but oddly enough—because it was a popular spot—they had never been. She said yes.

George had reserved a quiet table in the back, away from the bar and the piano. "Look, Tilda," he had started, after dessert, after the waiter had served them coffee. "I'm not going to waste words; I can't, really. It would be silly, wouldn't it? At our age, to waste anything? Here's the thing: We've spent some time together this year. Hell, we've spent the night a couple of times. Well, Cuba doesn't count, I guess. I left as soon as I undressed you and got you into bed."

Tilda raised her eyebrows and looked at him over her reading glasses.

"Okay, I made sure you were okay and in bed for the night before I left you to sleep it off. And the second time, I was on the couch. But technically, you get what I'm saying. We've shared some emotionally intimate moments, but you always seem to back away after. When I think we should be getting closer."

Tilda was about to offer an explanation, but he cut her off.

"Wait, just let me say one other thing, or two more things. I know this is your first year without Harold, but—and here's the second thing—but you've been open to me, whether you admit it to yourself or not. You're making yourself not want me. I think you could want to be with me if you let yourself."

Tilda wasn't sure she wanted this conversation, but she had accepted the invitation, and now she owed him an explanation, but what she said instead was, "You're right."

Now, on the bench at the beach, with her eyes on the horizon, Bev asked, "So how is everything with George?"

Tilda gave her a sideways glance. "It's as though you're reading my mind. I was just thinking about our dinner last week."

"Well?"

"Well, it was nice."

"Nice?"

"Yes, and George wants to take it to the next level. What a stupid expression. As though relationships were a competition, and only the really good ones get to advance."

"But that's kind of true, isn't it?"

"I don't know, but to his credit, that isn't how he put it. He just came out and said it. 'I think I'm in love with you, and I want to be more than an occasional date or a friend,' is how he put it."

"Wow. That put it out there, didn't it? And what did you say?"

"I told him I knew it wasn't fair to keep him waiting and that I knew at our age we didn't have that kind of time. I told him I had feelings for him, that maybe love was possible, but I just couldn't say it yet. I told him I hoped he could give me a little more time, and if he could, I would promise to be more open to him—and not 'emotionally unavailable.' Another term I can't abide. What is it about relationships that causes this psychotherapy language?"

"Hmm. As interesting as a linguistics lesson would be right now, I'd rather know how you feel about this," said Bev, who had turned to face her friend, who, deep in thought, was still looking at the horizon.

"You know, to tell you the truth, I felt a little pressured," she answered.

"Let me put it this way," said Bev. "If there is even a shred of a chance that you could love him, then maybe a new relationship in your life is possible."

Tilda turned to look at her. "Really?" She smiled, knowing what her friend was up to. "You are really going to turn my own words back on me?"

"Well, isn't that some version of what you told Darren about Amanda? And if it could be true for them, couldn't it be true for you and George?"

Tilda took a breath. "I'm thinking about it," she said. "But it has to be on my terms, my timetable."

"So your year of meddling hasn't turned out too badly. You rescued your granddaughter from Brooklyn, Lizzie still wants to play Scrabble with you, Darren has forgiven you—thanked you, even. And your advice to him can be applied to your relationship with George. Not a bad year. Well, a terrible year, I know. But look at you, in spite of it."

Tilda smiled. These things were true.

"But wait," said Bev, "before we move on, I still have to ask you what's new with Harper. When did you see her last?"

"I haven't seen Harper much since we got back from Portugal. She's busy with school, but I did have a long talk with her the last time I was over for dinner."

Tilda drew her arm out in front of her, pushed up her jacket, and scratched her elbow. "I think I told you everything was okay since she got her period."

Bev nodded.

"Well, not exactly."

Frowning now, Bev said, "I'm not surprised. After all, isn't that exactly what she was trying to avoid?"

"Yes, exactly." Tilda pushed her jacket back over her arm. "Sometimes I'm too close, or maybe I just say what I want, hoping I can make it be true. How could she be all right with it?"

Tilda felt herself close to tears now. "I think we've all missed how really hard this has been on her."

Tilda had known as soon as she saw Harper on Friday night two weeks ago that she was troubled, her green eyes dark, her gaze often downcast. She was grateful when Harper asked if she wanted to see how her Portugal souvenirs looked in her room. She knew Harper wanted to talk.

"She closed her door immediately and sat on the bed with her knees drawn up to her chest. I was frightened, but then she just told me about her period. She had told Dr. Bernstein she didn't want to get her period, but now it was too late. She would have to wait a long time before Dr. Bernstein or any doctor would agree to hormone therapy."

Tilda was trembling. The sun was beginning to dip behind late-afternoon clouds. But she pressed on with her story.

"I asked her if that was what she really wanted, to begin testosterone, and she waited a long time before she answered that she didn't know. I asked her what it meant to her to be Harper and not Tilly, and she said it meant she could be anything, or nothing different. Which left me a little confused."

"Well, it's okay, isn't it? She has time to decide. These are huge questions she's asking, and she's brave enough to admit that she doesn't know if she wants to be male. Maybe she doesn't want to be either, or maybe she'll be both. That's possible too, isn't it?"

"Yes, it is. It is possible."

"How did you leave it?"

"I told her what I always tell her, that we love her, will always love her, and that she has time to sort it all out. In the meantime, she will have to live with puberty. And I honestly think she will be all right. She told me she was glad we went to Portugal and that it was our connection to Grandpa. It was, you know?" Tilda said, turning to look at Bev.

She reached over and gave Tilda's hand a squeeze. They were quiet a moment and then Bev said, "It all sounds logical to me, but what's the professional opinion?"

Tilda wiped a stray tear away and said, "When I talked to Laura she said Dr. Bernstein thought Harper was on the verge of a breakthrough but that she wanted to wait until her next visit before reaching any conclusions. I think she tells Laura and Mark about Harper's progress, but then she also sometimes sees the three of them together. She says she's Harper's therapist and won't say anything to either of them, Mark and Laura, that Harper isn't okay with."

"Breakthrough. That sounds intriguing," said Bev. "Will Harper stay Harper, do you think, or might she someday go back to being Tilly?"

"Oh, I think one thing is certain: she's Harper, now and forever." Hearing herself say these words she knew in her heart to be true, she felt a slight twinge of regret. Her namesake. No more. *It's okay*, she thought, giving herself this brief moment of sadness.

And then, as if Tilda suddenly remembered the purpose of the trip to the beach, she turned to Bev and said, "Okay, now for sure it's your turn. What's going on in your life?"

Harper knocked on the door, and Dr. M said "Enter," the way she always did in that funny kind of accent, as though she were asking Harper to enter some exotic, unfamiliar place. She explained it to Harper on the day of their first meeting: "I want you to knock each time you come because then I know you are asking to enter, that wherever our session takes us, you have willingly chosen to go there. It's a kind of ritual that I think will be helpful."

Harper entered, took off her jacket and her backpack, and slowly took her place in the soft upholstered chair. She slipped off her boots and pulled her legs onto the seat, first hugging them to her, then gently swinging them beside her.

"How have you been since our last appointment, Harper? Last week was probably a little difficult—you cried, but I think it was worthwhile. Sometimes when things are hard there can be a good outcome. Do you remember what I asked you to think about last week?"

Harper shrugged her shoulders. "Not really," she said. "All I know is I cried a lot. And I cried at home, too."

"That's good. Sometimes crying is a good thing. It helps us to get things out of our system."

"All I know is that I can't believe Grandpa is actually dead and never coming back. Sometimes it's a shock all over again, like the first time I found out."

"And now?"

"Now I don't think it will be a shock anymore. Now I think I know it's really true. I think I cried myself into knowing it."

"I see. Maybe that's good, too, not having that shock every time, right? And what else about last week?"

"Well, I was mad that I was going to have to accept getting my period."

"Are you still mad?"

Harper shrugged again. "I know what you said was right. You told me from the beginning that the whole thing would take a long time."

"Anything else?"

"Not really."

"Well, we talked about being afraid and loving our family and hating that people we love have to die."

"Uh-huh. I remember."

"Okay. I'm going to ask you a hypothetical question. Do you know what that means?"

"Sure, it's a question about something that's made up. It can be a trick question that a good politician won't answer. That's what my social studies teacher said."

Dr. M laughed. Her head went back when she laughed sometimes. Harper liked it when she did that.

"That's a good teacher, I think. But this isn't a trick question. Sometimes a hypothetical question lets us explore possibilities that haven't or that won't happen but that we can learn from just the same. Okay, here it is. I want you to imagine being very fond of someone, someone not in your family. Can you think of someone?"

"Is it someone I know, or can it be someone I admire, like a famous person?"

"No. Someone you know."

Harper thought about it. She thought for a long time.

"I like my friends and some of my teachers, but I don't know about 'fond.' Is that like love?"

"Yes, like love. Someone you like to be with. Someone who makes you happy when you're with them."

Harper thought of Lizzie and told Dr. M.

"So it's a good thing, being fond of someone. I mean, you like being with her. When you think of her you have a good feeling. It's not scary, right?"

"Sure. Yeah. I guess so."

"Okay, now imagine you're older, maybe a few years from now, and you're fond of someone else. Maybe very, very fond, maybe you love this person. Wouldn't that be a good thing, to have those feelings for someone who isn't in your family? Wouldn't it be good to love someone?"

Harper thought about this. She knew Dr. M was getting at something. She didn't know what it was, but she knew the answer to the question. "Yes, it would be a good thing. I mean, to feel so strongly that you wanted to see someone, to spend time with them, and that that person made you happy. Yeah, that would be a good thing."

"You wouldn't want to grow up and live in a world where you couldn't feel that way, would you?"

"No, I guess not."

"You might even love someone as much as you love your grandpa, in a very different way, but just as much. And you wouldn't want to miss that, would you?"

Harper felt a place in her chest let go. It felt good.

"No, I wouldn't want to miss that."

Dr. M didn't say anything for a long time. They both just sat there, and it was okay.

"Harper, remember when I told you my mother died when I was a little girl, younger than you? Well, if I were afraid to ever feel that way about someone again, I would've missed out on my husband, who I love very much, and my two little girls. I wouldn't have them, and they're the world to me, the way you are to your mom and dad. It's so worth it, Harper. Loving other people is so worth it. What do you think I mean by 'worth it'?"

"Worth possibly losing. Losing them, the way you lost your mother and the way I lost Grandpa."

"Hmm," said Dr. M. She nodded, and they sat quietly some more.

When they did begin to talk again, it was as though Harper could breathe more deeply—and it felt good. The world was big, like the heavens and the stars and the moon and the sun. It felt too big sometimes, but it was also good.

"See you next week, then?" said Dr. M, rising.

"Yes," answered Harper.

Their time was up.

Harper walked into the waiting room and realized she had forgotten all about her decision not to see Dr. M again.

Chapter Fifteen

HER YEAR OF DISCOVERY

ᕲᘇ

April. The month of sweet flowers, with tender roots and leaves and young sun. April. The cruelest month, of memory and desire, dull roots, and spring rain. It was all this, new beginnings, the pull of the past, and more. This year as always there was Easter and Passover. But different this year would be Harold's Yahrzeit, the observance of one year of mourning on the Hebrew calendar.

Laura had taken care of all the arrangements for the unveiling, the graveside ceremony to be held on Tuesday. The observance would be a small family gathering, mostly, including only a few close family friends. Bev and George would be there, Darren and Lizzie, and several of Mark and Laura's friends from the temple, but that was all. Laura had laid it all out during a recent phone call. She had taken care of the headstone, planned the ceremony, and made arrangements for a reception at her house afterward. "It will be catered. Family Fare will deliver before we get there," Laura had explained. "My friend Madge has volunteered to set it up so everything will be ready for us when we arrive. Oh, and I forgot to tell you, Rabbi Hoffman will be out of town, so I called Rabbi Ross."

Tilda felt a flutter in her heart.

"At first he said he had room on his calendar, but then he asked if you had suggested getting in touch. When I told him I was making the arrangements and that you hadn't suggested anything, he said I should talk to you first. What's going on? Dad liked him. Don't you think he's the right choice?"

No response.

"Mom?"

Tilda didn't know what to say. She had blocked the whole Rabbi Don incident out of her mind. She couldn't even remember if she had told Laura about her encounter, and now it was apparent she had not. What to say? He had apologized. There was no real harm done, possibly not even any ill intent on his part.

"You've caught me off guard, Laura, let me think. I mean, technically we don't need a rabbi, do we?"

"No, but . . . don't you want a rabbi? I just thought it would be nice to include him because of his relationship with Dad, and I guess I thought Dad would appreciate having him there."

"And he wanted you to ask me, right?" Tilda sensed her daughter's rising concern that something was up. Next she would ask if Tilda's session with Rabbi Ross hadn't gone well, and Tilda would have to explain or lie, and neither option appealed. "Well, I'm sure it will be fine. And you're right, your father would be pleased," she added quickly.

"Good," said Laura, sounding relieved. "Then it's all settled."

Tilda did not respond.

"Right, Mom? It's settled?"

Tilda exhaled into the phone. She took a breath and began. "No, Laura. Not exactly." And she told Laura about the incident—about the wise words that had struck a chord, and then the leaning in, the cologne, the knee.

"Why didn't you tell me?" Tilda didn't answer, and Laura went on.

"I thought you had been comforted. You even repeated the things he said that had seemed right to you."

"I know, Laura. I guess a rabbi who does an inappropriate thing can still be a dispenser of wisdom. When is anything ever either completely black or white?"

They both paused to contemplate the complexity of fallen man, so like an angel . . . and yet.

Laura was the first to speak.

"Even so, it won't do to have him there. Dad liked him, but you're the one who has to look at him. No, it won't do. And Dad would've been horrified. No. That's it. Leave it to me."

Tilda nodded and smiled. Laura was more often than not, unflappable. About his daughter, Dad would be proud. "Thank you, Laura, for understanding."

"Of course. So, everything is pretty much done. And George is picking you up at eleven, right?" Tilda pictured her daughter adding and subtracting from her to-do list.

Tilda assured Laura that all her own plans were taken care of and not to worry. She hung up, once again marveling at her daughter's tendency to worry being overridden by her capacity to get things done.

⌒ ᴖᴖ

Tuesday morning Tilda woke to the sliver of light peeking in through the night shades. She lifted them up and opened the bay window to reveal a day of sweet flowers, tender roots, leaves, and young sun, indeed. It was glorious. Mark and Laura both had been gardening for over a month, the fruits of their labor in full view. Under the two cherry trees were daffodils and patches of trillium. Along the property line were rhododendron and azaleas in shades of light to dark pink. The visual display was matched only by the scent now filling her room. Under her window were thick clusters of hyacinths, in animated colors, their sweet smell pleasantly diffused before it reached her sitting on the window seat. There was still a chill in the air. She closed the window.

Her emotions were as mixed as the colors before her.

It was almost too much, this awakening, this quintessential visual ode to spring. She was at war with herself. She wanted to throw off the dull remains of the past season, embrace the new life teasing her, but still she held back. This was, after all, a ritual day, a day of remembering, not forgetting. But it was also a day of unveiling. A lifting of the veil . . . perhaps of her own.

She opened her closet and decided on her gray flannel dress because she would be able to wear it with the lavender cashmere cardigan Harold had given her for the last of her birthdays they had shared together. She dressed and waited for George, who had gone to the train station to pick up Bev.

The unveiling wasn't like the funeral. That had been a primal experience, as though she weren't present in a world she recognized. She recalled it as dense and heavy, as though she were deep underwater, so deep the pressure constricted her lungs. There was no space for the force required by tears. Around her were people she knew and loved, but they were too far away to touch, floating near and then away.

Today was different. She was present, standing by George, next to Laura, who was next to Harper, who was next to Mark. Bev, assuringly, was just a step behind her. She was in a familiar world, in the cemetery, standing near the plot of earth that held Harold, something she had come to accept. All was familiar.

Rabbi Geller, who had been Laura's teacher, spoke to each of them standing around the covered headstone. Tilda was first to put her hand out to her. "Thank you for coming," she said. As soon as the rabbi took her place at the graveside, Tilda breathed more easily. This would be a day of remembering, yes, but only of Harold. Thanks to her ever-thoughtful and capable daughter, all would go well on this, Harold's day.

Rabbi Geller began, "The Lord is my shepherd . . ."

When it came time for the family to speak, Laura, who had prepared a eulogy, found she could not speak and handed her pages to Mark. She pulled a tissue from her bag and turned to wipe away her tears. Tilda hadn't been fast enough to offer her own, several of which were within reach in the pocket of her dress. Mark looked lovingly at Laura and made a brief apology for not being prepared and said he would read but that the words were Laura's.

He began, "Psalm 15 asks, 'Who shall sojourn in Thy tabernacle? Who shall dwell upon Thy holy mountain?' The language is archaic, but the meaning is clear. It asks, who is fit to be with God? The answer is clear. It is the decent man, not the rich and powerful man, but the one who speaks the truth in his heart, who doesn't slander, who does no evil, who doesn't cheat, who is good to others. My father was this decent man. In his goodness, he made life better for all whose lives he touched. As a husband, a father, a grandfather, he was that decent man who made our lives richer through his love, who kept us near and in his heart while he lived, and who continues to keep us, as we keep him in our hearts today, in this world without him."

Tilda heard Laura softly weeping and Harper, too, crying. Tilda's legs began to weaken. She felt warmth coming up from her chest as her breath became labored. She needed to sit, but there was nowhere to sit. She remembered that she had brought a small bottle of water in her bag. As she fumbled to find it, George leaned in and held her while she extracted the bottle and handed it to him. He opened it and gave it back. She took several sips, remembering to breathe slowly. She pushed against George's side, letting him take her weight. He braced, ready to receive her.

Rabbi Geller came to the middle of the group again. "God, full of mercy, who dwells in the heights, provide a sure rest . . ."

Laura passed out copies of the Kaddish. It was a rendering of the Sephardic, she explained; they all would recite the transliteration. Laura, now in control, read aloud:

"Render greatness and holiness to the mighty name of God," she began. "May the great name of God be a source of blessing for all eternity," she continued.

When she came to the end, all joined her:

"May the One who creates harmony in all the worlds, in tender love create peace for each of us and for all the House of Israel, and for all of the world, and let us say, *amen*."

Rabbi Geller removed the veil. And there was Harold's headstone.

Beloved Husband, Father, Grandfather, it read. *He lived justly*. And in Hebrew at the bottom: ה"בצנת. *May his soul be bound up in the bond of eternal life*.

❧

After the reception, after the ride home, after George had left her at the door on his way to take Bev back to the train, Tilda took off her dress and got into the bathtub. Retreat was what she wanted most. It had been a good day, a fitting end to her first year without Harold, but now she needed to be alone, to let it sink in. What did it all mean? That was the question. But meaning eluded her. She had come to not expect answers.

After the bath, she snuggled into her robe and settled on the sofa with a light blanket and a cup of tea. And then the doorbell rang. Tilda thought first to ignore it. There were no lights on. Whoever it was would assume no one was home. But she was home, and it might be important. She threw back the blanket and went to the door. It was Harper.

In the doorway, without words, they clung to each other as the tears fell.

Soon they were seated next to each other on the sofa.

"Mom said she would drop me off but that you have to take me home. Is that okay?"

"Of course. You don't have to ask."

They took their usual spots on the sofa.

"Grandma, I have something I need to tell you," Harper began.

Tilda thought she could not take a surprise today. She didn't want to hear that Harper had decided to have her breasts removed, start on testosterone, grow a beard. Not today. Today she could not be that understanding and reasonable person she so wanted to be always for her beloved granddaughter. She held her breath.

"I want you to know what you did for me."

"What I did?"

"Yes. Our trip, what that meant."

"Okay."

"It made me not be afraid anymore."

"What were you afraid of?"

"I was afraid of how big and unknowable everything is, everything—the universe, God. What does it all mean?"

There was something different about Harper, something Tilda couldn't quite name, this new questioning person.

"But then I saw where the explorers stood. Where they left from, to discover how to cross oceans, how to read the stars in a new way, even. I saw the megaliths and realized that everybody has always tried to find answers to things they didn't know. Then I saw where people died, thousands of people, for what they believed, their faith. So it all in the end comes down to discovering your truth. It could be about the universe or about God. In the end it's the same thing. You helped me, Grandma, to see that truth really is beauty."

"I gave you all that?"

"You and Grandpa. He always said I had to figure things out for myself. The starting gun is when you're born, he said, and you have a lifetime to figure out your purpose before the finish line."

"Do you know your . . . purpose, then, Harper?"

"I haven't suddenly found religion or anything, but I do think people have to be strong to live in this world—to believe in something bigger."

"Something bigger," Tilda said. "I wonder what Grandpa thought his purpose was."

"Oh, I know. He told me. He said it was from a book. There was a quote he thought made sense."

"Do you remember what it was?"

Harper thought about it a minute.

"No, but I think it's here, in your office where all the books are."

"Would you recognize it?"

"I might. He took it down and showed it to me. He had it marked."

"Let's go see."

Tilda turned on the light in her office, and they began exploring.

"I think it was on the shelves on the left, about the middle."

"That's where his Vonnegut books are."

"Yes! That was it. It was Vonnegut, Kurt, right?"

"Right. Well, here they all are. He had every book he ever wrote."

"It was red, I think, with a sexy woman on the cover. Here it is. Yes, this is it," she said, handing the book to Tilda.

"*The Sirens of Titan.* I remember this book. It's about Martians taking over Earth."

"Look, here's his bookmark for the page."

It took us that long to realize that a purpose of human life, no matter who is controlling it, is to love whoever is around to be loved.

They read it silently. They read it aloud. First Tilda. Then Harper.

"That's the other thing, Grandma, that I was afraid of. Love. I thought it was scary and awful, because of how much I loved, love, Grandpa."

"But why was that scary?"

"Because he died."

"Are you still scared?"

"Are you?"

"Still scared?"

"Yes. You're scared. You're scared of George."

Tilda's heart raced a little, just enough to cause her to put her hand on her chest. She had to think about that. She thought she was holding back for Harold, not because of George.

"Maybe we were both scared, Harper. I think you might be right."

"You know, Mom loved Grandpa as much as we do. She converted for him, but she isn't afraid. What we don't have is her faith. I don't think you have to believe in God to have faith, but you have to believe in something, so now I'm going to believe in what scared me the most, love."

Per amore. Tilda shook her head and drew her grand-daughter into her arms.

"You continue to amaze me, my dear, dear Harper."

There was so much more Tilda wanted to talk about. She wanted to share her own fears and sorrows. She wanted to tell her about Anthony. She wanted to find meaning in Anthony's short and terrible life, something she never could.

You, dear Harper, have absorbed the entire history of your grandfather's family, of his people. You have found a way to make sense of it. And soon, I think, I will be ready to tell you about my family, about my brother, and he will not be forgotten. We will have faith together that, through our love, that child will not be forgotten.

She finally let Harper go, and, after some time together talking and laughing on the sofa, she got dressed and drove her granddaughter home.

❦

The next day, Laura called. "I'm glad you had some time with Harper yesterday. Did she tell you her news?"

"Her news?"

"That she's staying Harper for the foreseeable future. That she can't go back to being Tilly because she isn't Tilly anymore."

This was not news to Tilda, who had already surmised it. And it hadn't come up in their conversation last night, so Harper must have decided to tell her parents after her talk with Tilda.

"No. Not in so many words." Tilda didn't want to discuss the rest of their conversation. It was locked in her heart for her and Harper alone.

"She hasn't decided on her gender yet. And that's okay, according to Dr. Bernstein. We had a family session with her. She told Harper she didn't need to make any decisions about it yet. And she told us privately that at this point Harper isn't a candidate for hormone therapy, but she isn't ruling it out. Some kids take longer than others to know their true gender. She said if anything, Harper might be gender neutral and might in that case retain her primary sex assignment as female."

None of this worried Tilda. She knew that whatever Harper decided, she would have love in her life, and in the end that was all that mattered.

"Mom, your year is up, and so is our deal."

Tilda wondered where this conversation was headed.

"Do you remember our deal?"

"Yes."

"Well?"

"Well?"

"Okay. Here's what I think. What about George?"

"That's not an opinion. That's a question. Honey, George and I are okay. We're sorting things out."

"Mark and I think he might be a good partner for you."

"I don't need, I don't want, a partner. If George and I end up together, it will be because I love him."

"Do you think he might be that person, then?"

Tilda paused. "He might be." Tilda surprised herself when she realized the stress she had put on the word *be*, rendering the sentence, He might *be*.

"Good," said Laura. She noticed it, too. "So I guess you're going to stay in the house."

"Yes, I'm staying in the house."

"Also good. Now you can take over your own garden."

They both laughed, and Tilda was pleased at their ability to do so now, a year later.

"Mom. I know how hard this year has been. You've been great. You've handled everything with grace and love."

"Thank you, Laura."

"But I have something else I want to talk to you about."

Tilda heard that note of earnestness that led her to suspect trouble.

"It's a difficult subject. But Dad. Well, he's in our family plot. Our congregation accepts Jews and non-Jews. Have you given any thought . . ."

"Oh, dear. Can this wait?"

"Yes, of course. It can. But I just wanted to plant a seed."

Tilda found the whole idea of *planting* in this context to be funny but thought it best not to say anything.

"I know, dear. Yes, I'll consider it and let you know."

"Love you, Mom."

"Love you too." *My darling, Laura. She of great faith, who never saw a question that couldn't be answered.*

Tilda had considered the subject. She had told Harold years ago that she wanted to be cremated and to have her ashes scattered over the Long Island Sound. They had never decided what they would do. Of course not. They had years yet to sort their thoughts out. Only they didn't. And now Tilda still knew what she wanted, to be free of earth when her day came, to be floating on the waves of her beautiful sound, to catch a breeze, to float over Laura's house, over to see Harper, to visit Harold's spot of earth. She would tell Laura, but not yet.

❧

Still April. Still time for her own first-year observance, with Harold, at the Point, one of their special places, all seasons. They walked the trails in the summer, enjoying the fresh sea air and the warm sun. In fall, the colors buoyed their spirits as they anticipated the darker days to come. In winter, they bundled up and walked carefully on snow and ice, marveling at the frozen sound during the coldest days. And in the spring, they picnicked. And so on this fine April day, Tilda packed their picnic basket with a fresh baguette, a small wedge of Manchego cheese (Harold's favorite), and a bottle of Prosecco—with two champagne glasses.

She found a quiet spot, a table near the trees, with a view of the water, farther back from their favorite spot, but more private. She put down the tablecloth and put out the bread, cheese, and sparkling wine, including the glass for Harold.

She took her first sip. *To my Harold. I made it through this first year without you—and I suspect there will be at least a few more. You're happy, I know, that the little family we made is enduring. Laura is a wonder, who loves you with all her heart.*

She raised her glass again and took a second sip. *To Harper. She is beautiful and strong and will be the best of us one day if she isn't already. She gets a lot of her kind heart and her spirit and her love from you. It's a nature-and-nurture thing, I imagine, because she has your genes and your teaching to guide her in this life.*

And to me. I meddled in the lives of others and I did no harm. Maybe even some good. Darren is willing to try. He will open his heart and try to forgive Amanda. Emile will try to forgive Amanda for entering and then leaving his life, leaving him and Gregory. Lizzie's little stickies all over the house pleading for forgiveness did not go unnoticed or unheeded. Forgiveness is a wonderful thing, no matter where it comes from. Lizzie came over a few nights ago with Harper, and we played Scrabble. Lizzie beat us both with two words: petrichor *and* gibbous. *The smell of earth after rain and a moon phase. They are both such lovely things. That smell reminds us all, on some level, of what it is to be alive. It was all around me, that smell, after the last spring rain. And it made me happy to think of earth again in a new way, that it holds you, receives you. It isn't so awful anymore. And the gibbous moon is a less-than-full moon. We always think of the full moon as the moon of romance, of poets, but a less-than-full moon has its own meaning and beauty. It can be waxing or waning, new and full of future promise or in its final stage before leaving until its next appearance. Like the seasons, like life, all of it to be embraced.*

Now, after the wine, she was a mix of moon and rain. She had brought poems to read, and now she mixed them up in her soliloquy to Harold.

So, my darling. My first year of mourning is over. Some days I laugh and find joy in simple things again, the way I used to. Other days I am undone by you. Sometimes I'm so tired, I don't know if I can go on. I remember the white room with you when the curtain fluttered, and I am lost. But I accept that I must go on. The world will become interesting again, won't it? And I will be able to praise once again this mutilated world, won't I?

I will start anew and keep you with me always. Another toast.

To life.

❦

Still April. The next morning, Tilda tied her bathrobe around her and hurried to answer the door. There was George, holding a black Lab puppy that couldn't have been more than six months old. He was squirming in George's arms, and George was laboring to hold him.

As soon as the puppy saw Tilda, he started pulling out of George's arms, in her direction. Instinctively, Tilda put out her arms to the puppy, who leapt to her. Now holding him, she looked down to see his amber eyes searching her face. Then one pull up, and he was licking her cheeks, her face, bathing her in the scent of kibble and sweet warm milk.

"I put in the paperwork to adopt him a while ago. And he finally got here. I picked him up from the rescue truck at the park-and-ride lot in Stonington yesterday. It was quite a trip, but I think he's adjusting. He likes you, Tilda."

Tilda was distracted, enjoying holding the black mass of fur in her arms and being kissed.

His name is Anders, but can we call him Bully, BullyToo?

Tilda looked up.

"Yes, George, yes," she said, finally, breaking the silence that had hung between them, and she and BullyToo stepped aside to let George enter.

QUESTIONS AND TOPICS FOR
DISCUSSION

1. There are many themes running through the novel—loss and renewal, fear and triumph, discovery and acceptance. Which of these most resonates with you and why? Are there other themes in the book that you find interesting? If so, what are they?

2. How does Tilda handle her grief when she is with Laura? With Tilly? With Bev? Does she present herself differently to each of them? Which face of her grief is her deepest and truest?

3. For much of the novel, Tilda is grieving. How does she manage to cope? How does she develop and change?

4. Early in the novel, Tilda becomes involved in the Esmond family crisis. Is this reasonable? An overreaction? Why?

5. Two teenagers are depicted in the novel. How would you describe Tilly? Lizzie? How are they different? How would you account for the friendship that develops between them?

6. How would you characterize Tilda's best friend, Bev? How are she and Tilda different? The same? What do you think accounts for their friendship?

7. How would you describe Tilda's coming to terms with Tilly's gender uncertainty? What is her greatest concern? Does she initially ignore Tilly's attempts to come forward? If so, why do you think that is? When does she fully accept Tilly as Harper?

8. At one point, Tilly accuses Tilda of being afraid of George. Is this is an accurate assessment? Where do think Tilda's fear comes from?

9. After her initial reluctance, Tilda agrees to go to Cuba with George. There are references to *Guys and Dolls* during the trip. How is this fitting?

10. When do you think Tilda becomes aware of George as potentially more than a friend?

11. Why is Tilda's journey to Portugal with her granddaughter so integral to the novel's theme? How is it different but equally important for both Tilda and Tilly/Harper?

ACKNOWLEDGMENTS

With a full heart, I thank my first reader, Lori Dietrich, for her wisdom—and for sharing it so generously; Dr. Ralph Kaufman, MD, for his guidance in the chapters depicting the patient-therapist relationship; to childhood friend and adult advisor Cantor Karen Blum, for her eye on content relating to Jewish ritual and practice; to the ever-supportive team at She Writes Press—especially Cait Levin, for her skill in every phase of the publishing process; Julie Metz, for her patience and expertise in cover design; Barrett Briske, proofreader and copyeditor, for her eagle eye; and Brooke Warner, for her support from the earliest days in my effort to bring *Tilda's Promise* into the world. My love and thanks go, as always, to my husband, Steve, for reading, commenting, and supporting me in this as he does in all things. And, finally, my thanks to my granddaughters, Sienna, Maddie, and Lilly, who inspire me every day.

ABOUT THE AUTHOR

Jean P. Moore was born in Brooklyn, New York, and grew up in Miami, Florida. Her novel *Water on the Moon*, published in June 2014, won the 2015 Independent Publisher Book Award for contemporary fiction. Her work has appeared in journals and newspapers such as *upstreet, SN Review, The Timberline Review, Angels Flight Literary West, Fiction Southeast, Distillery, Skirt, Slow Trains,* the *Hartford Courant, Greenwich Time,* and the *Philadelphia Inquirer.* A memoir piece, "Finding Charles," appears in *Persimmon Tree.* Several of her poems are found in *Women's Voices of the 21st Century* (2014). Her chapbook, *Time's Tyranny,* was published in the fall of 2017. She, her husband, and their black Lab, Sly, divide their time between Greenwich, Connecticut and the Berkshires in Massachusetts.

SELECTED TITLES FROM SHE WRITES PRESS

She Writes Press is an independent publishing company founded to serve women writers everywhere. Visit us at www.shewritespress.com.

What is Found, What is Lost by Anne Leigh Parrish. $16.95, 978-1-938314-95-7. After her husband passes away, a series of family crises forces Freddie, a woman raised on religion, to confront long-held questions about her faith.

Stella Rose by Tammy Flanders Hetrick. $16.95, 978-1-63152-921-4. When her dying best friend asks her to take care of her sixteen-year-old daughter, Abby says yes—but as she grapples with raising a grieving teenager, she realizes she didn't know her best friend as well as she thought she did.

Shelter Us by Laura Diamond. $16.95, 978-1-63152-970-2. Lawyer-turned-stay-at-home-mom Sarah Shaw is still struggling to find a steady happiness after the death of her infant daughter when she meets a young homeless mother and toddler she can't get out of her mind—and becomes determined to rescue them.

Keep Her by Leora Krygier. $16.95, 978-1-63152-143-0. When a water main bursts in rain-starved Los Angeles, seventeen-year-old artist Maddie and filmmaker Aiden's worlds collide in a whirlpool of love and loss. Is it meant to be?

American Family by Catherine Marshall-Smith. $16.95, 978-163152-163-8. Partners Richard and Michael, recovering alcoholics, struggle to gain custody of their Richard's biological daughter from her grandparents after her mother's death only to discover they— and she—are fundamentalist Christians.

Magic Flute by Patricia Minger. $16.95, 978-1-63152-093-8. When a car accident puts an end to ambitious flutist Liz Morgan's dreams, she returns to her childhood hometown in Wales in an effort to reinvent her path.